I0673126

CURSED SPECIAL EDITION

BOOK ONE OF THE BEHOLDER SERIES

CHRISTINA BAUER

COPYRIGHT

Monster House Books
Brighton, MA 02135
ISBN 9781945723971
Second Edition

Copyright © 2019 by Monster House Books LLC
All rights reserved. This book or any portion thereof may not be reproduced or
used in any manner whatsoever without the express written permission of the
publisher except for the use of brief quotations in a book review.

DEDICATION

For All Those Who Kick Ass, Take Names
And Read Books

AUTHOR'S NOTE

Dear Readers,

Here are some thingy-things to know about this special edition:

Why I did this

Short answer: I'm changing distributors.

Long answer: Because of that switch, my first seven books need new back-end tracking numbers. In other words, I must deactivate the original CURSED (as well as some other books) and then republish it.

As in, the exact same book.

So there will be two versions floating around.

Again, of the exact same book.

Which will be hella confusing.

Now for some context. My day job used to be in software, and we have a saying: *it's not a bug, it's a feature.* So, I figured that if I must have two versions, one of them might as well include new content.

The special edition series was born.

What's in this special edition

An all-new honeymoon story! Boom. Mic drop.

More special editions ahoy

As I mentioned above, my first seven books need new product numbers, so they're also getting extra content. Here's an overview of all seven new special editions (SE):
- ANGELBOUND SE, Angelbound Origins Book 1
- SCALA SE, Angelbound Origins Book 2
- MAXON SE, Angelbound Offspring Book 1
- PORTIA SE, Angelbound Offspring Book 2
- CURSED SE, Beholder Book 1
- CONCEALED SE, Beholder Book 2

So there you have it: why I wrote this special edition and some other semi-random stuff. Hope you enjoy this new special edition!

Thanks for reading and being you,

Christina

CURSED

*M*y black cat, Lucy, tiptoed across the roof. I paused from hammering and gave her a hopeful smile. "Hello there. You here to keep me company?"

Lucy shivered and leaped away. I frowned. *Lucy's not afraid of me, too, is she?*

I leaned over the edge of the farmhouse. Below me, Lucy stalked past the front porch, her long tail flicking. "You don't think I'm scary, do you?"

Lucy looked up, bared her teeth, and hissed.

That's my answer, I suppose.

I was eighteen years old, owned my own farm, and could cast a little magick. Everyone I knew found that frightening. Well, everyone except Tristan, but he was away at sea right now. It felt like forever until I'd see my only friend again.

Don't think about it. There's too much work to do.

To keep my mind off my worries, I soaked in the view from my roof. An oak forest towered to my right, the leaves gleaming like they'd been dipped in emeralds. To my left, acres of golden barley rustled in the breeze. A broad road cut between the two sides—I'd widened that myself last month. I sighed.

I love this place.

At least, I did until I saw what was coming.

A wagon lumbered up the road. It had an open back for hauling crops, yet the cart was painted yellow and had tall red wheels. Fancy. A man in a straw hat flicked the reins of two gray chargers. With a ride like that, he could only be one thing.

Another suitor.

That made the third one this week. It was getting ridiculous.

Ever since the courts had confirmed that Braddock Farm was mine, men suddenly saw me as marriage material. It was doubly annoying because of all the years I'd spent as a social pariah. But now that I owned my farm outright, the law would give any man I married half my land.

No doubt, whoever was driving was well aware of that.

Too bad for him, I knew exactly how to deal with unwelcome visitors. I had some planks that needed breaking down, and splitting rails would mean using my Necromancer magick. That always frightened the locals silly.

Not that I made it a habit of scaring them. As a rule, I rarely used my Necromancer power. And I certainly had no desire to join a cloister for real training. What was the point of learning how to conjure skeletons and ghosts? Over the years, I'd just figured out a trick or two that made chores easier.

After I slipped off the roof, I stepped up behind the barn, lined up some planks, jammed iron wedges into each one, and hefted a mallet onto my shoulder.

Here we go.

I closed my eyes and reached out with my mage senses. The ghostly energy was everywhere, if you knew what to feel for. The echoes of things done in the past were all around us. Kisses, fights, birdsong... It never went away, really. Necromancers could pull that power into our bodies and transform it into other kinds of energy.

I summoned magick into me. The power worked the best when I focused it all into my left arm. Still, it came in through each pore and kicked its way through every vein. Power hurtled through my limbs. I gritted my teeth and kept up my concentration. Conjuring magick reminded me of riding a spooked horse —you needed just the right mix of firm grip and loose spine. If I lost control, I'd shake until I passed out.

Within seconds, the bones of my left hand glowed blue. Magickal strength flowed through my muscles. Now, hauling up the heavy mallet was no harder than lifting a teaspoon. I raised it high above my shoulders and then slammed it down with supernatural force.

Thud.

The first plank cracked just as my would-be suitor stepped around the barn.

I couldn't believe it. Of all people, Wyatt was here.

The very man who'd complained to the courts that I was using my rogue magick to summon storms and destroy crops. Never mind that Necromancers didn't control the weather. And never mind that my crops always got hit by the same storms.

When he'd last visited, Wyatt had been dressed in black from head to toe. His shirt had even been embroidered with pentagrams to deflect my evil eye. This time, he was dressed quite differently. His too-tight pants were tucked into his work boots and his white shirt was unlaced, showing off his firm chest. Clearly, he thought I was shallow enough to fall for a few muscles. *What a horse's arse.*

"Hello, girlie." Wyatt took a half-step closer, his gaze locked on my breasts. I had the sudden urge to vomit.

I hefted my mallet again, hoping he'd take the hint not to come any nearer. "Elea. My name's Elea."

"Didn't I say that?"

"Nope." I adjusted my grip to show my glowing bones. "Why are you here?"

"Some monk had a letter for you. Thought I'd help out." He slipped an envelope from his pocket. I recognized the seal—it was from the monastery where Tristan had trained as Necromancer. He'd given up the faith to become a merchant. Why would the monks write me of all people?

"Thank you." I reached for the letter, but Wyatt pulled it away. "Not so quickly. I want to talk."

Now, we get to it.

"So talk." My bones glowed more brightly as my swing took on extra power.

Thud.

Wyatt jumped when the hammer hit. I grinned.

"You've grown into a lovely young woman, Elea. Eighteen years old is only a decade younger than me." Wyatt clutched his hand to his chest the way that characters did in badly drawn illustrations of courtly love. "You're tall and fit with hair black as a raven's wing, smooth olive skin, and whiskey-colored eyes. A man could spend a lifetime looking at your sweet face."

I stared at him, slack jawed. Whiskey-colored? Did he really say that?

Wyatt's blue eyes narrowed slightly and he pursed his lips as if ready for my kiss.

Oh, no.

"Please, Wyatt. Ever since the courts ruled in my favor, I've had suitors darkening my door day and night."

Wyatt shook his head in surprise. He was really playing this up. "The finding of the court is merely a coincidence. You're a lovely maiden. I've been hoping to be sweethearts for ages."

"Sweethearts. Truly." I smacked my lips. "For ages."

"Of course."

I gripped my mallet tighter and imagined it was his neck. "When my parents bought Braddock Farm, you painted 'Death to Necromancers' on the side of the barn. Rosie told me all about it."

He waved his hand dismissively. "I was ten at the time. It was a joke."

"It wasn't funny. My parents died of the plague soon after that."

"I'm sorry for your loss."

"Now you are, perhaps, because you want something. But you weren't sorry back then. And you weren't sorry when my guardian, Rosie, died, either. I was fifteen and alone, and you petitioned the court to take the land away from me because I was a minor and rogue Necromancer."

"Mine was one of twelve families who signed the petition." Wyatt's shoulders slumped with sadness. With that, he switched from playing the handsome suitor to the mistreated man. "You must understand—"

"I've run this place for three long years," I said, cutting him off. "If Rosie hadn't left me the coin to pay servants, I'd have been lost. But lo and behold, as soon as I'm named the rightful owner, I'm overwhelmed with offers of love and friendship? Not likely." I hefted the mallet again and imagined Wyatt's face in the middle of the nearest plank.

Thud.

That was satisfying.

Wyatt pinched the bridge of his nose. "Fine, you win. I admit that I behaved poorly."

"Poorly?" This was beyond belief.

A muscle ticked on his jawline. "Terribly, then. Now, hat do you say to courting?"

Even on my best days, I was quick to anger. Today wasn't one of my best days. I lifted the hammer once more.

Thud. "Not a chance."

"Why?" He paced a line beside me. "That Necromancer sailor's already courting you, isn't he?"

"Necromancer sailor?" I pointed the mallet straight at his nose. "You mean merchant captain, right?" Tristan had trained as a Necromancer. That was a long time ago, though. I looked longingly at the letter Wyatt still gripped. It had to have something to do with my friend.

"So, are you courting or not?"

My cheeks flared red. "No, it's not like that between us." Tristan wanted more. I just didn't feel that way about him. We could talk for hours about my books and his travels, but it didn't go farther than that for me. There was just no spark.

Wyatt exhaled. "Then, you'll consider my courtship?"

Tristan would tease me to no end if he knew Wyatt were here. Thinking about Tristan calmed me a little. When I spoke again, my voice was surprisingly gentle. "Wyatt, I appreciate your interest. The answer is no." I stretched out my palm once more. "Give me my letter and leave."

"Any other woman would be honored to have me." Little bits of spittle flew out of his mouth when he talked. "Necromancers had no right buying land in our shire. Your family wasn't here a month before the plague struck them down. That was the judgment of the gods, Elea. You risk their anger merely by being here."

Rage had me seeing red. The only thing I had from my parents—outside of a few hazy memories from Rosie—was Braddock Farm. "I risk the anger of the gods by working my birthright? And why is that?"

"Be reasonable. As it is, you're a risk to good society. What if you marry another of your kind? We all saw the judgment of the gods last time. Your only chance is to choose someone like me. That way, you might even have normal children. Besides, I'm the largest landowner in the shire."

That did it.

"How about you give me my letter, oh largest landowner, and return to your wagon?" I raised my left arm, making my bones glow the brightest shade of blue yet. "Or, if you prefer, I'll rip out your spine where you stand. Your choice."

In truth, I had no idea if spine-ripping was something I could manage. But the threat sounded good, and if it got Wyatt off my farm, then I was willing to improvise.

"Your loss." He lifted his chin defiantly. "I'll marry one of the county girls."

I whipped the letter from his palm. "Good luck to you both." *Mostly her.* I gestured in the general direction of his wagon. "The road is that way."

Wyatt stomped off through the mud. I was never happier to see someone leave. Once he was well and gone, I tore open the envelope.

Dear Elea,

Come to the Bell in Hand tavern right away. Tristan needs you.

Quinn

My stomach sank to my toes. Quinn was Tristan's dyad, the monk who'd trained with him at the monastery. The pair had stayed close even after Tristan left the order. Quinn had never written to me before, though.

I rubbed my chin and thought. Tristan always stayed at the Bell in Hand when he was at port, so that was to be expected. But his voyage wasn't supposed to end for months. And Tristan never cut a trip short, especially when he was making a delivery to Tsar Dmitri, the ruler of the Necromancers. The two were good friends.

What if Tristan was sick? Or injured?

My body went numb. There were so many ways a sailor could get hurt. When storms hit, they could get washed overboard or caught in the rigging. The lucky ones escaped at the cost of an eye or a leg. And if pirates were the problem, then things got far worse. Those fiends always targeted the captain for extra torture. Some disemboweled their victims alive. My chest tightened with panic.

I have to get to Tristan. Now.

Turning on my heel, I rushed into the barn and saddled Smoke, my fastest mare. Normally, I'd pack food and a change of clothes, but there was no time to waste. If I left right away, I could be at the Bell in Hand by sunset.

As I galloped away, images of Tristan flickered through my mind. The two of us sitting in the tavern common room, playing chess and chatting about politics in the Tsar's entourage. Long days spent walking my fields, discussing books he'd brought from overseas. Mornings laughing in the barn while he tried to feed the baby goats.

As much as I loved Braddock Farm, it was a lonely life. After Rosie died, Tristan had become my sole company. When the locals saw me coming, they crossed to the other side of the street. Even my servants looked upon me with dismay. And now, I had false suitors trying to flatter me with lies. In some ways, that was worse than open terror, because I knew the fear remained, bubbling under the surface. Every day, I sensed dread pressing in around me like a vise. Then, I'd see Tristan and the world became friendly again.

Please, let him be all right.

～

Smoke and I galloped around the final turn to the Bell in Hand. The rickety wooden building bowed out at an odd angle. A square placard hung from the corner, showing a man's hand ringing a bell. Bands of anxiety tightened around my throat.

Tristan is in there.

I slid off Smoke, tied her to the nearest hitching post, and rushed inside. The tavern was packed with bodies, loud voices, and the stench of burned meat. I pressed through the crowd and toward the back staircase. Tristan always stayed in the same room.

Second floor, last door on the right.

I sped up the narrow stairway to an upper hall that was thick with shadows. A single window cast a sickly beam of moonlight onto the warped wooden floor. I sped to the last door and whipped it open.

"Tristan?" My pulse beat so hard my heart thudded in my ears.

The darkened room held little more than a tiny cot. A candle flickered atop a bedside table alongside a washbasin. Tristan lay asleep, his features drawn and skin pale. I hurried to kneel at his side.

I hurried to kneel at his side. "Tristan? It's Elea."

Tristan half opened his eyes. "You…"

I brushed the backs of my fingers against his soft cheek. Tristan was normally all high cheekbones, and long, jet-black hair. Now, his face had hollowed out, his skin looked so pale it was colorless, and his dark hair was almost gray.

"You…" Tristan let out a dramatic sigh. "Smell like a barn."

I couldn't help but smile. "I work in one every day, in case you hadn't noticed."

"I had." He choked back a cough. "Let's discuss the finer points of mating mules and mares—"

"Tristan." I knew what he was trying to do, and I wouldn't allow it. My friend looked too ill to pretend that everything was fine.

"It can be a rather lopsided business if the mule is too small—"

"Tristan!"

"What is it?" Tristan wheezed out a rough breath. Speckles of blood flared on his white pillow. *Oh, no.*

I yanked down my sleeve and used it to dab his chin clean. "You always try to soften the blow when things are serious. Don't." My voice hitched. "Just say it."

Tristan leaned back into his pillows. The shadows in his cheeks deepened until his face resembled a skull. "I'm dying, Elea."

The world seemed to freeze for a moment. *Tristan is dying.* That couldn't be true. I wouldn't let that be true. I'd fought for the farm when everyone said it was impossible. I could find help for Tristan. "What's wrong?"

"I'm cursed."

My skin prickled with alarm. "Who cast it?" If an Apprentice or Master Necromancer were behind this, then there was a good chance the spell could be broken.

Tristan's brown eyes dimmed. "It was the work of a Grand Master. The best I've ever seen."

A chill crept along my scalp. "Tell me exactly what happened."

He nodded slowly, as if each movement of his head was painful. "My last voyage was to Tsar Dmitri. He's dead. Viktor killed him."

The words made no sense. I knew all the players in the Tsar's entourage. "Viktor? I thought he was harmless."

"We all did. Turns out, the man's a Grand Master Necromancer. He took down the entire Imperial Guard with skull seekers."

Not good. Skull seekers combined the worst of a hungry ghost and a speedy will-o-the-wisp. They were whip-fast and their teeth could bite through almost anything. "Were you there? Is that what hurt you?"

"I was there, but no, the seekers didn't injure me." Tristan's breathing turned rough. Bits of white phlegm congealed at the corners of his mouth. "After Viktor proclaimed himself Tsar, he cursed anyone who didn't pledge fealty to him on the spot."

Cursed. Seconds ticked by before I could force the words from my mouth. "You didn't pledge fealty to Viktor, did you?"

"No." Bit by bit, Tristan pulled back his blanket. His muscular torso was ripped open. The white bones of his ribs poked through bloody organs. *By the gods.* Bile crept up my throat. Tristan spoke in a rough whisper. "The moment I got back to port, these wounds appeared. They're laced with magick." His arm flopped down with the blanket, covering his injuries again. "I'm so sorry." His gaze locked with mine, and all the regret in the world hung in his eyes. "You're next."

I must have heard him wrong. "What?"

"The curse will kill you, five years from this very day. The spell goes after whoever I love the most." His voice broke. "I'm so sorry. I wanted to marry you, Elea. Now, this is my legacy."

I clutched my stomach. How could this be happening? My entire body trembled with fear. I latched onto the one possible bit of good news. "But you still have some time, right? And if we kill the mage, we kill the spell. It's the oldest rule of Necromancy. I'll find some mage to help. We can get out of this, I know it."

"If we had more time and someone willing, the curse could be moved to another person."

I shrank back. "I could never ask that of anyone."

"My good-hearted Elea." He sighed. "I knew you'd say that." Blood seeped through the heavy blanket. A coppery tang filled the air. "There's something else—" His bloodied hand slipped from under the coverlet. A small silver band rested on his palm. "Dying would be less painful if I knew my band was on your finger."

This is really happening. Tristan is dying. My eyes pricked with tears.

Years stretched before me, a never-ending string of lonely days without my friend. "Yes, of course." I lifted the band and slipped it on. The ring glowed with a flash of blue. Magick had been cast. "What spell is it?"

"Joy. I spent the last hour casting it. Do you feel happier?"

In truth, I felt nothing, but I couldn't bring myself to tell Tristan that. Clearly, he was in no frame of mind to cast decent magick. "It's beautiful, Tristan. That's what's important." My hand shook as I eyed the blood-covered ring. "A perfect fit."

Suddenly, magickal energy charged the air, like the tingle of power before a lightning storm, only far more intense. Every inch of my body went on alert. Was this the curse?

Tristan's sickbed burst into angry flames. The power exploded, slamming me backward onto the floor. Panic sped through me. Heat pierced my body.

No, no, no!

The mattress burned brightly as coals while Tristan writhed under the covers in agony. Great shafts of fire licked around him and speared into the ceiling. Black smoke and flame billowed into my face. His pale skin puckered over in angry red boils. I gasped.

"Tristan!" I picked up the washbasin and tossed water into the flames. It had no effect. Gods-damned magick.

Tristan's flesh darkened and curled. I leaped forward, slapping at the fire with my bare hands. Agony burned into my palms while the flames climbed. Tristan screamed, a sound that pierced my ears and shattered my heart. Edges of bone jutted out from the fresh burn holes in his flesh.

Not my Tristan. Not like this.

The fire stopped as quickly as it had started. I panted, waiting for another onslaught.

Nothing happened.

The room showed no sign of flame or smoke. The charge of magick drained from the air. The spell was finished.

I knelt next to Tristan again. His body carried no mark of fire. My hands were free from burns and pain as well. Was he still alive somehow? I leaned in closer.

Tristan lay on his side, his body frozen in his last thrash of agony. His brown, bloodshot eyes stared emptily into mine. He was dead. I sobbed so hard I couldn't pull enough air into my lungs. I fell in a heap on the floor, gasping, weeping, and hopeless.

The room seemed to spin beneath me. My vision collapsed until I could only see Tristan. His lifeless face was frozen in horror. My insides twisted with grief. I wasn't sure how long I stayed locked in his dead gaze. At some point, Quinn appeared at my side. He gently touched my shoulder.

"I'm sorry." Quinn stood tall and silent in his black Necromancer robes. He was rail-thin, bald, and had a face crisscrossed with scars. His voice was deep and almost without inflection. "I was surprised when Tristan told me the curse struck you. I thought his feelings for you were more infatuation than love. It's unfortunate that you were drawn into this mess."

I slowed my breathing and wiped my face with my sleeve. "What does the curse do?"

"Our friend burns, even now."

My skin chilled over with shock. "So the fire followed Tristan into his next life?" *Where he'll burn for eternity... As I will, too.* "We need to stop it. Will you help me?"

Quinn stayed as unmoving as a statue. If any of this him, he didn't show it. That was all part of Necromancer training, but it still seemed cruel. "There is nothing to be done... For him, or for you."

I couldn't believe what I was hearing. "Nothing? We can get

rid of the new Tsar, that's what we can do. Kill the mage, kill the spell."

"Viktor's a Grand Master. There are few at that level of power, and those who are will never come to your aid. Word of the curse has spread. Too many of my Brothers have died already. All Necromancers are pledging fealty to the Tsar. Anyone with power and training is being asked to join him. I'm getting his mark, too."

Rage spiraled through my limbs. How could Quinn be so resigned? I hopped to my feet. "Viktor killed Tristan. You're going to leave your dyad to suffer in fire?"

"And protect the one *I* love most from this curse? Yes." Quinn sighed. It was the first time he'd showed any real emotion. "Tristan was—" He paused, choosing his words carefully. "*Unwise* to deny the new Tsar. When you pledge fealty, Viktor merely gives you a mark on your left shoulder. It's not so great a burden."

I opened my mouth, ready to argue the point. That mark was undoubtedly laced with evil magick. But the steely look on Quinn's face made me stop. There was no way I'd change his mind. And there was still a curse to end.

I laced my fingers behind my neck and tried to think. My legs shook with shock. If I couldn't rely on Quinn and his monastery, then I'd need to find someone else. Tristan always said I had the most raw power he'd ever seen in a Necromancer.

By the gods, I could get trained. "Do you know of anyone who's refused the mark? Anywhere I could learn to become a Necromancer?"

Quinn's still features melted into a placating look. "You'd need to reach the Grand Mistress level. That's years of grueling study. Few make it after a lifetime and you only have five years. I say live them to the fullest. Enjoy your farm. Think of your good memories of Tristan."

I set my fist on my hip. "If I were the type of person who gave up, I wouldn't have a farm in the first place. Now, do you know where I can get trained or don't you?"

Quinn looked to the ceiling, as if imploring the gods for patience. I was starting to really dislike him. "The Zelle Cloister sits isolated in the mountains. Its Sisters are elderly and weak. The Tsar isn't bothering to ask for their fealty. Maybe they could train you... If that's what you truly wish to do."

I paced the floor. My life teetered on a precipice. On one side was the life I'd carved out for myself. Braddock Farm was my legacy and first love. Maybe the Tsar would die of natural causes before my time was up.

On the other side, there was a chance to save Tristan. And myself. I could choose a new existence as a Sister in a cloister for Necromancy. Becoming a Grand Mistress Necromancer meant years of mind-bending work for possibly no reward. And I'd have to leave Braddock Farm behind, maybe to never see it again.

I ran my fingertips along Tristan's jawline. Images of his suffering flickered through my mind. His pale skin blackening with char. The mass of gore that was once his firm chest. His horrible screams. That was Tristan's existence now and for all eternity, and it could be mine as well. Unless I did something.

There really was no choice. "I'm positive. You can be on your way."

"Are you sure you don't want my help for the journey?" It was hard to tell if he felt anything. I thought I saw a flicker of worry on his face, though.

"No, you've fealty to pledge and no time to waste. Besides, there's a cloister agent in town. She can take me." Most towns had a recruiting agent for Necromancers. They were always someone who'd left the order, yet kept in touch with those they'd left behind. The one for my shire had been trying to get me to join up for years. She'd be thrilled when I stopped by. "Please. I've kept you long enough as it is."

"Best of luck to you, then."

"And you as well."

Quinn stepped away and closed the door behind him. I moved back to Tristan and gripped his hand. Already, the flesh was ice cold. My friend was gone, but still suffering. "Don't worry, Tristan. I'll try with everything I am. For both of us."

And I meant it.

2

ALMOST FIVE YEARS LATER

I leaned against a wall in the Zelle Cloister library and tried to hold back my temper. Good Necromancers always controlled their emotions. And now that I'd attained the level of Grand Mistress Necromancer? I shouldn't let anything upset me. Still, I wanted to tear every book in this library to shreds.

I couldn't find the *Master Atlas of Magick*, and that was thwarting all my plans.

After nearly five years of hard work, I'd finally tracked down the elusive Tsar. Viktor would visit the Midnight Cloister on Sunday.

The same day my curse ran out. I brushed my hand over my queasy stomach. In one week, my torso would get torn wide open, followed by fires that would consume me for all eternity. Panic tightened up my spine as I thought how hopeless my mission really was. Then, the words of my Mother Superior rang through my mind. She could always sense when my resolve was fraying.

Focus on what you can do. Not the curse.

I inhaled some calming breaths and tried to regain control. After all, I should be thankful for any chance to kill Victor and end my curse. No one had thought I'd become a Grand Mistress, let alone track down the mysterious Tsar. Those thoughts didn't help for long, though.

That gods-damned atlas stood in my way.

Why couldn't the Tsar be at a sanctuary fair or visiting some open city? Of all the places to find him, a cloister was the worst. Years ago, Viktor had magickally cloaked every cloister and monastery under his control. As a result, you wouldn't know the places existed, even if you were standing at the front gates. He'd also put hexes on any books that could unhide those spots. To see and enter the Midnight Cloister, I needed an incantation from the *Master Atlas of Magick*. Trouble was, Viktor's hex kicked in whenever I cast a finder spell to locate it.

Today alone, I'd tried seventeen finder spells. I wanted to scream. Too bad that would wake up the entire cloister.

I twisted the totem rings on my left hand. I'd carefully loaded each one of them with spells to kill Viktor. My plan was simple. I'd swamp the man with so much magick, so quickly, that he wouldn't know how to retaliate. That was the idea, anyway… If I could get to the Midnight Cloister by Sunday. My shoulders shook with rage.

I hated Viktor.

I hated that it had taken me so long to discover where he'd be.

And I really hated how he'd put a hex on that atlas.

But most of all, I hated that he was right. I'd finally pinpointed where the tyrant would appear. My kill spells were loaded and ready. So, Viktor was clever to hex the damned *Atlas* and its incantations. I kicked the floor with my sandal. Every time I thought I was a step ahead of Viktor, I found out I was wrong.

Think, Elea. There must be some way to break that hex.

I stepped around the library, hoping the movement would clear my head. This library was always my favorite place to think. The rest of the Zelle was hand-hewn out of a mountainside. The other rooms were so small, you'd clunk your head if you weren't careful. But the library? It was nothing but natural caves, starting with the massive one that I stood in. Brown rock towered above me, the jagged stone looking like the majestic columns of a cathedral. Niches had been lovingly carved in the walls and filled with rare books. Even better, this cavern was only the first in a long line of caves that wound for leagues.

So many books.

So much beauty.

Such a hike to find anything, even if it didn't have a hex.

My footsteps kicked up to an anxious pace. Time was running out. I brushed my finger along the only band I wore on my right hand. *Tristan's betrothal ring.* He suffered in fire. My turn was next.

I needed to find that book.

A Sentinel Spirit hovered nearby. These were Sisters who'd tied some of their life force to the Zelle, hoping to serve through eternity. Faith was our library Sentinel, and she was pretty intense for a ghost. Most Sentinels floated peacefully. Faith darted around, her wrinkled features always pinched with worry. She floated directly into my line of vision and pointed anxiously at my mouth. Sentinels couldn't make sounds unless they were singing hymns, so this was Faith's way of asking me to eat something. I shook my head.

Then, the idea appeared.

I motioned to Faith. "What if I let loose with everything I had? Pumped it all into the finder spell?"

She frowned, titled her head, and pretended to sleep.

Faith had a point. The other Sisters could sense my magick, and if I used that much power, I could wake them up. Outside of myself, the youngest Sister here was ninety-three. They all needed their rest.

"How about if I cast a regular finder spell, and then pushed more energy in? That shouldn't bother anyone."

Faith tapped her thin chin for a moment before nodding.

I exhaled. Good, I had a plan.

Raising my left arm, I focused all my energy. Power tore through my body. When I'd started training, the sensation would get so intense, I'd convulse. Now, after years of practice, it only tickled. My powers were no longer a wild animal that I simply tried to ride. Today, I could focus a droplet of energy onto the tip of my pinky, or set loose a torrent of magick from my palm. Within a few seconds, the bones in my left hand glowed with sapphire light, casting eerie shadows inside my flesh. I began the words for a finder spell.

Dust and bone, skull and stone, locate what I seek.
Dark from light, morn from night, strength from the words I speak.

Instead of giving my muscles power, the energy whizzed out from my left hand. The air became charged, reminding me of the promise of lightning before a storm. My magick grew heavier until an azure-colored mist appeared by the floor. I focused the flow of my power and the haze solidified into the shape of a skeleton that was covered in sparkling blue sapphires. *What beautiful sight.* So far, the spell was working.

"I summoned you," I said. "Get me the *Master Atlas of Magick.*"

The finder skeleton didn't move. Instead, its eyeholes flared with brightness as it inspected me from head to toe. Seconds passed. The skeleton should have responded already. That urge to scream came back with a vengeance.

This was where all the other spells had gone wrong, too.

The sapphires on the skeleton's body began to blacken. Its bones clattered and wobbled as more of the blue gems disappeared.

Damn, the Tsar's hex was kicking in.

Faith waved her translucent arms at me in a gesture that said 'now!'

"I agree, Faith." I drove fresh power into my finder spell, more than I ever had before. A tidal wave of energy washed out of me and into the skeleton. My body became drained and numb. The skeleton turned bright with blue sapphires once more. Excitement skittered across my skin. The spell was in action.

"I summoned you. Get me the *Master Atlas*."

"I heed you, Grand Mistress." The skeleton's teeth clacked as it spoke.

I bobbed a little on the balls of my feet. *I'm one step closer, Viktor.*

The skeleton turned on its heel and began scaling the cave wall.

Faith gestured wildly to the finder skeleton. It was clinging by one hand to the ceiling, like a monkey. With its free arm, it jammed its hand inside a deep niche.

I never would've looked in there.

The skeleton's legs swung beneath while its arm dug around the hole. Anxiety tightened across my chest. *This has to work.*

The skeleton dropped to the floor with a rattle and thud. The *Master Atlas* was in its hand. *Thank the Sire of Souls.* The skeleton offered me the volume. "As you requested, Grand Mistress."

"Thank you." I reverently slipped the atlas from his fingers. "You may go."

The skeleton vanished. My knees turned rubbery with relief. The *Master Atlas was mine.*

I quickly flipped through the pages. The book began with

maps of Nyumbani, the far-off continent where Creation Casters dwelled. While Necromancers controlled spirit and stone, Casters wielded magick over nature. I kept going.

Next, came Ausdauer, the continent that was my home. Here the maps began with the eastern side. These lands were home to the Forgotten, which was what we called men and women who didn't have magick. There were two kinds of Forgotten, and they lived in different types of places. Commoners held most of the small farms, while Royals ruled them from their vast estates.

I turned another page and there it was. The Midnight Cloister. It sat in the center of a vast desert called the Endlos. I tapped the spot with my fingertip. The words for a transport spell were clearly marked. After such a long search, it hardly seemed real to be this close. I quickly committed the incantation to memory.

Across the library, uneven footsteps sounded on the stone floor. Petra, my Mother Superior, hobbled into view. She was a tall and wiry woman whose dark mage robes contrasted with her pale, lined face, and long white hair.

"Greetings, Elea." Her features were perfectly unreadable. Necromancers never showed emotion. Petra was so good at it, I sometimes wondered if she was human.

"Greetings, Mother. Sorry if I woke you." The Sisters had given so much to me, I hated to take their sleep as well.

"I was already awake when I sensed your spell." Her voice was so controlled, it was almost a monotone. "No one else noticed, I'm sure." Her mouth thinned. "You worry far too much about your Sisters. They're tougher than they look."

"Yes, Mother." Petra was always warning me against emotional attachment. It wasn't easy. After Rosie and Tristan died, the Sisters at the Zelle became my second family.

"I came because I couldn't help wondering what you were casting." Her eyes widened for a fraction of a second before her face returned to its regular stony look. "Is that the *Master Atlas*?"

I handed it to her, pride swelling through me. "Yes. I finally found it."

"Excellent work. You may just be the one to free us from Viktor." As she said Viktor's name, the rare spark of hatred gleamed in her features. Petra loathed the Tsar almost as much as I did.

"I plan to, Mother." Her faith in me meant the world.

"You've been working on that spell for a week." Petra sent a quizzical look to the Sentinel Spirit. "Faith, has she been eating and sleeping?"

I stepped between Petra and the Sentinel. "I'm fine," I lied.

Faith started mouthing a tirade while gesturing wildly. Clearly, she didn't agree. Unfortunately, Petra was excellent at lip reading. "Faith says you're in desperate need of a meal and sleep." Faith waved her hand in front of her nose. "Oh, and a bath would be useful, as well."

Thank you for nothing, Faith. I steeled my features and addressed Petra with my best 'I'm a tough Necromancer' face. "I'm ready to go after the Tsar. If I leave right now, I'll have almost a full week at the Midnight Cloister before he arrives."

Petra scanned me from head to toe. I knew what she saw. Tired face. Long, snarled black hair. And my clothes? Grand Mistress robes were swaths of fabric held together by neatly tying hundreds of tiny ribbons. They were supposed to be perfect at all times. I was a mess. Petra shook her head. "You aren't leaving."

I glared at the Sentinel. "Faith is over-worrying, I don't think—"

Petra raised her hand and shot me a warning look. I quickly closed my mouth. "Why, Elea," she said slowly. "You sounded a little irritated just then."

When it came to reading my moods, Petra was worse than Rosie, and that woman had raised me until I was fifteen. She was right, of course. I was tired and cranky. "Apologies, Mother."

"You need to keep a tighter rein on your feelings. I know you weren't raised to our ways, but emotion is the enemy of a Necromancer. Remember that."

"I will, Mother."

Petra slowly lowered herself onto a bench made of rough-hewn wood. I swore I could hear her bones creak with the movement. "Come here and show me your totem rings."

I obediently stepped to her and pointed out each ring in turn, beginning with my thumb. "This contains a spell to block Viktor's magick." I touched my fingers next. "Protection from harm, strength of stone, skeleton sword, and cluster of fireballs."

Petra eyed them all carefully. "They look in order. You don't need me to say this, but guard your totems with your life. If you lose them, they could be used to track you." Petra drummed her nails on the bench. "Recite to me what you know of the Tsar's approach to battle."

I straightened my stance. "Viktor doesn't like to fight. He had a few skirmishes right after he killed Tsar Dmitri. In those, Viktor mostly used skull seeker spells. Since that time, he's kept legions of guards around. They've never engaged any major enemy, though. His warriors have no magick, either."

This was something I hoped to find out more about at the Midnight Cloister. Viktor was close with the Royals and their ruler, the Vicomte. The Royals supplied most of the Tsar's army. Still, it was odd for Necromancers to form an alliance with those who didn't have magick. Most of the Forgotten feared us.

"And those who aren't in his guard?" asked Petra. "What of the mages who wear his mark?"

"He allows some to roam the continent, but only so they can recruit fresh Necromancers for his monasteries and cloisters.

Since those places are magickally hidden, we never see if or how those recruits are trained. There's no telling how many Necromancers are left, either. After a mage gets a mark, they pretty much disappear."

It was wise for the Tsar to hide the monasteries and cloisters. As much as Commoners feared mages, they'd be enraged if the Brothers and Sisters were in serious trouble. Mages were the only ones who could tackle tough problems. We ended civil wars and stopped the spread of plagues. Even so, there had always been a love-hate relationship between Necromancers and the Forgotten.

Petra shook her head. "You didn't mention Viktor and his experimentation."

Damn, I always forgot that part. Petra was continually going on about it, too. She had all sorts of wild theories. I'd never run across any evidence to back them up, though. Mostly, I listed it to keep her happy.

"That's right, hybrid magick," I said quickly. "There's been information that the Tsar likes to experiment mixing Necromancer energy with that of Casters." I didn't add how that information only came from Petra. "In early history, there were a few documented cases of mages trying to combine magick, but none of those attempts resulted in anything useful. We don't know what the Tsar has been able to accomplish."

Petra sighed. "You always underestimate his obsession with hybrid magick. The mark, the Tsar's power… Both could flow from combining Caster and Necromancer energy."

"I'll try to remember that, truly." I never really understood her focus on this side of the Tsar. It was never mentioned in any writings on the man. I wasn't entirely sure that 'obsession' was the way to describe his interest. And there was absolutely no evidence to connect hybrid magick to the mark, either.

Petra's face took on a faraway look. "Since you're about to leave, I think I need to make that lesson a little clearer." She started untying the ribbons by her waistline. I couldn't believe it. Necromancers never exposed their flesh in public.

"You don't need to do that." *Whatever 'that' is.*

"On the contrary, it's beyond time that I did." Petra opened her robes and exposed her stomach. My brows drew together as her skin came into focus.

I fought the urge to gasp.

Petra's skin was pockmarked with scarred-over holes. The burrow-marks wound around her lower ribs as well. "Look on this carefully, Elea. It is Viktor's handiwork. Before he became Tsar, he was a rogue mage. He abducted me from a sanctuary fair while I was still a Novice."

There were always rogue Necromancers around, even now. My old enemy Wyatt wasn't wrong to fear them. They traveled with sanctuary fairs, selling their services to anyone with coin. If you wanted to find unusual spellwork, fairs were the place to look. They weren't places to visit without a good reason, though.

"Viktor put me under a blinding spell and secreted me into his study. He brought out tools..." She shivered. "Bone hooks covered in snake scales. He wanted to see how they affected a Necromancer."

My eyes widened. "That's why you fear hybrid magick." Necromancers used bone hooks to haul around enchanted ice. The instruments were laced through with our power—it should be impossible to layer a Caster skin on them. I tapped my chin and thought through this news. "Viktor might have used hybrid magick to make his mark. But why?"

Petra quickly redid her ties. "He uses that mark to control the Necromancers who pledge fealty to him. Of that I'm certain."

"Perhaps," I said. "But there are easier ways to control some-one. Viktor's already proven that curses get people to do his bidding. He must be trying to do something that regular spells can't accomplish."

"Whatever it is, *that's* what you need to discover before you attack on Sunday."

She was right. I couldn't fight what I didn't know. "I'll use my time before Sunday to investigate. Try to determine what he's using hybrid magick for."

"Good." Petra sighed. "I'm glad we understand each other."

Petra looked so thin and frail on the bench. I had the urge to hug her. She'd worked incredibly hard to get me ready for this moment. All the Sisters had. The Tsar had overlooked them as old, weak, and not worth the trouble of threatening into taking his mark. But every one of them was sharp as Petra. They'd trained me well. I took a half step forward and then stopped myself. "Uh, thank you, Mother."

She kept her features cool and composed, but I didn't miss the slight hitch in her voice when she spoke. "Viktor will pay." She pulled a small blue envelope from her pocket. "I brought you a letter of introduction. With any luck, old Berta is still Mother Superior at the Midnight Cloister. We exchanged letters as Novices. I wrote that you're on a pilgrimage to meet the Tsar and asked for her help. That used to be a very common occurrence. It shouldn't raise any suspicion."

No, it shouldn't. But I didn't know what truly awaited me in the Midnight Cloister. I took the letter anyway. There was only so much we could foresee without any insight into the cloister. "Thank you again. I'm not sure how I could ever repay you."

"How about getting a good night's sleep?"

"Yes, I promise."

"Excellent. Then you won't summon him?"

'Him' as in Tristan. If I spoke Tristan's name during the day, the curse summoned him into my dreams at night. He was always in flames, tortured, and screaming. It never made for a good rest.

"I have to. I've memorized the spell from the atlas. I'm on my way. He needs some hope."

"I wish you wouldn't. I won't stop you, though. You're moving beyond my care." She sighed. "You may leave the cloister at dawn. I'll ask the Sisters to skip our morning casting, so there will be no interference. We don't want any magick disturbing your transport spell."

She wasn't wrong. I'd heard horrible stories of Necromancers transporting themselves into trees or down to the ocean floor. Still, there was no need to disrupt the Sisters. "I can step outside the cloister grounds. It's no problem. Please keep to your schedule. The Sisters need their routine."

"If you insist."

"I do, and I want you to know... I appreciate you..." I shifted my weight from foot to foot, unable to find the words. "By the Sire, I know I'm not supposed to say these things, but I'll miss you terribly."

"And I will you." She stood quickly and fixed me with a serious look. I'd never seen such raw emotion on her face before. "Promise me one thing."

"Anything you wish."

"When you kill that bastard, tell him I trained you."

I couldn't hide my smile. "Consider it done."

Once I curled into my tiny bed, I expected my dreams to be about Tristan. After all, I'd said his name before I fell asleep. Normally, he and I met in my old farmhouse. Instead, I dreamt that I sprouted wings and flew into the starry sky. Wind flowed over my body, and I hummed with pleasure as the cool air caressed me. A vast and empty desert rolled below, a vista of golden sand that was patterned in delicate ripples.

All of which was very strange.

If my dreams didn't take me to Tristan, then they usually sent me wandering aimlessly through the Zelle, worrying myself sick over some nonsense question like 'why did I show up nude to breakfast?' But tonight, the pull across the desert was so strong it felt like a rope had been tied around me. There would be no meandering, and my nonsense worries were gone as well. I only had a real concern for my friend.

Why wasn't I with Tristan? Was our bond broken?

My wings kept driving me toward a lone figure crouched before a fire. As I flew in closer, I saw that it was a man dressed in Caster leathers. He was long-limbed with tousled brown hair and broad shoulders. I wanted to touch the ropes of muscle that wound down his arms.

Wait a minute. Where did that thought come from?

Only Necromancers who'd renounced the faith had the desire for a mate and children. Grand Mistresses weren't supposed to be attracted to the opposite sex at all. I certainly never had been, even before I joined the Zelle.

This man was dangerous. I wanted to fly away from him, but my wings only brought me nearer. Firelight cast deep shadows over the man's rugged face, highlighting his square jawline, light beard, and bright green eyes. He stared into the fire, repeating the words of an incantation.

"I call upon you," he said. The rest of his spell was lost on the wind. A haze of red mist swirled around the ground, the unmistakable sign of a Caster spell. One word carried above the noise. "Viktor."

I gasped. What would this Caster want with the Tsar? The man glanced up, his green eyes looking straight at me.

No, through me.

The man spoke the last words of his incantation—"so mote it

be"—and lowered his head once more. The red mist of his spell disappeared.

After that, the man, desert, and night sky all vanished. I found myself back in my old farmhouse. Now, this dream was familiar territory. I huffed out a relieved breath, knowing that Tristan would be here soon. Our connection was still intact.

My kitchen looked the same, which was even more reassuring. Everything was neat and clean with bare plaster walls and simple wooden furniture. Tristan instantly materialized before the hearth. My soul warmed to see him. Like always, he wore his captain's uniform—a long blue coat with bright copper buttons over short trousers and tall boots. The flames licked around him, close enough to warm him, yet not near enough to burn.

Not yet, anyway.

Gods-damned curse. Every dream started off this way. My friend would look fine and healthy, but all too soon, the flames from the hearth would turn deadly. A bitter taste filled my mouth. This was my friend's afterlife—burning to death, only to regenerate and burn again.

We didn't have long before the fire took hold.

"Elea?" Tristan's voice was low and ragged. "Are you really here?" His once-bright eyes stared blankly across the room.

"Yes, it's me."

The flames from the hearth burned hotter, setting the back of Tristan's coat on fire. On instinct, I reached toward him.

"No," Tristan said. "It's bad enough that I have to suffer. I won't have you burning yourself again." He gritted his teeth against the pain. My hands curled into useless fists. I wanted to take his agony away, but there was only one kind of comfort that I could offer.

"I found the *Master Atlas of Magick*. I'll be with Viktor soon."

His shoulders slumped with relief. "Thank the—"

Suddenly, fire burst from the hearth and enveloped Tristan

whole. Every muscle in my body tightened. Tristan cried out, the pitiful sound slicing through the roaring flames. His flesh melted off in strips, exposing the bone underneath. My eyes stung.

"I'll kill the Tsar, Tristan." I hoped he could still hear me. "You can count on it."

The fire and smoke thickened. Tears streamed down my cheeks as all too soon, Tristan was burned away.

3

I woke up the next morning in my cramped cot. Like most places in the cloister, the Sister's dormitory was a snug and dark space that had been dug out of the mountainside. A single wooden wall blocked out the elements while providing a window-hole for air and light. An external covered stairway connected this place to other rooms in the Zelle.

I rubbed my eyes and tried to get my wits about me again. That dream had been rough.

It was hard to see in the dim light. Still, all the other beds appeared empty. The Sisters must have left for morning spell-work already. My brows lifted with surprise. Most days, I was the first one awake. A gray-haired Sister stepped out of the shadows.

"Ah, you're up," said Sister Constance. She'd once been tall. Now, her shoulders were hunched with age. Her long silver hair hung in a thin sheet over her black robes. Like all the Sisters, she moved and spoke like an emotionless statue come to life.

"I overslept," I said.

"You summoned that Tristan. You shouldn't have tired your-self, today of all days."

The rooms in the Zelle were always chilly. Even so, the temperature seemed to drop another twenty degrees. "Mother Superior told you I was leaving?" I'd hoped to sneak out without any goodbyes. Otherwise, I wasn't sure if I could go.

"We all know," said Constance in her monotone. "We're casting spells for you this morning. Strength and wisdom. I was only to stay until I saw you off." A flicker of sadness tightened her face. "Good luck." For a moment, I thought she might say something more, but she turned on her heel and strode away.

"Thank you." My voice wobbled with emotion. I didn't want to leave my Sisters. They appeared detached and stiff. Underneath that, I knew any one of them would lay down her life for mine.

I watched Constance leave and my heart sank. *Time to kill the Tsar.* I'd dreamed of this morning, expecting it to be a triumphal day where I smiled from ear to ear. After all, I was a Grand Mistress Necromancer now. I'd tracked down the Tsar. I had a fistful of totem rings that were loaded with spells to destroy him.

But actually living this moment? It was a lot harder than I'd expected. What I really wanted to do was crawl under my covers and wait for everything to go away on its own. Maybe someone else would take on Viktor. Maybe my curse would just spontaneously end.

Maybe I needed to get out of bed and kill the man already.

I rose, dressed quickly, and skipped breakfast. My stomach was roiling enough without adding food into the mix. It felt like an especially long walk down the stone hallway that led to the cloister exit. Murals of happy skeletons lined the passage. The figures twirled, sang, and offered silly grins. The afterlife would be fun, or at least, that was how the Zelle saw things. They really were an amazing group.

As I reached the end of the hallway, the floor became slick with snow. My thin sandals slipped on the ice, and I tried not to think of it as a bad omen. Was my mission about to fall out from under me as well?

Focus on your task. One step at a time.

The passage ended in a ledge that jutted onto the exposed mountainside. Snow crunched under my feet. I stepped out and glanced up. A network of wooden stairways wound up the mountain's face. The soft voices of my Sisters filled the air. They were well into their morning spells now. Part of me wanted to race back and join them.

I turned around instead. Below me, a steep staircase zigzagged down the mountainside, the stone steps glistening in the sun. Not good. I'd forgotten how icy things got this time of year.

Why had I told Petra not to cancel morning spells again?

Oh, yes. I hadn't wanted to upset my Sisters further. I also didn't want my transport spell colliding with their magick, so there was nothing left for it than to walk down the freezing mountain. I debated going back for my furs, but worried that I wouldn't be able to leave the dormitory again if I did. Straightening my shoulders, I began the long climb down.

It was late morning by the time I reached the final flight of stairs. My teeth were chattering so hard my jaw hurt from the strain. Ice clung to my hair and made my eyelashes stick together. For the hundredth time, I considered casting a warming spell and decided against it. I'd never transported so far away from the Zelle before. I needed to conserve all my power for that incantation.

At last, I reached the final step. A small field of snow separated the staircase from the cloister's boundary line, which was a low stone wall covered in more painted murals. The tall and leafless trees of the Frost Forest stood a short distance away.

I made it.

Shivering from cold, I looked back up at the mountain. The Zelle was more than a league away from me now. That was more than enough distance to safely cast. Excitement warmed my soul.

I was about to truly begin my mission.

A little voice inside my head said I might only be making my situation worse. If I got caught, who knew what terrors the Tsar would inflict? As much as I wanted to turn back and return to my bed, I had no choice but to move forward. The curse would take hold regardless of what I did, so I refused to stand still and wait for it.

You can do this.

Lifting my left arm, I pulled Necromancer power into my body. The energy wanted to buck and reel through me. Even so, I concentrated it into my hand until the bones there shone blue. I spoke the transport spell from the atlas.

> *The greatest cloister of all*
> *Jewel of the Endlos desert*
> *Center of sunlight and sacred learning.*

I paused the incantation, giving the spell time to take hold. A blue haze formed around my feet. Perfect. All I had to do was recite the last lines, and I'd be off.

> *Sire of Souls, I call upon thee*
> *Transport me to—*

Suddenly, a red mist appeared on the snow. I blinked hard, not believing what I saw. Caster magick. Alarm rattled down my spine. This was why I'd hiked away from the Zelle in the first place. With this foreign magick in the mix, my spell could get ruined or worse.

I needed to end this incantation. Now.

Lowering my arm, I tried to cut off the power to my spell. It was too late. I was already being dragged in a new direction.

Darkness and pain enveloped me. It felt as if my body were being yanked in a hundred directions at once. Every joint and muscle was pulled to its limit. I tried to scream. No sound came out. At last, I was solid and standing on my own two feet. Every inch of me felt strained and boneless. I leaned over, balancing my hands on my knees, and gasped for air. What a mess. A full minute passed before I recovered enough to look around.

I scanned the horizon once. Twice. Nothing but sand and sunshine in every direction. The Midnight Cloister was nowhere to be seen. For a long moment, I stood stock-still as my black robes fluttered around me and the truth became clear.

My spell got thrown off. Gods-damn it.

A figure used magick to materialize nearby—a hulking man dressed in fitted brown leathers, which was the classic look for a Caster. Plus, he was positively bristling with their traditional weapons. Daggers were holstered onto his thighs. A pair of short-swords was strapped to his back. His face was rugged and surprisingly familiar. Brown hair, broad shoulders, and green eyes… I'd seen this man before.

He was the Caster from my dream. If this man's incantation were focused on finding the Tsar, then our magick could have crossed paths and thrown my spell off. Who knew how far I was from the Midnight Cloister. This was a delay I didn't need and couldn't repeat. I marched toward my unwelcome guest. "Hey, you!"

"Hail and well met." His deep voice rumbled over the sands. "I'm Rowan."

I stopped an arm's length away. "Elea."

"Your transport spell caught with mine, Necromancer." The way he said the word Necromancer, I might as well be dripping with the plague. "Why did Viktor send you?"

It was an effort to keep my voice low and features calm. Of all the people in the realm, I would never help Viktor. "It's not your place to question me, Caster. I'm going to transport away. This time, you won't interfere. Do you understand?"

"If you're an agent of Viktor's, then I'm not allowing you to go anywhere until you explain yourself."

After five years of monotones, his voice sounded positively wild with inflection. It made me even more anxious to leave this man behind. "I don't have time for your nonsense. I'm going and unless you want to eat a fireball, you won't stop me."

I lifted my left arm and pulled in some magick. My body still felt shredded from the last trip, but I had to risk it. I had to transport to the Midnight Cloister right away. Energy streamed into my torso. My limbs shook.

Quick as a heartbeat, Rowan stepped forward and grabbed my wrist. How dare he? Anger made my vision collapse until all I could see were his determined green eyes. This man had a lesson to learn.

Well, I warned him.

I started the incantation for a fireball spell. My bones glowed blue with power. Rowan began some kind of counter spell. I didn't recognize the words. Still, there was no mistaking the surge of foreign energy that coursed through me. The hold I'd kept on my power shattered. My magick drained away.

I locked gazes with Rowan. Not even Petra had been able to block my spells so well. "You're a gods-damned menace."

"Interesting comment, coming from an agent of the Tsar."

"I am not aligned to Viktor."

"You know how many times I've heard that? Your kind does nothing but lie."

"My kind?" This mindless thug was calling my sweet Sisters a pack of liars? Well, I had more than one way to cast a fireball. One word would launch the magick from my totem ring. It angered me to waste my weapon on some brute in the desert. It might be my only way out of here, though.

I raised my left fist. "Fire!"

Five balls of blue fire shot out from the ring. They slammed into Rowan's chest, knocking him onto his back. Good. I'd feel sorry for the dolt, but he had it coming. They whirled through the air to come around for another pass.

Before I could do anything else, the veins in Rowan's right hand glowed red with Caster power. Giant worms burst from the sand, gulping down my fireballs and then burrowed under the ground once again. I stared in shock. Sure, I knew Casters could control nature. Even so, I'd no idea they could make something strong enough to swallow a fireball.

The next thing I knew, I was pinned to my back with Rowan's bulk on top of me. Panic skittered down my spine. I tried to summon power into my body. I couldn't since his damned counter spell was still in place. With his right arm, Rowan held both my hands above my head. His torso and legs pinned down the rest of me. That got my blood boiling and how.

I writhed and kicked. He was so huge, my movements barely made him shift his weight. "Get off me, you sick son of a bitch!"

"You serve the Tsar, I know it." His left hand gripped the neckline of my robes and tore down. The Sisters had warned me about men like this. Why didn't I transport away the moment I saw him? I'd never so much as kissed a man, and now I'd be ravaged in the desert.

I fought harder, not that it did any good. Well, there were spells that could make him pay, now or later. "Leave me alone or you'll regret it!"

Rowan's warm fingers brushed the bare, smooth skin of my

left shoulder. "You were telling the truth." His eyes widened. "You don't have a mark."

I bucked underneath him. "Of course, I was telling the truth. Get off me or I swear, I *will* find a way to kill you, in this life or the next."

Rowan's voice turned pleading. "I'm so sorry I did that, it's just—"

"I said, off!"

"I'll get up slowly. No need to keep fighting." He gently rolled his massive bulk away. Why would anyone need so many muscles, anyway? It was bad enough the guy could cast like he did. I'd never seen anything like it.

The moment his weight lifted, I hopped to my feet. My throat tightened with rage and hurt. The Zelle worked me hard, sure, but no one had ever raised a hand against me, let alone pinned me down.

This is the big, bad world, Elea. If you're going to kill the Tsar, then you have to get used to such things. Maybe even worse.

With trembling hands, I tried to retie the ribbons on my shoulder. I didn't want to transport to the Midnight Cloister looking like this. A real Grand Mistress never let her robes get messed. But there were too many torn ribbons, and my coordination was shot. I couldn't risk casting a spell to fix my robes when I needed all my strength to transport. I redid my shoulder into some semblance of proper form and then focused my attention on Rowan. "You're a bastard."

His green eyes were filled with regret. "Once again, my heartfelt apologies."

"So you said. I'm casting my spell now. Since I'm not an agent of the Tsar, you're going to leave me alone, right?"

"It's not that simple. You're a Grand Mistress Necromancer. You're the first one I've ever met who isn't a pawn of the Tsar."

His gaze intensified. "There are things you need to understand before you go. We must talk."

"No, I must leave." This conversation was going nowhere. I raised my left hand and started to pull power into me.

He gripped my wrist again and blocked my spell. "I'm sorry, Elea."

"You keep saying that while acting like a fiend."

"I can't let you go. You're about to cast a transport spell to the Midnight Cloister."

"That's rather obvious." Our spells had crossed, meaning we were both headed to the same location. "Why do you care?"

His grip held tight. "You have no idea how rare you are. I doubt there's another independent Grand Mistress Necromancer of your skill left on this continent."

"Still doesn't explain why you're keeping me here."

"Transport to the Midnight Cloister and you'll be dead in an hour."

My eyes narrowed. "Why would you care?"

"I could use your help."

I pulled at the torn fabric on my shoulder. "And attacking me is how you get it?"

"Let's put that behind us." His face turned pleading.

I glared at him. "Let's not."

"I'm offering you a trade. In exchange for your help, I could give you some information. I've been spying on the Midnight Cloister for months. Aren't you at all curious how I know that they'd kill you?"

The thought that the cloister was unsafe had occurred to me before. Why else would the Tsar close off the cloisters and monasteries? I eyed the man warily. Maybe he really did want my help. Not that he'd get it, but I was curious what he knew. A mage of his power could uncover all sorts of things. "What's wrong with the Midnight Cloister?"

"My team and I have been watching the gates all day and night. Young women come in. Old bodies go out."

I was proud of how I controlled my urge to roll my eyes. "Last time I checked, that's how life works."

"It's the same women, Elea. Only, they're aged and dead in a matter of months. The better the mage, the faster they're killed. My spies have only seen one Grand Mistress go in. She lasted less than an hour."

"Why?"

"I don't know. That's why I could use your assistance. We need someone inside the cloister."

I stared pointedly at his hand on my wrist. "If this is how you recruit help, then you're terrible at it."

Rowan released my hand and took a pointed step backward. "The way I've behaved hasn't inspired much confidence, but you *are* about to transport to your death."

"You're right. I have no confidence in what you say."

"Let me prove my honesty to you. There's an oasis near here where my team is camped. The Midnight Cloister has recruiting agents there. Low-level Necromancers, all of them. You can ask them about the Sisters yourself."

I rubbed my neck and thought through my options. *That could work.* I was powerful enough to cast a truth spell on a low-level agent and they'd never guess the difference. And if the Grand Mistresses were being killed at the Midnight Cloister, then I'd need to change my plans. I'd be much better off acting as a Commoner who didn't know magick than arriving in my Sisterly robes.

I needed help and a change of plans. The question remained, though… Was Rowan the one to team up with? Something about him didn't add up. "What's your interest in Viktor?"

The corded muscles in his neck tightened. "The Tsar's been working hybrid magick on my people. Let's just say I want him dead." Based on the determined look on Rowan's face, that was all he'd say on the subject. "And what about you?"

"He cursed me." Someday, I'd be able to say those words without my voice breaking.

"You're one of those, then."

"Yes." Everyone knew about the Tsar and his infamous timed curses.

"How long?"

"Five years." I didn't say that the five years ran out on Sunday. That kind of information would give Rowan too much power over me.

Rowan let out a low whistle. "Viktor must have hated your loved one."

"He did." The Tsar saw it as a comfort to send your loved one to burn with you. The longer the curse, the more he hated those concerned.

Rowan's gaze intensified. "I'm sorry."

"Don't be. I'll kill him before it strikes me down." *Hopefully.*

"So, will you go with me? Meet my team?"

"Not a chance. You're asking me to follow you to an oasis where your people are waiting. I've a better shot to fight you here." I lifted my hand and showed off my totem rings. "I haven't brought out the bad magick yet."

Rowan scrubbed his hands over his face. "You're not making this easy."

"I didn't mean to."

Rowan paced in a circle. Was he about to attack me again? I pulled some magick into my body, just to be safe. Rowan didn't make another assault, though. Whatever he was considering, it had his handsome features hard with worry. At last, he stopped and raked his fingers through his hair. "This will sound crazy."

"That won't be too different from the way you've acted."

Rowan sighed. "Maybe this will convince you anyway. Last night, I prayed to the Sire of Souls for help."

My breath caught. He'd seen me in the dream, too. I kept my features still as stone. "Go on."

Rowan gave me a sad smile. "I warned you it would seem insane. Casters follow the Lady of Creation, but I went out into the desert and prayed to the Sire. I asked him to send someone to help, and I could have sworn I felt him answer that prayer. Elea, I think he sent you to me."

Our gazes locked. I remembered how drawn I'd felt to Rowan in the dream. And then, he'd fought and stopped me. If he were trying to drag me away, he could have done so already.

"I'll tell you something else that's crazy," I said.

His features turned unreadable. "What?"

"I'll go with you to that oasis."

One side of his mouth lifted into a crooked smile. The grin softened his rugged face. "And you'll help me kill the Tsar?"

"It's a little early to say that. Let's meet this agent of yours. If your story is true, then we'll talk some more." My stomach tightened into worried knots.

Please, let trusting this man be a good idea.

With that, we started our long walk toward the western horizon.

hen will this hike be over?

We'd been marching for hours. Why had I thought I could walk across a desert in a black robes? I'd become a hot and sticky mess who refused to waste any magick on spells for comfort. But that wasn't the worst part of all this. My quiet walk had given me time to think… And that was far more painful than the heat.

The past five years had been a whirlwind of action. Every waking hour, I'd trained my powers, loaded spells onto my totem rings, and sought out the Tsar. When I saw Tristan in my dreams, it gave me a frightening preview of my future, but afterward I'd dive right back into work and forget. In all that time, I hadn't really thought about an eternity of being burned alive.

Now, I couldn't stop picturing it. *Pain. Flame. Forever.*

"Lovely sunset," said Rowan, interrupting my thoughts.

"Oh, yes," I said quickly. I'd barely noticed how the sun touched the horizon line as we neared the oasis.

"I thought every woman liked a sunset." He gestured at the red, yellow, and orange painted across the sky.

"Not me." Tonight, the colors reminded me of the shifting shades of the fire that would eternally burn my skin.

This was how the entire walk had gone. Every so often, Rowan would try to make conversation and I'd answer with one or two words. I knew he was trying to make up for tackling me, but I wasn't in the mood.

Finally, we closed in on the oasis. A small forest of palm trees surrounded a still blue pool. Hundreds of tents clustered around one side of the water, while the opposite bank was crammed with a busy market. The low murmur of voices echoed over the sands. It was much larger than I'd expected.

Rowan gently touched my shoulder. I almost jumped out of my skin. "Yes?" My voice came out harsher than I'd like.

"I didn't mean to startle you."

"Don't worry, it's easy to do. I've lived the last half decade in a cloister."

Rowan nodded. "Ah, touch and Necromancers." This time, the word 'Necromancers' didn't have as much hatred tied to it. "My team is over there."

Rowan gestured toward a small group of conical tents by the water. The structures were formed with bent poles, so the shapes swirled upward, reminding me of the twisted spires I'd seen on some churches. Anything curved was a classic design for Casters. Rowan even had swirls embossed along the seams of his jacket.

As we stepped closer to the group, I could feel the protective energy of a magickal ward surrounding the camp. It was some serious spellwork, too. If I hadn't been a Grand Mistress, I might have turned away in fear.

Rowan set his fingers in his mouth and whistled. Two pairs of men and women came out from the tents. I shook my head. These four could've stepped out of an illustration of Casters from one of my library books. The men were bulky and tall, while the ladies were petite and pixie-like. All of them wore brown leathers like Rowan's—fitted pants and a matching jacket. They paused outside their tents and eyed me warily.

Rowan pointed at the four Casters in turn. "This is Flint, Laurel, Orion, and River."

"Pleased to meet you." I noticed that they all held leather helms at their hips. Traditionally, those were only worn when their king was close by. "Is Genesis Rex here?"

The other Casters looked wide-eyed. Rowan seemed to care less. "Why do you ask?"

"You all have your helms." From what I knew of Caster culture, Genesis Rex was a very hands-on ruler, which made him an easy target of assassination attempts. Nothing like leaving your tower to make you a target. The helms were one way to protect him. It was harder to kill the right person when you couldn't see anyone's face.

"Force of habit, I suppose." Rowan leaned in closer and grinned. "And if he were nearby, we certainly couldn't tell you."

"Force of habit, eh? What are you, a member of the Imperial family?" A painfully long silence followed. That intense look returned to Rowan's green eyes. All the other Casters suddenly found other places to focus their gaze.

"You were the one who tackled *me*, Rowan." I pulled on the torn fabric of my shoulder. "A little truth would be welcomed here."

Rowan nodded slowly. "I'm his nephew. Unless Rex has a child, I'm next in line for the throne."

"Oh." I'd never met someone Imperial before. Was I supposed to curtsey or something?

Rowan turned to the other Casters, and I was grateful he ended the awkward moment. "Everyone, this is Elea. She's a Grand Mistress Necromancer and an independent one, too."

Laurel paled. "She is?"

"Are you sure?" asked Orion. "We haven't met one yet, unless you count the corpses."

"That's what I heard." And I'm here to see if it's true.

Rowan scanned the tents. "Where's Jakob?"

"Ale tents," said Orion. "Where else?"

Rowan muttered something under his breath.

"Who's Jakob?" I asked.

"The Necromancer in our number," said Rowan. "We needed a mage who understood Necromancer ways. Jakob is the finest independent we've met."

Interesting choice. Life in a monastery was very different from that in a cloister. The Brothers made us Sisters look like wild women. They had regulations on how you could walk, talk, or even use a chamber pot. "Is that working out?"

"Not well," said Rowan. "Not yet, anyway. Jakob learned magick in a sanctuary fair. His knowledge of cloister life is limited."

I stifled the urge to roll my eyes. A sanctuary fair was hardly a fit training ground for Necromancy. They were places where rogues cast sloppy spells for desperate people. Someone who grew up there would be next to useless in understanding a cloister. "So, where are you getting your intelligence?"

"Most of what we've learned has been from infiltrating the traders who make deliveries to the back gate."

"Which is why you need me."

"Correction. That's why we need you *alive*. But you'll see for yourself soon enough."

I shifted the torn neckline of my Necromancer robes. "I can't see an agent of the Midnight Cloister dressed like this."

"Right. We've all manner of disguises here." Rowan turned to Laurel. "Help get Elea dressed as a Commoner. Then I'll take her to the marketplace."

Laurel jumped forward. After such a long day, she seemed like a chipper blur with her hazel eyes, golden hair, and a bright smile. If dressing Necromancers for market was strange to her, she didn't show it. "Let's get you ready." She reached for my hand. I pulled away quickly.

"Apologies," said Laurel. "I forgot how you Necromancers are."

I hugged my elbows. Back in the cloister, you never made physical contact with another Sister. But being around people who weren't in Necromancer robes? It reminded me of my life back on the farm. Commoners used to give and receive hugs all the time. If I were going to play the part of a Commoner, then I'd have to seem a little less controlled. Laurel might be a good person to practice on.

Laurel gestured toward one of the tents. "In here, when you're ready."

I stepped into a snug space that was filled with waist-high baskets. Laurel followed. "The things in there should fit you." She pointed to one of the baskets, and the motion highlighted a silver ring on her finger. The jewelry seemed like such a normal thing for a Commoner to have. What would a typical girl of my age say to something like that?

"That's a, uh, pretty ring." The moment the words left my mouth, I wanted to pop them back in. Trying to act normal wasn't a good idea for me.

"Thank you." Laurel stared at me expectantly.

I searched for something else to say. "Are you a mage?" Totem rings were the only kinds of bands I knew much about.

"No, it's not that kind of ring." Laurel beamed. "This shows that Orion and I are mated. Our bonding animal was a ladybug." She held out her hand for closer inspection. "See?" She tapped the tiny rock. "The stone is carved into a ladybug shape." Laurel gripped my hand and gasped. "You have rings, too!"

I was very proud of myself for not pulling my arm away. "Yes, I do."

"They're so interesting—silver with little white skulls." She touched them all. "Oh, and the skulls are made from real bone, too. What are your rings for?"

The words fell from my mouth before I could stop them. "Killing people. Well, a person."

"Oh, I..." Laurel kept blinking at me. "Oh."

"But I won't kill you, of course." My cheeks turned red. It served me right for trying to act. "I need to change." Laurel kept staring and blinking. "By myself."

"That's fine." Laurel snapped back into being chipper. She nodded toward the brown basket. "You'll find what you need in there. Do you know what a Commoner dresses like?"

"Very much so."

"I'll leave you to it, then." A few seconds later, the tent flap closed behind her with a swish of fabric. What a disaster. *I'm not playing a normal girl again any time soon.*

I turned my attention to the brown basket and began sifting through its contents. There was a simple green dress that looked like it would fit, along with a pair of matching slippers. I put them on and almost moaned with pleasure. The loose fabric felt so cool and smooth against my skin.

How strange to wear a robe without ties again. On the farm, I'd dressed like this constantly. For the first time in years, it felt like I could really breathe. I hadn't realized how all those ribbons were pulling on me. I slipped my totem rings into my pocket—no need to advertise that I was a Necromancer with my jewelry—and stepped back outside.

Rowan looked me over from head to toe. His expression was unreadable. The man was as bad as Petra.

"What? Don't I look like a Commoner?"

"You look fine." I thought I saw an odd heat in his eyes, but it disappeared too quickly to be certain. Perhaps I'd imagined it. "We need to get going."

"I couldn't agree more. Where are the agents?"

"In the marketplace. This way."

We stepped along the edge of the pool and through more clusters of tents. Most were tall and elaborate constructions made of heavy tapestry and covered in gaudy colors. Royals. I choked on the heavy perfume wafting out of each one.

Soon, we left the Royal tents behind for the busy marketplace. The scent of burned meat and unwashed bodies hung in the air. The place was a warren of cramped streets and simple tent-like stalls. Some were nothing more than four tall poles with fabric tied between them. Simple wooden tables were piled high with exotic fruits. Other stalls were strung across with ribbons, cloth, or strips of drying meat.

And the people. I'd never seen such a crowd. Strange faces were everywhere. Now, I understood how a jackrabbit felt in a snare. I wanted to run away. The press of the mob only held me more tightly in place.

Rowan touched my shoulder again. "You all right?" he asked.

I didn't jump as much this time. "I think so. This is…" It was an effort to organize my thoughts. "Unusual for me." I scanned the crowd and the stalls. "I don't see any Necromancers."

"You have to know where to look." Rowan nodded toward a far corner. "That's her."

I shot a discrete glance over my shoulder. A woman sat at the end of a cramped row. Her rug was covered in large, empty-looking bowls. Unlike the other stalls, hers seemed pretty bare. There weren't even any poles draped with fabric to block the sun.

I turned to Rowan. "She's dressed like a Necromancer, but there isn't a banner or statue to the Sire of Souls. Most agents have those."

"She's not that kind of agent, Elea. Her recruits aren't willing. Who would volunteer to become old and dead?"

"We'll see." I hope you're wrong.

"What's your plan?" asked Rowan.

"I approach her, play the Commoner with untrained powers, and then cast a truth spell or compulsion. Based on her robes, she looks like an Apprentice-level mage. She shouldn't be able to detect a thing."

"I'll stay here." Rowan folded his arms across his chest and frowned. Something was upsetting him. I didn't have time to find out what. "Be safe."

"Thank you."

As I approached the stall, I couldn't miss how the woman reminded me of Tristan with her elegant bearing, high cheekbones, and pale skin. Close-up, I found that her bowls were half-filled with fruits, nuts, and dried meats. There were no sacks of dried marrow for making pudding, though. That was odd. Strict Necromancers only ate the nourishing gel made from bones.

"Hungry, sweetling?" The woman had a lovely alto voice. "Come get something from Hestia."

My stomach rumbled in reply. Buying food seemed as good a way as any to start a conversation. "The dates look delicious, but I've no coin. May I work in exchange?"

Hestia looked up at me through long lashes. "Depends what you can do."

I crouched over and spoke in a whisper. "I can turn milk sour. You know. If you have any enemies you want to harass." This story was true enough. When I was five, I'd soured all the milk on the farm by mistake. That was when Rosie knew I'd inherited my parents' magick.

"No one keeps milk at the oasis." She pursed her full lips. "But you may have some magick, so I could find another use for you."

My jaw fell open in pretend shock. Hopefully, I didn't overdo the emotion. It wasn't like we had acting classes at the cloister. "You think I might have real magick?"

"I wouldn't be surprised." She patted my hand. I took that as a sign that my ruse was working.

"I can't believe it."

Hestia waved to a small boy. "Go tell your uncle that this nice young lady deserves some of our best dried yak."

The boy bowed at the waist and then ran off.

Hestia patted the spot beside her. "Come, sit for a spell while we wait for my brother. Tell me more about yourself. What other strange things can you do?"

I sat down and fidgeted on the blanket. "This will sound silly."

Hestia's voice turned silky. "Not to me."

"Sometimes, I can feel my bones move inside me." It was another thing I'd complained about to Rosie, back when I was six.

A hungry look twisted her pretty face. The muscles in my neck tightened with alarm. I was back to feeling like that jackrabbit again, and this woman was trying to pull me into a trap. "How much does it hurt?" she asked.

"Only a twinge now and then."

"Well, that doesn't sound silly at all. Have you ever thought of joining a cloister? You could get trained properly."

I slipped my hand into my pocket and set it against my thigh. I couldn't speak an incantation, so I'd need to cast by focusing power in my palm. That meant a small flash of light, which could give me away. But by setting my hand against my skin, Hestia shouldn't see anything. "I'm not so sure about that."

"Why not?"

"I've heard stories." A second later, my palm flared against my thigh and my spell was cast. Hestia didn't so much as glance at my arm. *So far, so good.* "They say Necromancers disappear from the Midnight Cloister. Grand Mistresses and everything."

"Whatever gave you that idea?" As the spell took hold, I could see Hestia's soul separate from her body. A transparent blue version of her became an exact overlay on her mortal form. It was a sight that only I could see. *Perfect.* While the body could lie, the soul could not.

I leaned in closer. "I heard they go in young and alive, but they come right back out, only they're old and dead. Is that the truth?"

Hestia spoke one word. "No."

At the same time, her soul mouthed 'yes.'

All of a sudden, I couldn't pull enough air into my lungs. Rowan was right. Sisters were being murdered. I couldn't walk in as a Grand Mistress and hope to live long enough to kill the Tsar. My only chance was to enter as a recruit. And since Rowan was telling the truth, it wouldn't hurt to have him as an ally. We needed to talk.

Hestia set her hand on her chest. "Are you all right, sweetling?"

"I'm fine. I was just wondering how one might join a cloister."

She tilted her head and her long black hair fell in a neat curtain over her shoulder. "Well, I happen to know the Mother Superior at the Midnight Cloister. I could take you there, if you'd like to look around."

"Perhaps. I need to think about it first." *And make a plan with Rowan.*

"Don't wait too long. We leave tonight, sweetling." Something in Hestia's eyes reminded me of the foxes that circled my old henhouse.

She'd take me there, but only as a prisoner. Maybe there were better options. Every agent couldn't be as foul as this one.

"I don't know if I can make a decision so quickly. If I miss you tonight, are there others who could take me?" *Please let there be others.*

"No. I'm your only way. I'm what you call their exclusive

agent. Every so often, another Necromancer tries to step in. They don't last long." Her soul said the very same things as her body. Even so, the spirit's eyes glinted with evil as she spoke the words about other agents not lasting. No doubt they ended up as dead as the Grand Mistresses.

"Ah. Thank you for telling me. I'll return before you know it." I slowly rose and backed away, careful to keep my eyes on her. I'd seen enough predators to realize that running away was the worst thing I could do.

Once I was deep into the crowd, a heavy hand wrapped around my right wrist. *Hestia had sent someone after me already.* On instinct, I began the words for a bone melter spell. Another magick blocked mine.

"Wait, Elea. You can't cast here."

I exhaled. "Rowan."

He scanned my face carefully. "Are you all right?"

"Fine." I guided us to a secluded spot between tents, taking us out of Hestia's line of vision. "I spoke with her."

"And?"

"You were right. She's an agent of the Midnight Cloister, and they *are* killing Sisters there. They're definitely kidnapping girls and she wants to take me tonight." I laced my fingers behind my neck. "We need a plan and quickly."

"Let's talk back at camp. That place is well warded." He angled his huge frame to block my view of the market. "Look over my right shoulder. Be careful not to be seen."

I moved onto my tiptoes and peeped past Rowan. A huge man with a bald head, round belly, and tanned skin pushed through the crowd. He was wearing the black robes of an Apprentice Necromancer.

"The woman said she was calling her brother." I stepped out of view. "That's him, I'll bet. He's coming for me."

"Her type doesn't take chances. She gets paid for every Novice that she brings through the door." His gaze intensified once more. "Are you sure you want to enter the Midnight Cloister this way?"

"Absolutely." *Maybe.*

A muscle ticked along his jaw. "No need to decide right now. As long as you stay in this oasis, they'll find you."

I hugged my elbows. They'd find me and then...

Rowan leaned in closer. "Elea, look at me."

I forced my gaze to meet his. His eyes burned with an intensity that I'd never seen before. "This doesn't have to be your fate. You have a choice."

Images flashed through my mind. Tristan standing in my dreams. His skin burning down to the bone. The screams from his deathbed. Those terrible words.

You're next.

There'd never been a choice for me. "I must kill Viktor. There may never be another chance like this."

"You don't know that."

"Yes, I do. My curse runs out on Sunday, Rowan."

Rowan's features softened. "I'm so sorry."

"Not as sorry as I am."

"Let's discuss this at the campsite. They'll have a hot meal ready for us by now."

I let out a ragged breath. "I'd like that."

Rowan scanned the marketplace. "The man has left." He stepped away and motioned for me to follow. "The other Casters are excited to spend time with you, by the way. They haven't met many independent Necromancers who aren't—" He bobbed his head, searching for words.

"Dead?"

He chuckled. "That's it."

I'd never heard him laugh. It was a deep and rolling sound that I liked very much. "Your mood has lightened."

"Was I in a stern mood?" He raised his brows. "Me?"

"Oh, yes. Constantly, but particularly once we reached the market."

"I suppose I was worried."

"You're over six feet tall and large as a barn. Plus, you can cast spells that affect me, so you're strong in magick as well. I can't imagine what you'd have to worry about."

"I wasn't worried for myself, Elea."

The impact of his words seeped in. He was worried about me. The realization made my chest warm in an unusual way.

What? A Grand Mistress getting all warm and emotional? That only led to trouble.

I straightened my shoulders. Rowan may be able to help my mission, but I had to be careful around him. If he made me stray from my learning, I'd end up worse than dead.

*R*owan and I closed in on the Caster camp just as the first stars appeared in the sky. Already, the air was starting to cool. His team sat around a small fire, roasting meat on skewers. Bits of their traditional armor—full helms and shields—lay around them. Laurel rushed up to meet us.

She was smiling so hard I thought her face might split. "How was the market?"

Laurel was also standing awfully close again. I took a half step backward. "It went well, thank you."

Rowan stepped between us, making a nice barrier. "We can discuss the market later. Elea needs to eat."

My brows lifted. I wasn't used to people telling me when to eat. Or rather, I was used to the telling part… Not to actually listening. I was about to say that, but Rowan started examining each skewer of meat over the fire, searching out the best bites for me. This wasn't like Mother Superior ordering me around in never-ending lessons. Rowan was treating me as his revered guest. I worked hard to ignore how nice his attention felt.

Rowan finally plucked a stick from the fire and handed it over. "How's this?"

A mouth-watering smell wafted through the air. My stomach rumbled. "Thank you." Taking the skewer from Rowan, I sat down beside him and took a bite. I'd never tasted anything so tangy and delicious. I wasn't sure I could look at another bowl of nasty marrow pudding.

A tent flap opened and another man stepped into the firelight. He wore Caster leathers, but had the lean frame, shorter height, and darker coloring of a Necromancer. He stilled when saw me. The fire cast dark shadows on the elegant lines of his face.

"Why's she here?" His words were a bit slurred. Clearly, this was Jakob, the man who'd been in the ale tents. He was stinking drunk. *And he called himself a Necromancer? What of his control?*

"She's my guest." Rowan's no-nonsense tone said that was the end of the discussion.

Jakob plunked down by the fire. "Is this the same one Laurel dressed up?"

My eyes narrowed. Dressed up? I'm not a doll, thank you very much.

"Quiet, Jakob," said Laurel.

"So, *it is* the same one. How many Necromancers do you need to talk to before you believe me? They're all useless."

I was rapidly starting to dislike Jakob. "I'm not an 'it.'"

He ignored me, which made my blood heat up even faster. "Well, Rowan?" asked Jakob.

"Elea is an independent Necromancer who cast a transport spell from the eastern steppe."

The other four exchanged looks of disbelief.

"Impossible," said Laurel.

"You're the only mage powerful enough to do that," added Orion.

"And she's a woman," said Flint.

"You think female mages are weaker?" I asked. Everyone nodded except for Rowan. I shook my head. I'd read that Casters didn't have many women mages, but I had no idea it was like this.

Jakob turned to Rowan. "So, what do you want with this one?"

"*This one* is right beside you," I said. "And I'll discuss my plans with Rowan, and Rowan alone."

Jakob narrowed his bloodshot eyes. "I'm Rowan's right-hand man."

I glared right back at him. "Clearly, the team needs improving."

"And that will be you, eh?" Jakob looked me over from head to toe. Twice. His mouth wound into a wicked smile. Right. One of the grain merchants I'd traded with had loved this tactic. Leer at the girl and get her flustered. That wouldn't work on me.

"You're quite pretty, you know that?" asked Jakob. The Caster ladies groaned and rolled their eyes. "In fact, you're the first pretty mage we've met who isn't the Tsar's pawn. You're what, twenty or so?"

Rowan's voice lowered. "Leave her be."

"Maybe she doesn't want to *be* alone." Jakob leaned in closer. "You got yourself a man?"

I stared at the flames and kept my features level. I wouldn't acknowledge such a question. It broke about ten different Necromancer customs even to ask it.

"I can see the answer for myself." Jakob pointed to my right ring finger. "You *do* have a man. And since he's not here, I'm thinking he left you high and dry. What a shame."

I shot him a cold look. "Why don't you sober up?" My words were meant to be tough, but my voice wavered with pain. *Damn.* Never show a bully your weak spot. I might as well have offered a raw side of beef to a wolf.

Jakob grinned. "Why don't *you* answer my question about that man of yours?"

"I have nothing to say to you." My voice was calm this time. Even so, the damage was already done.

"Knew it!" Jakob pointed directly at my nose. "You're holding back on us." He rose to loom over me. "I heard how you were snooping around. Asking questions about Genesis Rex."

Snooping? I'd merely asked Rowan an honest question. Still, I wasn't going to play this game. Jakob was baiting me to fight. "I won't justify myself to you."

"You're really in league with the Tsar, aren't you? Say it!"

I rose so we stood toe to toe. All Petra's warnings about emotion vanished. I raised my right fist to show off my betrothal ring. "The man who gave me this is dead. Viktor cursed both him and me. Now, he suffers in flame and unless I kill Viktor, then I'll die, too. Does that satisfy your curiosity?" I turned to Rowan. "Him or me. One of us leaves."

"What?" Jakob spread out his arms. "What did I do?"

"What you always do," mumbled River.

"That's quite enough," said Rowan. "Everyone, take Jakob for a walk. Elea and I have things to discuss."

Jakob groaned. "But, Rowan—"

Rowan rose to his full height and yanked Jakob up by his collar. "Walk it off. I mean it. This is my last warning."

Jakob's head wobbled as he tried to meet Rowan's gaze. "But you need me."

"Not enough for this." Rowan tossed Jakob to the other Casters, who bolstered him off into the night.

Once they were gone, I sat down and hugged my elbows for warmth. When had it gotten so cold? Rowan wrapped a soft blanket around my shoulders and seated himself beside me. "I'm sorry for how he acted. I should have stepped in earlier. Trouble is, we need a Necromancer for our plan. He's the best one we've met so far, except for you."

"It's fine." Except that it wasn't.

"I don't believe you."

I stared off into the darkness where Jakob had disappeared. *What a mess of a man.* That said, I had bigger things to worry about than a drunk. "Believe it. You and I are here because we have the same goal. Kill the Tsar. That's it. I don't want Jakob to distract us."

Rowan stared into the fire for a long time. His face turned immobile as stone. "True."

"Good." It didn't feel good, though, which was ridiculous. I still wanted to throttle Jakob with my bare hands. And I couldn't stop wondering why that Necromancer was here. Jakob didn't know what happened inside a cloister. I stared into the flames and thought of Petra's final words. "Hybrid magick. That's why Jakob's really here, isn't it?"

Rowan nodded. "Viktor's developed special weapons." Rowan pulled a dagger from the holster on his thigh. "Viktor made this. We found it in my homeland. It will cut through anything, including enchanted armor. We've nothing to stop it. The same goes for Viktor's magick. His incantations are immune to counter spells."

Rowan handed the dagger to me and I turned it over. The blade had the look of whittled bone. "This is a Necromancer weapon."

"Look more closely."

I angled the dagger into the firelight. A delicate pattern of snake scales covered the blade. The small hairs on my neck bristled. "This has a protective Caster skin. I've heard about weapons like this."

From Petra. Viktor had used something like this to torture her.

The blade's handle vibrated softly in my hands. I'd felt this before, when I was replacing beams in the barn. "This has a jump mite inside it."

Rowan raised his brows. "How'd you guess?"

"I grew up on a farm." And too many jump mites can literally bring down the roof.

"This one has glowing red legs and a bony outer shell."

Glowing red meant Caster magick, while a bony outer shell indicated Necromancer spellwork. "So, hybrid magick."

"That's the key to Viktor's most powerful spells."

I ran my fingertip along the flat of the blade. "Necromancer magick is singular. It should be impossible to layer Caster skin on top, let alone to place a hybrid animal inside. What happens when you remove the mite?"

"Nothing, as far as we can tell."

That didn't seem right. Viktor must use the animals for a purpose. "And has Jakob created anything like this?"

"Not yet. We've tried hundreds of animals. Jakob tries to push in Necromancer magick while I use Caster power. Nothing has worked."

I tapped my chin. "But that's with animals that haven't been touched by magick, right?" Rowan nodded. "Have you tried pushing more power into the mite?"

"Many times. Nothing happened."

I frowned. The longer I held this dagger, the more its magick called to me. My own power responded. The desire to press my magick into the weapon became strong.

This had to mean something. Why else would it call to me?

Only one way to find out. I pulled Necromancer magick into my body, focused it in my left hand, and then pushed the energy toward the blade. A flash of purple light sparked from the weapon. Hybrid magick slammed into me, hard as a fist. I fell backward and dropped the dagger.

For a few long seconds, I could only stare at the play of stars overhead. The back of my skull ached. Before I knew what was happening, Rowan scooped me up and pressed me against his side. It must have been the shock of the magick, because his touch felt comforting.

"Are you all right?" he asked.

I leaned into the warmth of his shoulder. It seemed to have been made to cradle my cheek. I forced my breathing to slow. "I'm fine."

"What happened?"

"I tried pushing my power into the mite. The hybrid magick pushed back at me."

"Like a rush?"

"No, it wasn't fluid at all. Normally, when I cast, the energy flows."

"That's how it acts for me, too." He moved his thumb in small arcs on my shoulder. I tried to convince myself that I hated it.

"When our spells crossed, I felt that same fluidity from your magick, as well."

He nodded toward the dagger. "And that?"

"It was like being hit with a stone wall of power. Necro-mancer power doesn't act that way. Has that ever happened to Casters?"

"No. I've never heard of anything like it." Rowan stared into the fire as if the solution were written in the flames. "Are you recovered enough? Do you mind if I try?"

"Go ahead."

Rowan shifted so he no longer held me. My body chilled without his touch.

Must be the night air.

Rowan rested the dagger on his opened palms and began a formal incantation. The veins in his right hand glowed red as a crimson-colored mist appeared on the ground. Rowan stood as he pushed more energy into the spell. I'd read that Casters often did energy transfer spells like this.

Contain my power.
Hold my soul.
Consume my light.

Caster spells were never very wordy. Rowan kept repeating the spell, but no matter how much energy he summoned, there was no flash of purple light. No wallop of magickal force. The weapon didn't react to him at all.

A weight of worry seeped into my bones. Why would I be affected by the dagger while Rowan and Jakob weren't? Had I become somehow aligned with the Tsar without knowing?

Rowan stopped his incantation and tossed the dagger onto the sand. "Nothing."

Firelight flickered across the blade. This was beyond strange. "Do you think it's my curse?"

"Possible."

I'd seen bone daggers before. This one looked and felt strange. I remembered our conversation when we first met. "If that's what Viktor's doing with weapons, what's he doing to your people?"

The lines of Rowan's face became hard and firm. I had the crazy urge to reach out and brush the back of my fingers along his cheek, just like I used to do with Tristan. I picked up the dagger instead. "I know this is hard, Rowan, but for our plan to succeed, I need to understand everything I can about Viktor."

Rowan gave me the barest of nods. "That knife was transformed with Caster and Necromancer power." A muscle ticked along his jaw. "Viktor did the same to my people."

A chill of worry crawled up my neck. "I don't understand."

"Casters can create animals with magick. The ones we pour the most power into become our familiars."

"Those can take your power when you die, right?"

"Yes. Mine are a pair of snow tigers, Radi and Umeme." His features softened a little. "Viktor uses a Caster's familiars against them. Some years ago, he began kidnapping our mages and their familiars."

"I heard about the kidnapping part." *From Petra.*

"Their stories all ended the same. They were brought into his study under a blinding spell. A few days later, they woke up changed. If the Caster's familiar was a wolf, then the Caster might wake to find her hands had been replaced with that animal's paws."

How horrible. I'd loved all the animals on Braddock Farm. It broke my heart to take any of them to market, and I hadn't even made those creatures. Even so, that was just the beginning of this horror. "I can't imagine waking up to find a body part—" I couldn't finish. It was just too awful. "The people Viktor changes—"

"The Changed Ones. That's what they call themselves."

"So he murders their familiars and combines them. Why? Aren't they strong Casters?"

"Because the Changed Ones have teeth and claws just like that dagger. Unstoppable."

"Wouldn't the Changed Ones just attack Viktor?"

"The magick won't let them turn on their creator. They won't fight on his command, though. Viktor tried to brainwash the Changed Ones, but my people are tough. Eventually, they fight back. Caster power rebels against being controlled."

"And Necromancer energy thrives on it." My eyes widened. "He's looking for some way to use Necromancer magick to control the Changed Ones."

Rowan shook his head. "I wish I had you on my team months ago. You wouldn't believe how long it took us to figure that out. You got it in less than a day."

His praise made me feel like the cleverest Necromancer in the realm, so I kept right on going. "Let me guess. Five years ago, Viktor left your continent. He stopped abducting Casters and running his experiments. Instead, he came here to work on the next phase of his plan... Getting the Changed Ones to do his bidding. That's when Viktor killed the old Tsar."

Rowan nodded. "After Viktor left, we tried to move on and heal our people. Then, a few years ago, one of our seers saw that Viktor remained a threat. I was sent here to investigate."

"You're an awfully high-ranking man to send."

"Viktor went after all our top mages." A long silence passed before Rowan spoke again. "I'm one of the few mages who still looks like a man, Elea. The rest of my party are all warriors, not magick users."

Oh, no. I hugged my elbows. "I'm sorry."

"We all have our troubles." He poked at the fire with a stick and sent tiny embers flying up into the night sky. "Not all my top mages are accounted for. I'd been hoping to find some of our lost Changed Ones on this continent. But we haven't had any luck yet."

"The easiest place to keep them would be at a cloister or monastery."

He offered me a sad smile. "Something for you to investigate in your spare time. See if any of my Changed Ones are at the Midnight Cloister."

"I'll try." I picked up the dagger and flipped it from hand to hand. The thing was so light and innocent-looking to pack such a magickal wallop. This kind of power wouldn't be easy to go up against. I pictured the totem rings in my pocket and frowned. "Viktor will have weapons like this one on Sunday, won't he?"

"Yes. And there's no way to block that blade, let alone break it."

"We need hybrid weapons, then." And I didn't feel confident that Jakob would come up with anything soon. There had to be another way. "I take it you've visited the sanctuary fairs."

"My agents have contacted some Necromancers who may be able to help us."

"Who?" I thought through the most powerful Necromancers in the realm. "Mother Starlight? The Monk of Longmeadow?"

"Ocie and Yuri."

I almost dropped the dagger, I was so shocked. According to the stories, Ocie and Yuri were mages, a man and a woman, and they wielded unbelievable power. Hybrid spells should be no problem, assuming Ocie and Yuri actually existed. But no one thought they existed.

I certainly had my doubts. "That's your plan? I hate to tell you this, but those two are stories for children."

"All stories start somewhere."

"They supposedly live on a magickal plane that's gated from this reality. That's pretty outrageous stuff."

"Ocie and Yuri are real." Rowan was using his 'no discussion' tone again. "They made contact with Jakob two weeks ago."

Sure, they did. Jakob must have been pretty drunk to dream that up, but I didn't want to push the point with Rowan.

"Ocie and Yuri want to help us," Rowan went on. "But they have conditions. I expect to find out what those are soon. Trust me, they'll make contact again, and when they do, they'll give us the hybrid magick we need to fight the Tsar."

I scratched my head. Rowan's plan sounded like nonsense. That said, it wasn't as if my original plan was all that solid. I needed a new approach as well.

"How about you?" asked Rowan. "What are you thinking now that you know how Grand Mistresses are greeted at the cloister?"

"I'm still planning to pretend to be a Commoner with untested powers. That agent will take me to the Midnight Cloister fast enough."

"And what will you do on Sunday?"

Is he kidding? "Kill the Tsar."

"Assuming I can find you a weapon."

"I understand what we're up against with the hybrid magick." I pulled the totem rings out of my pocket. "But these are charged with spells and ready to go. I'll have the element of surprise on my side. With any luck, I'll kill Viktor before he has a chance to fight."

"If anyone can do it, you can."

"Thank you." I hated the blush that heated my cheeks. "We'll need a means to communicate once I'm inside. What level Necromancer is Jakob?"

"Master, more or less."

"Then, he can help us." I pulled off my betrothal ring. "This has a joy spell on it from Tristan. Jakob can use it to track down his magickal signature. That signature will be activated when Tristan and I communicate through our shared curse. When that happens, Jakob can join in and talk with me as well."

"Aren't the cloisters warded to block outside magick?"

"Our curse is Viktor's own magick, so it shouldn't be affected by his wards. Just tell Jakob that we need to communicate through a dream on Wednesday at midnight. He'll know what to do." I set my hand in my pocket and gripped my totem rings. "Is it a plan?"

Rowan nodded toward my hand. "What about those?"

I stilled. "Those what?"

"Your totem rings. What are the chances they'll let you keep them after you arrive at the Midnight Cloister?"

"I was planning to hide them in my hair." This was something I'd been thinking about. The plan didn't sound as fine when I said it aloud, though.

"All five?" He shook his head. "If they find them, they'll know you for a Grand Mistress. You won't live long."

"I'll be fine. They may not even inspect me."

Rowan's face lit up with indignation. "I don't like this. You'll be acting all alone."

"The Sisters at my old cloister were elderly. They trained me as best they could, but they couldn't offer any help. I'm used to being alone."

"That's not what I meant." Our gazes locked. "I'm here now."

"But... I barely know you."

"You can trust me. I proved it to you at the marketplace."

"That was one time, Rowan."

"Let me put it to you another way." He leaned in closer. "When you first looked at me, I could have sworn you recognized me."

That's because I did. The dream. Damn, I hadn't thought he noticed that.

I cleared my throat and stalled for time. "I have no idea what you're talking about."

"Don't lie, Elea." He gave me a lopsided grin that warmed me to my toes. "You're terrible at it, you know."

I couldn't help but chuckle. "Fine. Yes, I did recognize you."

"The Sire of Souls showed me to you, didn't he?"

I nodded.

"So I'll ask you again. What's really holding you back?" Rowan set his hand on my shoulder and I didn't pull away. "Take my help. The Sire and Lady want us to work together, and I want it, too. I believe this to the marrow of my bones... I can't defeat Viktor without you. And it won't work if you're an aloof mage who keeps running her own plans. I want you as a true partner."

The words affected me like magick. My pulse sped at the thought of having someone who really was at my back.

Yes, I want that, too.

Bit by bit, I reached into my pocket and pulled out my totem rings. The skull patterns were familiar as friends. The fireball totem was empty since I'd used its magick up on Rowan, so I quickly loaded it with a spell to break enchanted bindings. If Rowan was right, I was certain to be bound with manacles.

A long silence followed. Rowan watched me with intense interest. I clenched my hand into a fist around my rings. Was I really going to give these to an almost stranger? My hand didn't want to open. "If I give these to you, how will you get them back to me?"

"My agents have infiltrated the traders who bring deliveries to the back gate. We'll hide them in a package."

"You might try a shipment of Grand Mistress robes. They won't be used, but they won't be refused, either. And in my cloister, we all had access to the cloak room."

"Consider it done."

My hand still wouldn't move. Why did this have to be so hard? Finally, I forced my arm forward and gently set the rings onto Rowan's outstretched palm. My hand felt so empty without them. "I worked five years on those rings."

Rowan held them against his chest. "I'll guard them with my life."

"All right." *Hopefully.*

"Do you need to take a break?" asked Rowan. "There's more to eat, if you like."

"No. We should focus on planning." I straightened my shoulders. "How will you get inside the cloister?"

I can't believe I said that out loud. Rowan and I were really attacking the Tsar on Sunday. Together.

"The Vicomte is already planning to visit the Midnight Cloister on Sunday, along with the Tsar. The two of them are—"

"Allies, I know."

"Genesis Rex asked for a formal meeting with them both. The reply is due back any day now."

"And if they say no?"

"We'll storm the delivery gate." His gaze met mine, and all the determination in the world was set in his eyes. "Either way, this will be over in one week."

Possibly with me burning in eternal fires.

I hopped to my feet, my limbs buzzing with nervous energy. "Unless there's anything else you can think of, I want to go and get myself abducted. Tomorrow is Tuesday and I need time to look around."

"That's all I can think of. Good luck, Elea." The lines of Rowan's face became hard. I'd seen that look before—he was worried about me. I wanted to shake his hand or even worse, share an embrace.

Don't Elea. Now most of all, you need to stay in control.

I forced my face into a mask of calm. "And good luck to you as well." With that, I turned on my heel and stepped off into the darkness. I wasn't fifty paces from the campsite when a heavy set of arms wrapped around me from behind, holding me in place. The rough touch made me freeze with surprise.

And so it begins.

6

The man's paunchy belly pressed into my back as his thick fingers dug into my stomach. How I itched to cast a bone melter spell. This fiend could be a pile of gelatinous goo in seconds.

Don't fight it, Elea. You knew they'd do this. It's your best way in.

Still, it was one thing to think about being attacked and dragged away, and another to have whiskey-foul breath oozing down my neck.

Hestia stepped into a patch of moonlight in front of me. "Hello again, sweetling."

I writhed against the man's grip and tried to look like a frightened country girl instead of an enraged Grand Mistress Necromancer. "What's this about?"

Hestia forced on a false smile. "All we want is a friendly chat, now that you're gone from the Casters." The moonlight created a halo of light behind her dark curtain of hair. "We don't want you running away again."

Let her have her say, Elea. Then the goon will let you go.

"Why would I run? I was coming to find you." I blinked a lot, hoping it might help my illusion of frailty.

"Ah, I see." Hestia waved to my captor. "Our error."

The man released me and I quickly stepped closer to Hestia. "I truly wish to join the Midnight Cloister." *And get away from your henchman.*

"Good. There's just one little test we must perform before we go." Hestia pulled back her robes to reveal her left shoulder. The skin there was raised in the shape of a letter V. *The mark.* "You know what this means?"

I guessed this was the part in her little play where I gasped in awe at the symbol of her beloved Tsar. In truth, it might be better for me to grovel, but I wasn't that good an actress.

So, I played the simpleton instead. That much, I could manage. "What *is* that?" I did a lot of squinting. "I can't see in the dark, you know." *And I want a better look at your mark.* I'd never seen one close-up before.

An evil grin rounded Hestia's mouth. "It means that I serve Tsar Viktor the Great. And this mark is how I will test you." She grabbed my wrist and set it against her bare shoulder.

I froze with surprise. This encounter was becoming weirder by the second. "What are you doing?"

"This is the test, sweetling. You may have imagined your powers. It's not worth my time to work with someone with no raw Necromancer energy. The cloister won't accept you." She pressed my fingertips against the V of raised skin. Her flesh was clammy and slick. My stomach roiled. "Give it a moment. I'll soon know the truth."

Please, not the truth. If my real power was exposed, I was good as dead.

Seconds passed as I pictured this situation turning into a disaster. Touching the hybrid magick in Rowan's dagger had ended with a flash of purple light and me blown six feet away. Of course, I'd tried to pump power into the weapon, which I wouldn't do now. Still, who knew what would happen when I interacted with a real mark?

All of a sudden, a wall of magick slammed into me. On reflex, I firmed up my footing. Lucky thing, too. If I hadn't, I might have toppled over. More brick-hard power pummeled into my hand. If I let this go on, there might be another blast of light like earlier. That could expose my true identity.

I yanked my arm back with force. "There, I did it."

Hestia closed her eyes, her nostrils flaring as she inhaled deeply. "Hmm… I can sense the Necromancer power in you. You're strong. The Midnight Cloister will pay well for that." She opened her eyes and glared at me. "You'll have another test when you arrive at the cloister gate. Don't muck it up and try to run away. You'll end up dead and I won't get a farthing."

I fluttered my lashes at her. "I'll do my best. I realize what a great chance this is for a girl like me."

"Quite right." Hestia pulled some loops of metal from the folds of her robes. It took everything I had not to bat them out of her hands.

Enchanted manacles.

"All Novices are required to wear these," continued Hestia. "They're merely a safety precaution." She snapped the thick irons around my wrists.

I'd known this was coming. You don't abduct mages without stifling their powers. Even so, I wasn't prepared for the sensation. The steady flow of soul magick that normally poured into my body evaporated, leaving me feeling hollowed-out and miserable. I hadn't felt such fierce grief since Tristan died.

"She's not taking 'em well," said the man behind me.

"Then, put her to sleep," said Hestia. "She'll journey better that way."

I was wondering what kind of spell they'd use when the man slammed his fist into the back of my head. My skull exploded with pain as the desert night disappeared into perfect darkness.

7

J woke up to a heavy pounding noise. At first, I thought
someone was knocking on a door. Then I realized
that the thumps came from inside my head.

It was my own pulse.

I cracked my eyes open—even that tiny movement hurt—and
I found myself encased in semi-darkness. My eyes slowly
adjusted to the dim light.

I was trapped inside a boxy wagon as it rumbled along an
uneven road. Horses whinnied outside. Inside the stifling-hot
box, my body had turned so sweaty, my back felt stuck to the
wooden wall behind me.

What I wouldn't give for a gulp of water.

Thin tendrils of light peeped through the seams along the
wagon's roof. It was daytime now. *Tuesday, most likely.* The Tsar—
and my curse—arrived on Sunday. And this wagon was taking
me to the Midnight Cloister.

Five days left. I can do this.

I shifted my weight and felt a rope tighten around my waist. I was secured in a line with five other girls, three of us seated on each side. Everyone looked bedraggled and covered in sweat. The wagon hit a deep rut in the road, jostling us off our seats for a moment. One of the girls started pounding on the wood panel that separated us from the driver. She was willowy, about my age, and had blonde curls that cascaded down her back.

"I won't repeat myself again," she said. "I'm Mademoiselle Veronique Adeline Josephine de Haverville. I'm second cousin to the fourth family line of the Vicomte himself. I don't belong here. Release me before you pay the consequences."

Consequences? I was stunned. She was one of the Forgotten and a Royal. The worst she could do was pound on the wall, and she'd done that already.

The other girls took up her cry anyway.

"We're all under her protection," said one.

"Tell him, Veronique," added another.

"You have to set us free," cried a third.

All four girls stared doe-eyed at Veronique, absolutely convinced that she'd soon save them all. I almost felt sorry for them.

Once again, Veronique slammed her palm against the wagon panel behind the driver's head, one pound for every word. "Set! Me! Loose!"

A girl tapped Veronique's arm. "Set *us* loose, you mean."

"That's what I said." Veronique rolled her eyes. "Set us loose."

I slumped further back against the wall. If my plan were to succeed, it'd be good to have allies inside the Midnight Cloister. Veronique wasn't an option, though. She was everything I distrusted when it came to Royals. Whining. Entitled. Not too bright.

Veronique's friends continued to congratulate her for the clever threats against the driver. The girl tied beside me watched the show with interest. She had ebony skin, long braided hair, gold-colored eyes, and an air of confidence despite her ragged dress. She turned and offered me her hand. "I'm Nan."

I shook Nan's hand without so much as a wince. "I'm Elea."

"You all right, Elea? You look like you're about to lose your larder."

"My head's been better. I'll be fine, though."

She lowered her voice. "You know where they're taking us, right?"

"To the Midnight Cloister."

Veronique kicked at the wall behind the driver. "I am one of the Forgotten. You know what that means? I don't have any magick. And more than that, I'm not just a lowly Commoner. You carry a Royal in your carriage. You'll pay for this outrage. Set me loose, I say!"

Nan shot me a sly look. "Right proper ninny, ain't she?"

Veronique rounded on Nan. "How dare you call me names, you gutter wench? I'm the ward of the Vicomte himself. You're nothing more than a street thief and penny whore."

Nan leaned back. "You'd know a whore, I suppose. Heard all about the Vicomte and his wards, I did."

I smiled. Nan seemed cool under pressure and a sharp judge of character. Fine ally material.

Veronique's blue eyes turned wild. She lunged for Nan, but the ropes held her back before she could get too far. Since we were all connected, the movement yanked on everyone else, pinning us against the wall. My back slammed with enough force to knock some air out of my lungs. Everyone wore looks of shock except Nan, who'd had the foresight to lean against the wall in the first place.

I lifted my brows, impressed. "That's quite the trick."

Nan shrugged. "Been trapped in here for a day or so. Not

much else to entertain meself besides finding new ways to stop that one's mouth."

Veronique rolled her eyes, but she did remain quiet.

"Well done," I said.

The ladies huddled together and spoke to Veronique in soothing tones. Nan elbowed me. "I'm looking to escape," she whispered.

I lifted my brows in surprise. "Are you sure we should talk about it here?"

"Ah, once they start cooing at Veronique, they won't hear a thing for ages. Watch." Nan spoke in full voice again. "The Vicomte Gaspard is a fat old blowhard who eats worms and wears ladies under-drawers."

I cupped my hand over my mouth to hide my smile. Veronique and her friends didn't so much as glance in our direction. "Well done, again," I said.

I took a closer look at the woman I'd been tied to. *I can't believe those words came out of her mouth.* Eating worms? Wearing ladies under-drawers? She wasn't even blushing. "You seem rather calm."

Nan shrugged. "Oh, I've been in much worse scrapes. Goes with the territory."

I squinted, like I could see through her words somehow. "Territory? What does that mean?"

"My job, you might say. I find folks like Veronique here—those who have far more money than sense—and then I even things out a bit."

I kept my features still as stone, but on the inside I was jumping with surprise and excitement. "You're really a thief?"

"Cat burglar. I specialize in jewelry."

I angled my body toward her. The rope cut more tightly into my waist. I didn't care. "Have you been in many tough spots?"

"Like this? Oh, sure. Can't tell you how many times I've been bundled up in the back of a sheriff's wagon. I was all set to hang one time, too. Now *that* was a close call."

In my eyes, Nan's ebony face took on a radiance all its own. While I'd spent years poring over books and learning how to focus magick into my pinky, she'd been living free in the city, stealing from fools like Veronique and escaping from one adventure after another. "How wonderful."

The chatter from Veronique started to slow down. Nan leaned in closer, speaking in a voice that only I could hear. "We don't have much longer before they start paying attention again. Here's the thing. I'm not the planning type. More of a foot soldier, if you know what I mean. You've got a clever glint in your eyes, though. What do you say? Interested in teaming up to escape?"

I tapped my chin and considered. I wasn't looking to escape, but I couldn't exactly announce my assassination plans here. Still, I definitely wanted Nan for an ally. "I'm not sure what I can do. How about we agree to watch each other's backs?"

"I like it. Let's make it official." She spat on her hand. "Shake again?"

This was a new level of touching. For Nan, I was ready to try. I spat on my palm and shook. "Deal."

The wagon hit another rut in the road, and I fell backward, slamming my skull against the wood panel behind me. Hurt tore through my head, like a knife plunging into my temple. I leaned over and wrapped my arms around my torso. Nan patted my back. "Are you all right?"

"I'm fine. Just not feeling my best."

"You want me to tell the driver? He's awful obsessed about us not making a mess back here. He'll stop if you tell him you're about to get sick."

"No, I'll be fine. I need some quiet, that's all."

Nan leaned away and gave me some breathing room. I tried to focus past the pain, but I couldn't. No matter how awful I felt now, this was only a sampling of what waited for me on Sunday.

I had to end this curse.

8

The wagon wobbled along for hours before jostling to a rough stop. The driver's gruff voice sounded from outside. "Time to get out and piss, girls."

Nan elbowed my arm. "Got a way with words, don't he?"

"As long as he allows us out, he can say it however he wants." I'd never been afraid of small spaces, but the walls of this wagon seemed to press in closer by the second. Add to that my headache, and I was beyond ready for a breath of fresh air.

The driver stomped around to the back of the wagon and flung the wooden doors open. Blinding light seared into my eyes. I couldn't see the driver yet. Still, I could feel him tugging on the rope tied around my waist.

"Get out, you."

Following his pull, I stumbled too quickly from the wagon. Nan fell along behind me, slammed into my back, and sent both of us tumbling into the driver. Now that I was up close, I could see the man just fine. He was short and paunchy and wore the plain trousers and laced-up shirt of a Commoner. Before I knew what was happening, he'd opened his mouth, stuck out his tongue, and licked my cheek.

I stepped back as far as I could go without pushing Nan over again. *Who licks someone's face?* I'd handled frogs less slimy than that tongue.

My rage got the better of me, and I glared at the driver and plotted revenge. No, I couldn't cast a spell with these manacles on, but that didn't mean I didn't have other options.

"What was that for?" I asked.

"Not supposed to touch the merchandise," he said with a dark chuckle. "But that didn't count." He clicked his tongue at me like I was one of his horses. *Unbelievable.* I half raised my fists, ready to slam my manacles into the side of his head.

"Don't mind him," said Nan quickly. "Just move along."

I forced myself to take in some calming breaths. Remember Sunday and your curse. This driver is your best way into the Midnight Cloister.

The man scratched his dirty cheek and eyed me warily. "You've a sassy mouth. What type of Commoner are you?"

Nan stepped protectively to my side. "She's a thief, like me. We've gutted bigger men than you for a laugh, so watch yourself."

"Sure, you have," said the driver. Still, the words came out as more of a question. He took a step backward and pretended to find the horizon line fascinating.

I liked Nan more by the minute.

The other girls started mumbling behind me, and I realized that I was blocking them from leaving the wagon. I marched forward and scanned the desert around us. Golden sand stretched off in every direction. Not a soul in sight.

"You're not here to enjoy the view," said the driver. "Do your business and get back on the wagon."

Along with everyone else, I started the work of shimmying off my underclothes, hiking up my skirts, and relieving myself on the sand. We were tied in a line, so it made for an odd picture.

The driver watched everything with a level of interest that could only be described as creepy.

"Where's our food and water?" asked one of the girls.

"I'm a driver, not a tavern. You'll be at the cloister in an hour. They can take care of you there."

My heartbeat sped knowing we'd our destination so soon. Five years of work were behind me. An eternity of pain stretched forward as my possible future. Five days remained to fight it. And in only an hour, the real work started.

"Make sure you do your business." The driver sniffed and spat on the ground. A disgusting blob of white goo landed by his boot. "I don't want no piss or puke in my carriage, you hear?"

Nan groaned. "What did I tell you?"

I stared at the nasty little man. "And you were right."

We all shuffled back into the carriage. The driver threaded the rope ends through holes in the wagon's wall, knotted them tight, and slammed the doors shut once more. Soon, we were rumbling on our way. With every passing league, my pulse beat faster.

Almost there.

The hour flew by and before I knew it, the wagon was wobbling to a stop once again.

The Midnight Cloister. I made it.

Footsteps and voices sounded outside. There were men out there, and a lot of them. Guards, maybe? A sinking feeling ran down my rib cage. This wasn't a good sign. There were never guards at the Zelle. With all the magick guarding this place, why would they need warriors?

The back doors swung open. Late afternoon light flooded into our small space, revealing a woman who stood framed in the doorway. She was wiry and petite, with pale skin, long silver hair, and the black robes of an Apprentice. She scanned each of us each with almond-shaped eyes before gazing over her shoulder. The quick, bird-like movement reminded me of a mother hen. No question about it. This woman was looking out for someone.

Which was puzzling. Did she think the other girls and I were a threat? And who was she trying to protect, anyway?

One of the guards marched up to the Sister's side. He looked ridiculously tall and armored next to her tiny frame.

"We finished our search," he said.

"And?" The lines of the elder woman's face were drawn tight with worry.

"We found no one."

"Which is what I said would happen." The Sister's concern drained away. "Now, I must return to my duties." Her voice and manner suddenly became hollow and rote. Like Hestia, she'd clearly done this many times before.

The Sister refocused her attention on us. "Welcome to the Midnight Cloister," she said in an empty voice. "I'm Sister Sophia. I'll be in charge of you while you're here." She untied the rope from the carriage walls. "When I ask you to do something, you perform. Step down from your carriage."

We all shuffled outside and stood in a makeshift row. There were more guards along the wall, but only one stood near Sophia. Like all the rest, he was in full black armor with his face covered by a helm. He untied the rope from my waist. I was too distracted to care about a stranger being so close. This was my first full look at the famous Midnight Cloister.

It wasn't at all what I expected.

The Midnight Cloister was legendary for having the prettiest architecture, the best Novices, and the most Sisters. Its four white towers were famous, with one standing at each corner of the grounds. Everyone knew of the great blue basilica that loomed by the front gate, as simple and lovely as a gemstone. The low wall that encircled everything was a marvel of delicate crystal.

I blinked hard, hoping what I saw was some illusion of the desert sun. It wasn't. Viktor had changed things here, and not for the better.

The Midnight Cloister before me was nothing more than a fortified pile of rubble. To my left, the crystal barrier was gone, replaced by a massive guard wall. Soldiers in black armor patrolled along the top, glaring out at the desert like an opposing army might appear at any second. Those were the voices I'd heard before.

To my right, the changes were even worse. A cluster of dilapidated buildings stretched off into the distance, all of them rickety and off center. Many of the windows were boarded up. There was no one around, unless I counted the Sentinel Spirits who lurked in the shadows, their shoulders slumped.

This was wrong. Very wrong.

The deep bong of church bells filled the air, attracting my attention to the huge basilica. The building was supposed to be elegant and spare. The basilica before me was covered in statues of terrifying skeletons. There were hundreds, all carved from black rock. Unlike the ones at the Zelle, they weren't dancing to celebrate the joy of eternal life. These figures seemed to prowl along the rooftop, their arms outstretched and jaws opened. Hundreds of empty eye sockets glared at us, watching our every move. A shiver rolled down my spine.

This wasn't a welcoming cloister. It was a frightening prison. And that meant my experiences at the Zelle wouldn't be as useful as I'd hoped. A place like this would have different rules, schedules, and ceremonies. A ball of dread weighed down my stomach. They might even have us sleep in the dungeon rather than the Sisters' dormitory. A fresh sheen of sweat covered my skin, and it wasn't from the heat.

Sophia stared at us blankly. "So you all wish to become Novices?"

Veronique lifted her chin. "I've no desire to do anything of the sort. I want to go home."

Sophia sighed. "Don't be rude."

"I am a Royal. I'll be whatever I want."

"Guard. Silence her."

The guard stepped up and slammed his gloved fist into Veronique's temple. She shrieked and fell to the ground.

"Up," said the guard.

Veronique clenched her fist to the side of her head. "No."

"Get up or he'll strike you again," said Sophia. Her words had all the heat of a Novice reciting a practice incantation for the hundredth time.

Veronique rose unsteadily to her feet. A thin trickle of blood rolled down her cheek. I cringed in sympathy. Sure, I'd been wanting to punch her for hours. Seeing it really happen was something else entirely.

"As you can see, our guards don't have magick, but they have other abilities that make them just as powerful. Do you understand?" Veronique nodded. Her ladies stared submissively at the ground.

Interesting. For all their proud talk in the back of the wagon, Veronique and her ladies sure gave in easily. No wonder they'd been captured in the first place.

"Excellent." Sophia kept on droning. "Now, you will all undergo a brief ceremony that will make you Novices in this cloister. Novices are provisional members. In a few days, our Mother Superior will make each of you a full Sister. The initiation ceremony is when you'll receive the Tsar's mark and officially become part of our community. Any questions?"

No one said a word. My blood boiled. How could they

pretend this was any kind of legitimate ceremony? I'd practiced spells for six months before the Zelle took me on as a Novice.

"The Tsar will arrive soon," continued Sophia. "When he comes, there will be another ceremony, the Examination. He will review all of you. Some may be chosen to join his entourage."

I frowned. *Join the Tsar?* Was that some kind of code phrase for being turned into an old woman and killed? Whatever it meant, it couldn't be good and it was unsettling how easily Sophia rattled off a lie. I'd liked the fact that she was acting as mother hen, but I was starting to rethink what I'd seen. Maybe Sophia wasn't looking out for anyone but herself.

"One final item," said Sophia. "If you are not chosen, then you will stay behind to serve this cloister. Are we all clear?"

Another guard marched up to the first. The delicate wrinkles on Sophia's face crumpled with worry as the two guards started to whisper. Sophia was back to being a mother hen once more.

That was when I noticed movement along the roof on one of the covered walkways. A little girl peeped over the edge, caught my gaze, and grinned. She was about six years old with shiny black hair and almond-shaped eyes. Every inch of her radiated joy. She was like one of the baby goats the farm enjoyed each spring. I could only marvel at their boundless energy.

One of the guards snapped his attention to the walkway and the girl popped down out of sight. A nervous tic moved by Sophia's mouth as she stepped into the guard's line of vision. "What's with all this chatter? I'm conducting a ceremony."

Suddenly, I knew who Sophia was protecting. She cared for the little girl on the rooftop.

"Mother Superior wants everyone inside today," said the first guard. "You can't let your favorites run around."

"No one is running around. I already told you that."

The second guard stomped forward. "It's time someone taught that imp a lesson."

Sophia's mouth thinned to an angry line. "If she was out of her dormitory, then I'd be the first one to administer punishment. But she isn't, is she? If you don't mind." She gestured to us girls. "I have a task to perform."

"We're only following Mother's orders," grumbled the first guard.

"As am I."

Something moved in the corner of my vision, catching my attention. *Oh, no.* The little girl was shimmying down the side of the walkway. Her gray Novice robes were caught on a nail and she was yanking them loose. Old wooden crates were piled on the ground below her. If the child could get down, then she'd have a safe enough hiding place.

If she could get down.

My eyes widened. That poor girl. Sophia followed my stare and a shiver rolled across her shoulders. Her gaze locked with mine. A panicked question hung in her milky eyes.

Will you expose the child?

I didn't know what kind of person Sophia was used to joining this cloister, but I'd never throw an innocent child before one of those monster guards. I shook my head.

A small ripping sound echoed through the air as the girl finally tore her dress free, followed by a thunk when she hit the ground behind the crates.

"Did you hear that?" grumbled one of the guards. Alarm rattled along my nerves.

They're going to find her.

I'd normally cast a disappearing spell, but my powers were cut off. So, I said something instead.

"Hold it right there!" I cried. Every eye in the courtyard turned toward me. Even the guards along the wall stopped their ceaseless inspection of the desert.

The second guard clomped closer. His gravelly voice reverberated through his helm. "Want do you want? Trouble?"

No, I wanted to distract you from the girl.

Sophia stepped quickly to my side. "This potential Novice only wants to get on with the ceremony, don't you?" Her previously dead voice held an animated and encouraging tone.

I couldn't believe it. Sophia was stepping in to save me. "That's exactly it," I lied. "Mother Superior said this ceremony would make me a Novice, and I want that to start." Every cloister had a Mother Superior who ran everything. In truth, I had no idea if she cared about the ceremony, but I figured it sounded convincing.

"As you should," said Sophia.

Out of the corner of my eye, I saw the little girl slip around the back of the building. *Thank the gods.* Her exaggerated tiptoeing was so cute, I couldn't resent that she'd almost gotten me beaten or worse.

"Back to work." Sophia snapped her fingers.

The first guard stepped forward holding a small blue box. Sophia turned to me. There was a flash of some emotion on her face—regret, maybe?—before she went back to her old sleepwalking self. With half-hearted motions, she opened the box and pulled out a tiny snake about two inches long. My shoulders tightened. The serpent radiated the same solid energy that I'd felt from Rowan's dagger and Hestia's mark. More hybrid magick. I couldn't guess what it was for. I knew it couldn't be anything good, though.

"Raise your left arm," Sophia ordered. I did as she asked and was proud when my hand didn't shake too badly.

Sophia gripped my wrist. Her papery skin felt cool against mine as she set the tiny snake on my palm. I froze. What if I had a reaction like the one I'd had to Rowan's dagger? My true power would be exposed.

My heart pounded so hard it felt like it had crawled into my throat. I watched speechlessly as the snake wriggled to wind itself around my thumb. My own liquid magick stirred within me. The solid hybrid magick pushed back from the creature. Purple light flared on my palm.

"Is that right?" asked the guard. "Usually, that light's blue."

"I've seen purple before," said Sophia casually. "You keep to guarding and leave the magick to me."

She had? Necromancer magick was always blue. I'd only seen purple when I touched Rowan's dagger. When had Sophia seen something similar? Once I got the chance, I'd have to ask Sophia what it meant.

The tiny snake chilled my finger as it solidified into a metal ring. At the same time, the metal loops around my wrists took on the texture of snake scales.

Sophia pulled off the ring and held it up. "This now contains some of your magick. If you ever attempt to leave the Midnight Cloister, we'll be able to track you."

"Yes, Sister."

"And these." She tapped my manacles. "You can only get a few leagues from the wall before your irons will start to kill you. Don't bother trying to escape." She stepped to the next girl in line.

The others went through the same so-called ceremony, but I could only focus on the changes in my enchanted manacles. I'd placed a spell on my totem ring to break any magickal bindings. Sadly, that incantation wasn't likely to work on a hybrid spell. That meant that even if Rowan got me my totem rings, they'd be useless.

I needed another way to get these manacles off.

I scanned the cloister, desperate for anything that might be of use. There were boarded up windows. Sentinel Spirits. The stacked boxes the girl had jumped behind...

Hold there.

The crates were weather-beaten and cracked. Even so, the image of a red swirl was clear on one of them. That mark meant Casters.

My pulse picked up. Even back at the Zelle, we kept herbs and animals from the Casters as part of our library. The Midnight Cloister should have an even better collection. The most likely places to look were the library or storehouse.

Sophia's voice snapped me out of my thoughts. "Congratulations. You're officially Novices of the Midnight Cloister. I'll take you to the dormitory now. The other Novices await you."

Turning on her heel, Sophia marched us into a long covered hallway that led through a maze of buildings. I kept watching for other Sisters. There were none to be seen. How could that be? We hadn't heard from other cloisters in years, but that didn't mean they were all empty. A place like the Midnight should be mobbed with Sisters. So, far I'd only seen Sophia.

Who was left to sing at morning spellwork? Who celebrated the gifts of the Sire of Souls?

At length, Sophia led us to a bright blue door that was flanked with guards in black armor. "Go inside," said Sophia. "We're done with you for today."

The guards ushered us into the dormitory. The space was long and rectangular with a low ceiling. One tiny window looked out over the floor. Cots lined either wall. It reminded me of the Zelle, only everything was larger. At one time, this room had been nicer as well. Now the wooden bedframes were cracked, the mattresses were torn, and the blankets all had holes.

A few dozen girls milled, all of them in gray Novice robes. None looked older than twelve. The realization made me ill. What was the Tsar doing with so many children? A voice broke through my thoughts.

"Hello." I looked down to see the little girl from the courtyard. She blinked up at me with huge brown eyes.

"Greetings," I said.

"I saw you before."

"I know you did."

Nan whispered in my ear. "Watch yourself, now. If we're going to escape, we can't go picking up strays."

"It'll be fine." I knelt down closer. "I'm Elea."

"I'm Ada. This is Wulf."

I looked from side to side. "Where's Wulf?"

"He's invisible. He runs off all the time, too. Let me show you where he hides." Ada gripped my hand, dragged me along, and told me all about Wulf's adventures. I tried to enjoy her sweet tales, but I couldn't stop thinking about everything that had happened today.

Sophia said we'd receive marks at the initiation ceremony before the Tsar's arrival. But what did the marks do for the Tsar? I thought through every spell I knew, but nothing explained what Viktor was up to.

I only hoped I could figure it out before Sunday.

9

"*E*lea, what's wrong?" It was Ada. Judging by the curious look on her face, she may have been asking that question for a while. We'd been sitting in the Novices' dormitory ever since Sophia dropped us off.

"Hmm?" The last time I'd paid attention, Ada had been saying something about her invisible friend.

"We have to get your Novice robes," said Ada. "Everyone's going."

"The guards don't take us?" I asked.

"No, silly. You have your irons on now. Besides, the guards block all the places we're not supposed to go." She lowered her voice to a kid whisper, which was to say, no whisper at all. "Wulf and I know ways around them, though. It makes the guards so angry."

I couldn't stop my chuckle. "I noticed."

Nan stepped up. "We better get going. There's dinner after this and I'm hungry."

Dinner. At the Zelle, the Sisters always joined the Novices for meals. This place was so huge, there had to be some Sisters around. And I needed a chance to talk to them. Dinner might be my best chance. "I'm hungry, too," I said. "Let's get going."

Ada showed us to the cloakroom. The other new Novices were already there, toying with their garments. At first, Necromancer robes seemed like an impossible puzzle of ties and fabric. The previous group of Novices was trying to help, but from what I could tell, they were only making the new arrivals more confused. This was my chance.

While everyone tore through the armoires of robes, I grabbed the right size robe, quickly got dressed, and headed off for dinner, hoping to get some quiet time alone with a Sister or two.

The feasting hall was a cavernous room made with wooden pillars, plaster walls, and an arched ceiling. Row after row of long tables and benches stretched across the floor, all empty. Cobwebs swung lazily from the ceiling. This place could have seated two thousand Sisters easily. Right now, there was only me and a few Sentinel Spirits who lurked in the corners. Maybe these knew something that could help me.

I strode over to the spirits. Every movement I made seemed to echo loudly through the empty space. It made the lack of other Sisters here all the more noticeable.

The two Sentinels were tall, middle aged, and wearing Mistress-level robes. In life, they'd had the classic Necromancer look with their long black hair, pale skin, and elegant features. They also held themselves board-straight with carefully controlled faces. If you didn't look closely, it would be easy to miss the gleam of hatred in their eyes.

I paused before them. "Greetings."

Their serene faces contorted with silent screams. One crumpled to the floor in pain. Bit by bit, both of their mist-like bodies faded away.

Soon, they were gone.

I set my hand on my throat. *How horrible.* They'd been cursed.

The spell prevented them from interacting with the living. It was only done to punish a Sentinel who'd done something especially evil. In this case, I feared that Viktor didn't want the Sentinels communicating with anyone.

Rage tightened up my neck. Sentinel Spirits gave up their eternity to serve a cloister. This was a terrible misuse of their trust.

A shuffling sound echoed in behind me, followed by the low warble of elderly female voices. Some actual Sisters were coming into the feasting hall. I straightened my robes and tried to relax my cramped shoulders.

You only have until Sunday, Elea. Don't let anger stop you from getting the information you need.

I carefully approached the pair of Sisters who'd entered. They were frail and stooped, with gray hair and twitchy movements. The first set out wooden bowls while the second ladled in marrow pudding.

"Greetings," I said. The first Sister gave me a blank stare and continued with her work. I tried again. "Would you like to eat with me?"

She shot me a wary look from under heavily lidded eyes. "You've no mark. It's against the rules."

I glanced around. "There's no one's here but us. I won't tell."

"It's the mark." She scratched at her shoulder. "It'll hurt."

"So if you break the rules, the mark hurts you?" I lowered my voice. "What does it do, exactly?"

The second Sister grabbed the first. "Over here. I need your help."

"But I need your help, too," I said lamely.

The pair hurried away. I tried to follow, but they slipped behind a servant's door that locked soundly after them.

I stared at the closed door and tapped my foot. So, the mark knew when a Sister was doing something against the rules, and it somehow hurt them as punishment. Necromancer spells that could do that. You needed to be connected to the master mage, though, and that kind of magick had limits.

The connections were like magickal strings that tied mages together. There was only so much cord to go around. The master mage could either make a lot of connections that only worked over a short distance... Or create a handful of ties that stayed in place no matter where the other mage went.

I thought about pounding on the door, but the other Novices trudged into the room first. I'd never been around many young girls, let alone a few dozen at once. I'd expected them to have more life about them, like Nan and Ada. Instead, they all had the same hollow and hopeless look as the Sisters. Veronique and her friends looked as sad and frightened as the rest. They slowly filled up a few lonely tables in the vast hall.

Then Nan and Ada burst into the room. The empty space reverberated with their energy and life. Nan had clearly given up on ignoring Ada. Now, the girl clutched Nan's ankle as Nan dragged her around, asking, "Where's Ada?"

It was ridiculous. Nan knew we'd all been kidnapped under a dark purpose. That was why she'd asked for my help escaping. It was insane to be playing around with a child right now.

It was also wonderful. I couldn't help admiring the two of them for seeing something to laugh about in this prison.

Nan walk-dragged Ada to the table. "Have you seen Ada?"

"Why no, I haven't. Wherever could she be?"

Ada hopped up to stand. "I'm right here, sillies."

"So you are." I patted the stretch of bench to my left. "Why don't you have some marrow pudding?"

Ada slipped in beside me and Nan took the seat across from us. We all dove into our bowls. I didn't even mind the foul taste, I was so hungry.

Ada scooped a mouthful of pudding and I considered what

she'd said in the dormitory. She and Wulf could go anywhere they wanted. What had she seen? When I spoke again, I took care to keep my voice low. "Ada, what do you know about the Tsar's marks?"

All the color drained from her round face. "Nothing."

Nan lowered her voice. "Come on, now. You can tell us."

"No. Sophia says no talking about that." Nan's lower lip trembled.

A pang of guilt tightened my chest. "It's all right. Maybe another time."

A Sister marched into the room. "Greetings," she said in a clipped tone. "I am Marlene, Mother Superior of this cloister." She was middle aged, tall, and lean with a single lock of white hair striped along her temple. Her robes were Grand Mistress level and every inch of her was focused and intense. She wasn't controlled in the classic Necromancer way, though. Something greedy and overpowering bubbled behind her smooth facade.

Marlene waved to the door. "Sophia! Come here." The elder Sister shuffled to stand at Marlene's side. "Sophia tells me that you've all completed the ceremony to become Novices. My congratulations. I'll initiate you as Sisters on Thursday night."

Sophia's eyes widened. "Not Sunday morning? We always do it right before the Tsar arrives for the Examination. And... Everyone?" She shot a glance at Ada.

"We're holding the ceremony Thursday night." A hungry look gleamed in Marlene's eyes. "It pleases me."

"But only the elder girls?"

The more Sophia worried, the brighter the gleam in Marlene's eyes. I'd seen that look before. My barn cat Lucy used to get that gleam when she had a mouse on her claws. Some creatures just liked to torture others.

"Things are changing," said Marlene. "The Novices will be

initiated on Thursday." She smiled at Ada. "And it will be everyone this time."

Sophia's eyes glistened. "You can't mean that."

Ada bounced a little in her chair. "I want to be a real Sister."

"Shh," I said. "There's no rush to get the Tsar's mark."

"We'll discuss this later." Marlene returned her attention to the room. "Greetings once again. I'm sure Sophia has given you an introduction, but you Novices are a brainless lot who rarely listen. Best if I repeat things now."

The young Novices looked crestfallen by her insult, and Marlene seemed to like that even more.

"Thursday night, I will give you all the Tsar's mark. You'll then become full Sisters. The Tsar himself will arrive soon afterward for the Examination. If he examines you and finds you strong enough, then you may join his entourage." She clapped her hands with glee. "The Tsar graces us on every equinox. Still, this next visit is very special."

Interesting. Novices always practiced spells on the equinox because that was when their powers were strongest. The phenomenon faded as you learned to wield your powers more efficiently. I wondered if the Tsar wanted a performance of some kind.

"I have important news," continued Marlene. "For the Tsar's next visit, the Vicomte will be joining us in person, as will Genesis Rex himself."

I forced myself not to smile. *Rowan's missives had worked.* He'd be here on Sunday. And I wasn't the only one who was pleased with Marlene's news. At the mention of the Vicomte, Veronique visibly brightened.

Marlene's nose flared with disdain. "That is all I have to say. You may all sup now. Don't be gluttons." She sashayed out the door with Sophia following closely behind. I was sorry to see Sophia trapped with that kind of evil.

Once we were alone again, Veronique rose to speak. "Ah, I can only imagine how worried the Vicomte is right now." She fluttered her hands by her throat. "Imagine. Me, his beloved ward, torn away from him!" She exhaled a dramatic sigh. "I wouldn't wish to be Mother Superior when he learns what's happened to me."

"Be quiet." A Novice leaned closer to Veronique. "We don't speak ill of Mother Superior."

"She's giving us a chance to join the Tsar's entourage," added another. "Once we're Sisters and have his mark, he may choose us."

I shook my head in disbelief. Their faith in Mother Superior and the Tsar seemed absolute. This could only cause more problems. It would be harder to murder him with loyal subjects nearby.

I tapped my spoon against the wooden tabletop. Things were becoming trickier by the second. I needed more information and fast. "Ada, you know how to get places, don't you?"

"Oh, sure."

I lowered my voice. "If I wanted to get into the library or the storehouse, how would I do it?"

"Forget the library, you're too big to climb in."

"What about the storehouse?"

"Oh, Sophia might assign you to work there."

Nan looked up from her bowl of pudding. "They make us work?"

Ada nodded. "The storehouse is one of the places you can go. I'll ask Sophia. Maybe the three of us can work there together. It will be so fun!"

"The storehouse," Nan said slowly. "That's by the back gate, right?"

"And the back wall." I didn't need to add that the back wall was the same as the front, complete with guards.

"I like the storehouse," said Nan.

I knew what she was thinking. *Escape.* My thoughts were elsewhere, though. I needed some Caster magick so I could break these manacles.

Ada grinned. "Sophia will let us. You'll see."

"I hope so." Because right now, my many years of planning all came down to whether a six-year-old could get me into a storehouse.

10

I lay on my back and stared up at the dormitory ceiling. Everyone else was asleep, based on all the soft snores and creaking bedframes. I closed my eyes, whispered Tristan's name, and quickly drifted off.

My dreams took me back to the kitchen in my farmhouse. Tristan stood before the fireplace, his face looking more pale and haggard than ever.

"Tristan, I'm here."

My friend only stared blankly ahead, not seeming to notice anything. I rushed over and brushed the backs of my fingers against his cheek. "Tristan."

His bloodshot eyes locked with mine. "Elea, it's you." The fires of the hearth leaped higher.

"We don't have long. I want you to know that I'm at the Midnight Cloister. When the Tsar arrives, I'll kill him."

"Good." His mouth trembled with anguish. "Remember, the Tsar favors skull seeker spells. He may have taught them to his followers."

"I'll remember." I offered him what I hoped was an encouraging smile. "Petra grilled me on the Tsar and his tactics."

"If only you weren't alone in this."

"It's not only me anymore. I've found a mage to help."

"But you're in the cloister. How will you plan?"

"The next time you and I speak in a dream, he'll tag onto our magickal connection."

"What?" The back of Tristan's coat caught fire, but he barely flinched. He only stared at me, wide-eyed and alert. "You gave a mage my betrothal ring?"

"It had your joy spell on it. It's the only way to communicate with my allies while I'm inside."

The flames around Tristan burned hotter. My throat tightened. Tristan was about to burn again and he didn't seem to care anymore. How had it come to this? I couldn't stand by and do nothing. I scanned the kitchen. Sometimes, if I grabbed a blanket and snuffed at the flames, it could slow the fire. I turned to the side chest of drawers, ready to pull out a quilt. Before I got close, Tristan gripped my upper arm. "This Necromancer who will be tapping into this magick... What level is he?"

"Master level, supposedly. But he was trained in a sanctuary fair, so who knows what he can really do?"

"That's good." Suddenly, the fire engulfed Tristan whole, blocking him from view behind a wall of flame and smoke. Heat slammed into my body, sending me tumbling backward. My thoughts were reeling, too.

Tristan was acting so strangely. He seemed more concerned about his ring than my getting help. What was good about Jakob being an untrained Necromancer? Could Tristan be hiding something?

Nonsense. The one truth I knew was that Tristan was a loyal friend. However he acted was because of the years of pain he'd suffered.

Now it was time to free us both.

11

I spent the morning pacing the dormitory. We Novices had been awakened, fed, and dressed. Now, we were waiting for Sophia to come and assign our jobs for the day. Most of the younger girls wanted the kitchens. Although the only official meal was marrow pudding, the cook let the girls make whatever they wanted after chores were done. The draw was obvious.

For my part, I wanted to get into that storehouse and find some way to practice Caster magick. I was good as dead if I didn't get these gods-damned manacles off my wrists.

Ada padded up to my side and pulled on my robes. "Sophia will be here soon. You don't have to worry." She waved me in closer so she could whisper in my ear. "I told her everything at breakfast."

I leaned back to look at her. "You did? I didn't see the two of you talking."

Ada folded her arms over her chest. "I can't tell you how we talk. It's a secret."

"You don't have to say a word. I understand." I just wish

Sophia would get here. It was Wednesday. Only four days to go and I had no way to kill the Tsar.

At last, the door swung open and Sophia stepped inside the dormitory. Everyone fell silent. "Greetings, Novices. I'm here to round up volunteers for daily chores. Who's for the kitchens?" A dozen girls raised their hands. Sophia looked them over and pointed to certain Novices. "You can go." The girls almost skipped out of the dormitory.

"Next, the laundry?" asked Sophia. More Novices volunteered.

I twisted the skirts of my robes with my fingertips. I'd grilled Ada all about the storehouse during breakfast. It was closed and guarded except for whoever Sophia chose to work there. I needed her to assign me.

"We also have cleaning duties in the storehouse." She turned to me. "How about you, Elea?"

Thank the Sire.

"Yes, Sister."

Nan stood at my side. "Sign me up."

Ada raised her hand. "I'm going too, right?"

Sophia pursed her lips. "Yes, the three of you may go. That's all, though." She scanned the room. "Everyone's accounted for. You're all dismissed." She looked between Nan, Ada, and me. "Not you three."

My shoulders slumped with relief, followed by a pang of worry. Now that I was going to the storehouse, how would I find what I needed?

Once we were alone, Ada slipped to Sophia's side. "Can I hold your hand now?"

Sophia's face warmed. "Yes, Ada."

I glanced between the two of them. They both had the same shade of skin and matching almond-shaped eyes. Sophia's kindness started to make more sense. "Are you two related?"

Ada gasped while Sophia kept her features carefully even.

That's a confirmation.

"Follow me." The way Sophia said the words, it was clear that the conversation was over.

The two of them are definitely related. It explained why Sophia was so protective. I wonder how far she'd go to keep Ada safe from the mark? If I promised to set Ada free, would Sophia get the manacles off my wrists? It was worth a try. I only needed the right moment to ask.

Sophia led us through a maze of hallways until we reached a simple low structure that was shaped like a great rectangle. "This is the cloister storehouse," said Sophia.

We followed her inside to find a massive mess. Carrels, casks, and crates were crammed into every inch of space. Ada began climbing a wall of chests. Nan and I looked at Sophia, who shrugged. "It makes her happy. That's what matters." She seemed very frail and human as she spoke.

Ada ran off to scale another pile of boxes. Nan followed to watch that she didn't fall. I smiled. Nan was quickly becoming more attached to Ada than I was.

One Nan and Ada were out of earshot, Sophia turned to me. "There are important matters we need to discuss." She winced in pain and scratched at her shoulder. She was somehow breaking a rule and it was hurting her. "I'm not supposed to speak with you this way. I can only say things once."

"I learned about those marks." I looked warily at the door to the storehouse. "But if you're connected to the Tsar, will he know that we're talking?"

"No, only that I'm in pain, not what particular rule I broke to get hurt." She sighed. "And I'm connected to Marlene. She knows I suffer when I break rules for Ada's sake, and I do that all the time." A world-weary look dampened Sophia's lined face. "She enjoys it."

"I'm sorry."

"I'm not here for your pity. Why do you really want to work the storehouse? Do you want to escape? Ada seems excited to play. I won't have you two putting her in danger, though."

My Necromancer training came back with a vengeance. I kept my features schooled and calm. "I like unpacking things. Any deliveries this week?"

"None until tomorrow. And don't plan on smuggling anything past either gate. The Tsar himself cast dozens of wards there. Anything that can be used to help you escape won't make it in or out."

It took an effort not to pound the wall in fury. *My totem rings will never make it through.* "I understand."

"You've got some kind of plan in your head." She tapped her knobby finger against her cheek. "Well, if you're looking to escape, then it's true that the back gate is a short walk from here. I'd tell you not to try, but you won't listen. All I ask is that whatever you're planning, you leave Ada out of it. She likes you and Nan." Ada's giggled echoed through the air. "I haven't seen my girl smile in months."

"She's a sweet child."

"And I've precious little to make her happy. Which is why I'll let you kill yourself any way you choose... So long as you make Ada smile before you're gone. Do we understand each other?"

"We do."

Sophia turned to go, and I remembered another question I'd meant to ask her. "Wait. When you pulled my magick into that ring, the power flashed purple. You said you'd seen it before. Where?"

"That's one question I'll never answer." She looked at me over her shoulder. "Whatever you're up to, good luck."

"But, I was wondering—"

"I can't push it too far with Marlene." Sophia gripped her shoulder. "Too much pain will be suspicious."

"I understand. Thank you." Sophia nodded and stepped away.

Once she was gone, I scanned the massive space crammed with boxes. Where would I find something with Caster magick in all this confusion?

It's a good thing she wished me luck. I'll certainly need it.

12

I crawled toward the top of a high stack of wooden boxes. I'd kicked off my slippers hours ago—it made climbing easier. My stomach growled. How many meals had I missed? One? Two? It was hard to keep track. Another splinter dug into my ankle and I ignored it. I had far worse pain coming to me if I didn't get these manacles off soon.

I stood up on tiptoe so I could see the tiny containers that had been stacked up top. Did they have red swirls? I strained my neck enough and I could see at last.

No swirls. Damn.

I'd been at this all day and I'd yet to cover a fraction of what was stored here. I'd also yet to see Caster red on anything. Frustration tightened my neck and shoulders. By now, I'd hoped to find something I could test out.

"Elea!" Ada raced to the base of the stack I was climbing. "Come see what we found."

Nan strode up behind her. "Any luck?" She didn't know what I was looking for, but she must have guessed it had something to do with getting out of the cloister, because she'd been keeping Ada busy.

I hopped down and landed on the dusty floor. "Nothing."

Nan patted my shoulder. "How about you take a break?"

"I really shouldn't."

"You've worked straight through lunch and dinner."

Ada pulled on my skirt. "And you have to see what we found." Her face looked so bright and happy, I couldn't refuse.

"Show me," I said.

Ada raced to an open box that was about shoulder high to her child frame. She dug into the contents and pulled out a handful of long feather quills. Her face looked so bright, it could have been shining. "Look at this! Can you imagine the birds these came from? They must be as tall as the basilica."

Nan chuckled. "I told her they were for writing. She's more interested in the birds, though."

"What else have you found?" I asked.

"Oh, all sorts of strange things," said Nan. "Acorns. Sea shells. Barrels of ribbons. It's amazing, the things Marlene pays good coin for. The woman's a magpie." Nan lowered her voice. "How about you? Found what you need?"

"No." I couldn't hide the disappointment in my voice.

"You want to tell me what you're looking for?"

I huffed out a breath. My heart told me to trust Nan, but I didn't want to draw anyone into the mess of my curse. Still, I supposed it wouldn't hurt for her to keep an eye out. "I'm looking for boxes with Caster markings."

"Casters? Why do you care about them?"

The more people who knew about my plans, the higher the risk that everything would get exposed. "I just do, Nan. Sorry I can't say more."

"I get it. When I'm casing my next house, I never tell anyone which place I'm after. Just invites trouble." She winked.

"It's something like that."

Ada pulled on my skirts again. "Hello."

"Do you have something else to show me?"

"I know where there are red swirls."

I dropped down to knee level, my eyes wide. "You do?"

"I didn't mean to listen in. People just forget I'm there and I hear things."

"It's fine," I said quickly. "You're not in any trouble. Where are the red swirls?"

Ada crawled up a stack of boxes, quick as a squirrel. She disappeared along the top of the wooden shelves. I wouldn't even know she was there if I didn't hear the occasional creak of wood.

"Where are you, Ada?" asked Nan.

"Over here!"

That little girl was fast. Her voice now sounded from the other side of the huge storehouse. Nan and I sped to a far corner where Ada stood holding a small lacquered box. The outside was polished white with red swirls. "What about this?"

My heart leaped in my chest. The contained had Caster marks as well as the sun and moon symbol of Ocie and Yuri. That was good. It meant that someone was sending packages in their name, which meant there was hope for Rowan's plans. "That's perfect, Ada."

"It's one of my favorite boxes." Ada opened the lid. "Look, rings!"

I practically tackled the girl, I moved so quickly. Rings of power? I couldn't imagine a finer treasure.

I lifted the box from her outstretched hands and sifted through the bands inside. All resembled the band that Laurel wore. The rings were always in pairs with matching stones carved in the likeness of animals. I counted frogs, herons, and even pigs.

"The ones with peacocks are my favorite," said Ada.

Nan picked up a pair of matching hawks. "These magick?"

My shoulders slumped. These were mating rings. According to Laurel, they didn't have any magick at all. *Useless.* I turned to Ada. "Do you know of any other boxes like this one?" I hated the pleading note in my voice. I should be able to control my disappointment more.

"This is the only one I've ever seen," said Ada. "And I look around here all the time." She pointed to the box. "Eew!"

A scarab beetle crawled over the tops of the rings. I was so shocked I almost dropped the box. Where had it come from, anyway? It wasn't here a moment ago. As it crawled across the top of the box, the edges of its black shell glowed red with power.

Caster magick. This little thing must have been someone's familiar. I leaned in for a better look, excitement coursing through my bloodstream. Casters shared energy with their familiars. There were about twelve different incantations I could use to try tapping into the beetle's power and hopefully one of them would allow me to break the manacles. The insect's back opened to reveal crimson wings as it fluttered out of the box and onto the dusty floor.

"We should kill it," said Ada. She lifted her foot to stomp on the insect.

Nan held her back. "No, I think Elea wants to keep it."

Ada's eyes got big. "Like a pet?"

"Yes, but we have to keep it a big secret," I said. "Can you do that?"

"Not from Sophia. I promised her first that I'd tell her everything."

"What would you tell her?" asked Nan.

Ada shrugged. "Elea has a gross bug as a pet."

I chuckled. "That's fine."

The basilica bells rang through the air. Ada bounced on the balls of her feet. "Time for bed! Before we go to sleep, we can sit together and talk about all the things Nan and I found." She slipped her hand into Nan's. "Is that right?"

Nan mussed the top of Ada's head. "That's a plan." She looked at me. "I think Elea's not feeling well, though. She'll probably do something else, am I right?"

"Yes, I want to play with my pet." The little beetle was leaning back on its hind legs and looking up at me from the floor. Its antennae twitched in my direction.

"I think it likes you," says Ada.

Once a Caster died, they could give their power to their familiar so the animal lived on. It wasn't something Necromancers could do, but I'd read about this kind of spellwork. Sometimes, the familiar even chose a new mage to follow.

I hoped the beetle would pick me. There was one way to find out—I had to give it an order and see if it obeyed. I knelt down. "I'm going to find someplace quiet. I'll call for you when I'm ready."

Tiny antennae bobbed up and down before the beetle spread its insect wings and took off.

"My goodness," said Ada. "That might be a good pet after all."

I watched the creature flit away on its glowing wings. With any luck, I'd figure out a way to channel that power and soon. "I certainly hope so, Ada."

I stepped into the cloakroom. This was one of the few places the guards allowed us to go, yet the other Novices and Sisters rarely visited. In other words, it was the perfect spot to try casting spells with my new pet.

The cloakroom's maze of armoires offered many places to hide. I found a spot behind a particularly large set of freestanding bureaus. Sitting down, I leaned against the wall and stretched my legs out.

"I'm ready," I whispered.

The scarab crawled from under a nearby bureau and paused beside me. It perched on its hind legs and angled its antennae toward my face. Maybe it was my joy at finding Caster magick, but the bug seemed sweet looking.

I couldn't wait to test out some magick with it, either. I began by reciting the basic incantations for unlocking. Nothing happened. I'd expected as much, though. My magick was blocked after all and these were Apprentice-level spells. Hopefully, as I reached he higher levels, the Caster magick would set my powers free.

Next, I launched into the Mistress and Grand Mistress forms of the incantations. I threw my heart into every word. Nothing happened. Once in a while, my beetle twitched its antennae at me, nothing more. That wasn't good. If an unlocking spell didn't work, I couldn't imagine what would.

So, I tried them all again. And then, a third time. Still nothing. My forehead beaded with sweat. This had to work.

Maybe I needed a new approach. I tried spells for summoning, second sight, and detecting magick. Prying eyes, breaking walls, and raising the dead. I even recited ones for instant love, everlasting joy, and charming monsters. There was no response from my little insect friend.

Darkness grew heavier around me. Soon, the basilica bells would toll that we needed to return to the dormitory for the night. I couldn't recite incantations around the other girls, though. If I could tap into the scarab's magick, it had to happen here.

I pressed my palms against my eyes. What were the words for that incantation of greater joining? It was a Grand Mistress spell meant to repair complex things like millworks or clocks. It wouldn't be my first choice for a casting like this, but everything else had failed.

Soft footsteps sounded in the cloakroom. My torso tightened with alarm. I waved the little scarab off. The thing definitely had magick because it understood my intentions completely. It spread its wings and flittered away. I leaned my head against the wall and pretended to sleep.

"Hello, Elea." It was Sophia.

I slowly opened my eyes. "Greetings. You found me napping, I'm afraid."

"No, I haven't." Sophia flicked her fingers and an azure mist surrounded us.

I frowned. Why was Sophia casting? "What's that?"

"Privacy spell. Marlene knows I cast these to talk to Ada." She gripped her hands so tightly her knuckles turned white.

"Did it hurt you to cast this?"

"Everything hurts me when it comes to Ada. Marlene sees to that."

Because she enjoys Sophia's pain. "I'm so sorry."

"That's not important now. Ada told me about your adventures in the storehouse." Sophia scanned the room. "Where is the creature?"

"I don't know." I had a good suspicion, though.

Sophia knelt in front of me. Sadness was etched into every line of her face. "Any progress finding an escape?"

What was her game? Did she really think I'd announce my plans to her? "I don't know what you're talking about."

"You misunderstand my intentions. I'm not here to trap you. I want to help you." Sophia hissed, sucking in a pained breath and gripped her shoulder.

I could only stare in shock. Maybe Sophia had lost her mind. "You shouldn't talk to me like that. It's clearly hurting you."

Sophia smiled, but there was no happiness in her wrinkled face. "I just came from my chat with Marlene."

The one she promised yesterday at dinner. I could picture Marlene's hungry eyes as she threatened to give Ada the mark. "What happened?"

"We discussed Ada and the initiation ceremony."

I shouldn't be so emotionally attached to the child. With Ada, I couldn't help it. "Is she getting the mark?"

"Not until next season, which is why I need to know about your plans. If you found a magickal insect from the Casters, then you may have a real chance to escape. I want Ada to go with you."

It was foolhardy to answer her questions, no matter what kind of spells she said she'd cast. "We can't have this conversation."

Sophia sighed. "I understand why you'd be wary. This is no time to be cautious, though. I made a bargain to protect you and Ada. Neither of you will get the mark." She inhaled a long breath. "That bodes ill for me."

I didn't want the Tsar's mark, but Sophia shouldn't be making sacrifices on my account. I could take care of myself or live with the consequences. "What did you promise?"

"Nothing that wouldn't have happened anyway." Sophia offered me another sad smile. "All I want is for Ada to escape. From where I stand, you seem to be her best chance."

I sat up straighter. If Sophia had told Marlene something that made me look suspicious, this could end in disaster. When I spoke again, my voice was low and serious. "Sophia, what exactly did you say?"

"I will give Marlene my life and in exchange, there will be no mark on you and Ada until next season. During that time, you will be her guardian. It's all set. You needn't worry for yourself, Elea. Marlene suspects nothing beyond the fact that you'll watch over the child."

I raked my hands through my hair. This was undoubtedly a magickal agreement. "I wished you'd told me what you were planning to do. There might be other ways to protect Ada than losing your life."

"No, this is the only way."

"I can't believe that." I lifted my wrists. "Could you get these off me? Maybe we could team up."

"I couldn't, even if I wanted to. Only Marlene can remove those."

"Is there a key?"

"No, it's a hybrid spell. If you've found a source of Caster magick, then you've a far better chance of unlocking those than I do." She shuddered. "We don't have long and there is much I must tell you." Sophia raised her trembling hands and untied the left shoulder of her robes, exposing the raised V on her shoulder blade. "Viktor's mark punishes us for breaking the rules."

"I know. Sophia, we need to talk about the alternatives to you dying."

"Absolutely not," Sophia's face turned fierce. "You need to know what you're really up against. Watch." She inhaled a long breath. "I want you to help Ada escape."

With the word 'escape,' the mark moved.

Shock froze every inch of my body. Something was crawling under Sophia's skin. Whatever it was, it shifted under her flesh, skittered up her neck, and buried itself into the back of her head. *Oh, no.* I stifled the urge to vomit. Sophia gritted her teeth. "Do you understand now?"

I gasped. "By the Sire."

"Marks are creatures that connect us to the Tsar or a member of his entourage. Mine links me to Marlene."

The creature under Sophia's skin slithered back into place. *How disgusting.* I'd suspected that the marks linked the bearer to the Tsar in some way. But for them to be actual creatures? It was unthinkable. It was foul.

And it was also brilliant magick, much as I hated to admit it. Damn that Viktor.

Sophia's face turned pleading. "I'm not saying this to entrap you. I genuinely want to help you and Ada." She groaned in pain and then, something unexpected happened. The blue mist around us grew dimmer.

I froze. Once a spell was cast, it should stay in full force unless the mage who'd cast it died. But the mark was doing more than hurting Sophia for breaking the rules. Her magick was changing, too. "This does more than cause you pain, doesn't it?"

Sophia looked away. "I can't speak of such things. I have to save my strength."

Without meaning to, Sophia had answered the question I'd been asking ever since I left the Zelle. What did the Tsar want from Caster magick that he couldn't get from Necromancy? The true nature of the mark held the clue.

Only Casters had familiars. And only Casters could share their power.

I leaned in closer to Sophia. "Marlene takes away your magick, doesn't she?"

Sophia didn't reply. A single tear rolled down her wrinkled cheek. That was confirmation enough. With that, another part of the puzzle fell into place.

The equinox.

It was one of the few times when untrained Necromancers had extra power. If Viktor wanted to drain Novice magick, that was when to do it.

I slumped against the wall, my mind reeling. This explained why the young Novices came out old and dead. Draining magick was the same as taking away someone's life force. It would age them, body and soul. But what would Viktor want with all that power?

The Tsar was a schemer. He must be gathering energy for a particular spell.

By the gods. The Changed Ones.

Once Viktor had enough power, he could control the hybrid Casters. An eerie feeling crawled up my spine. With the Changed Ones behind him, Viktor would be able to control everyone and everything in the realm.

Sophia moaned and curled her body forward. "Please, help Ada." Her eyes turned wild. "You must. Ada is special. You see, she's my Sister."

I must have heard her wrong. "Sister?"

"I'm only twenty years old, Elea. Whenever I break a rule, it drains my life force as well. Marlene's constantly setting up traps where I have to break a rule or Ada will die. You see, she likes—" Sophia choked on a pained sob.

"I understand," I said quickly. "You don't have to say it again." I wrapped Sophia's hands in my own. Her skin felt papery and cool beneath mine. "Know this, Sophia. You have my word. I will do everything in my power to ensure that Ada will be free."

"That's all I needed to hear." Sophia slowly rose and retied her robes with shaking hands. "Farewell, Elea." Her spell vanished as she shuffled toward the door.

I caught up to her and stood in her path. "One last question. This is important."

"I'll answer if I can."

"When I arrived at the cloister, my magick interacted strangely with the ceremony. It flared purple instead of blue. You said you'd seen that before."

"I had."

"Where? Who?"

"No, Elea. I can't answer that. I'm sorry."

"It's fine." She'd already risked so much. "Thank you for everything." Sophia nodded before hobbling out of the cloakroom.

She's only twenty. That's three years younger than me. And Marlene had slowly drained her life away. It was another kind of curse. Sophia's would end tomorrow with the ceremony, and I only had a few days more.

The basilica bells rang through the air, startling me out of my thoughts. I was expected in the dormitory within minutes, or the guards would come looking. Now of all times, I didn't want to attract any attention.

I started to make my way back. Any way I looked at things, the conversation with Sophia made my chances for killing the Tsar look worse than ever. How much power had that man already gathered?

What chance did I have to stop him?

13

I stared up at the dormitory ceiling, pinched my thigh, and tried to keep myself awake. All the Novices were asleep. My scarab had stopped moving hours ago, too. Now, the beetle lay almost motionless on my pillow. I'd passed the time by thinking up new spells for tapping into its Caster power, but even that wasn't keeping my eyes open anymore.

It had been a long day, and I wanted nothing more than to sleep. It was a risk I couldn't take, though. I needed to wait for the crier to call out the change of guard, which always happened at noon and midnight. Rowan was still expecting to start our conversation when the clock struck twelve. I couldn't start my dream with Tristan too early or too late, especially since I wasn't sure how long Jakob could connect me to Rowan.

"Twelve o'clock and all's well."

At last.

I whispered Tristan's name and instantly fell into a deep sleep. My dreams took me back to my old kitchen once again. Tristan was waiting for me, standing by the hearth. His face looked more alert than ever before. I stepped in or a closer look. Tristan's mouth twitched, something that only happened when he was worried.

"Elea, you're here." Tristan raised his arms, reaching for me. He'd rarely done that when he was alive, and certainly never had in my dreams.

I stayed firmly in place. "What's wrong?"

Tristan dropped his arms. "I just want you to know. If there were any way the curse could have passed you over, I would have made that happen." The flames burst higher behind him. "You know that, right?"

"Tristan, why are you telling me this? Of course, I know you wouldn't have wished this on me."

"Yes, that's right. I love you, Elea. Please know that." The fire and smoke burst around him in a heavy sheet. His keening moan sounded loudly above the roar of flame. I stepped back, my hand on my throat. Tears welled in my eyes. Over and over, this was Tristan's eternity.

And soon, it would be mine as well.

It's not over yet. I must find Rowan.

I wiped the tears away with my palms and turned toward the door. Rowan and Jakob stood there, their faces still and eyes cold.

"What happened? Did you find Ocie and Yuri yet?" I set my hand on my throat. "Did something happen to my totem rings?"

A long silence followed. Rowan's face stayed grim. And Jakob? He'd worn the same look when he first heard about my soft spot for Tristan. The man was gloating.

"What a performance!" Jakob looked to Rowan. "Wouldn't you say?"

Rowan barely moved when he spoke. "State your piece to her and be gone, Jakob."

On reflex, I took a protective step backward. "What's all this about?"

Jakob held up his hand. My betrothal ring glittered between his thumb and pointer finger. "You tell me. What is this?"

"My betrothal ring." *This was too much.* Was he really going to try to upset me again by forcing me to speak of Tristan? It wouldn't work. I met his gaze straight on. "You know that because I gave it to you myself."

"You did. And I expect you didn't think I could cast a history spell on it."

"I didn't think much about it one way or another."

"Wrong!" Jakob's face lit up with pride. "You never suspected that I had enough power to look into the layers of magick on this ring. All because you're the Grand Mistress and I'm just a Master." He pointed to the hearth. "That's why you put on that convincing little performance with your accomplice." Jakob gripped his fists below his chin, batted his eyes, and spoke in falsetto. "Oh, Tristan. You couldn't have freed me from this awful curse."

What is this nonsense? "Speak plainly, whatever you have to say."

Jakob chuckled. "You're good, I'll give you that. You missed a life as a traveling player."

"She's right," said Rowan. "Out with it, Jakob."

The dark lines on Rowan's face gave me pause. Something was wrong, and it was more than Jakob and his petty jealousies. I shifted my weight from foot to foot. What had happened while I was in the Midnight Cloister?

Jakob held up the ring. "This has your so-called lover's spell-work on it. Yes, it binds you together, but the one he loves most is a mage named Quinn. They're related by blood. You had to willingly accept the curse in order to take Quinn's place. Who would do such a thing?"

What a pack of lies. "No one."

"Precisely my point. You accepted the curse because you knew your friend the Tsar wouldn't ever let you burn. This was all an elaborate ruse."

I reached for the betrothal ring. Jakob snatched his hand back.

"I'm not giving you the chance to hide your crimes," he said.

Could Tristan have put layers of spells on the ring? I'd never cast any history incantations on it. Tristan had placed a joy spell on it. Sure, the spell hadn't worked, but Tristan had cast it while he was dying. Could there have been another spell hidden on the ring? It was possible.

But to have accepted the curse?

I pressed my fingertips to my temples. What had I said back then? I'd answered 'yes' to his betrothal, of course. And Tristan had said something about transferring the curse to another and I'd refused. My blood chilled. That might have been enough to activate a spell. But Tristan wouldn't do that. Jakob must be getting his information from shoddy spellwork.

"You don't know what you're talking about."

"Tell the truth," said Jakob. "This has all been a game. You never meant to kill the Tsar. You're in his employ and think he'll spare you long before the curse comes due." Jakob almost snarled as he spoke. "No, this is a ruse to catch better prey. You seek to kill a member of the Caster Imperial family."

"You're mad."

Jakob laughed in a tone that was too brittle to be real. "That's why you asked about him when you first set foot in our camp." He took on a fake female voice. "Oh, look, you have helms here. Is Genesis Rex nearby?"

"I can read a book, Jakob. I know you wear your helms around your king. You're making something out of nothing. And I don't trust your spellwork."

"Oh, let's count off all the odd coincidences. You didn't know that you accepted someone else's curse... You didn't realize your spell would cross paths with Rowan's... You didn't know that

Rowan was Rex's nephew, yet you quickly guessed his real identi-ty." He raised my betrothal ring again. "You're guilty."

"So, cast a truth spell on me."

"Oh, but we can't, can we? Not in this dream. And even if you *weren't* in a dream, you're a strong enough mage to hide the truth." He shook his head. "What a beauty of a plan. What better way to ensnare Rowan's attention? He already had a Master Necromancer in his company." Jakob pounded his chest once. "But you toss out a *Grand Mistress*."

"I didn't toss myself anywhere."

Jakob kept talking as if I hadn't said a word. "You think you're so much better than me. Who wouldn't be interested in your skills, right? But that's where you failed. I'm a far better mage than you took me for. I found you out. What do you say to that?" Jakob glared, his features wild with triumph. Rowan assessed me carefully.

A heavy quiet filled the air. This conversation had gone completely out of control. My mind was humming with every-thing Jakob had said. Still, I could tell that however I answered, it would change things for me. This was somehow like the moment that I'd decided to go to the cloister.

I'd only seen one path then. I only saw one path now.

I set my emotions behind a wall, just the way they'd taught me at the Zelle. I needed to face this situation with logic or it would only get worse.

"Look past your petty jealousy, Jakob. This is about more than entrapping Rowan. I've gotten confirmation that the Tsar is using his mark to drain Necromancers. Once he has enough power, he'll control your Changed Ones. No matter what spell you cast, that truth remains the same. And I remain under Viktor's curse. No one in their right mind would think the Tsar would spare them." I looked to Rowan. "No offense, but I couldn't give a horse's arse about you and your Imperial family."

The edges of a smile curled Rowan's mouth. The expression was gone quickly, though. "Wait outside, Jakob."

"You can't be serious," Jakob said.

"As the plague. Ocie and Yuri already said that it has to be her."

I lifted my brows. *They'd contacted Ocie and Yuri?* At last, there was some good news today.

Jakob kicked the floor with his boot. Even sober, the man was no pleasure to be around. "Only because you won't give me a chance."

"This isn't up for discussion." Rowan pointed to the door. "Outside."

Jakob stomped out of the kitchen and slammed the door behind him. *Good riddance.*

Rowan stepped closer. "I'm sorry about that. It isn't as absurd as it sounds. There have been many attempts on my life. Rex still hasn't recovered full use of his leg after an attack last spring. Viktor is a little obsessed with my family."

"I can understand. After I was slated to inherit my parent's farm, I'd suddenly become a target. And that was only the local farmers, not an evil Necromancer."

Rowan chuckled, making a low and rumbling sound that I liked very much. "Glad we settled that." He rubbed his palms together. "About the totem rings—"

"I have bad news there. The gates all have wards. Nothing with magick will pass by without triggering an alarm."

"Excellent work. What else have you discovered?"

My chin lifted with pride. "I got access to the storehouse and found a box with Ocie and Yuri's mark. There were some rings in there like the one Laurel wore."

"Mate bands don't have any power outside the pair."

"They looked useless, but there was a scarab familiar in the box too. I've been trying to cast a hybrid spell with it. Nothing has happened so far. It keeps following me around, though."

Rowan shifted his weight from foot to foot. "It's been following you."

"Yes."

"And it came out of that box."

I narrowed my eyes. "That's what I said." *What was he getting at anyway?*

"That's very unusual for a Necromancer." He cleared his throat. "How many of us do you know?"

"How many Casters? Why would that—"

Oh, no.

I took a half step backward. "You don't think this has something to do with a…" I couldn't get my mouth to say the words 'mating ritual.'

"No, of course not," said Rowan quickly. He changed the subject and I was happy to let him. "I have news for you as well. Ocie and Yuri made contact again."

"Excellent." If I didn't kill the Tsar, there'd be no future for me. I didn't need to waste time and thought on odd Caster rituals. "What did they say?"

"They'll give us hybrid magick to fight the Tsar." Rowan frowned.

"That's good news, right?"

"But only if they can give it directly to you."

"Me? How do they even know me?"

"My spell in the desert. They say they were the ones who heard it. They want us to work together."

"They want us together?" I thought back to the little scarab beetle. "Do you think they're playing supernatural matchmaker?" A blush colored my cheeks. "That's a little crazy."

"Who knows what mages of that level are after?" He cleared his throat, loudly. "The fact is, they're our best chance to get the power we need by Sunday. Think about it. The fact that they got a Caster familiar into the Midnight Cloister? That's a sign of serious power, even if they were a little odd about it. We can't pass this up."

He had a point. "Are they going to break into the cloister somehow?"

"No, you need to escape and go to them."

"Escape?"

Rowan nodded and I paced a line by the hearth. Trying to steal away from the Midnight Cloister right now was just too much. There had to be another way. I raised my wrists. "I can't get out with these manacles on. If I did, I'd be dead within in a day."

Rowan stared at the manacles. "Ocie and Yuri gave me a spell to help you. Once you're out, they've arranged to attend a sanctuary fair not far from the Midnight Cloister. They said that you wouldn't be able to cast a transport spell."

"They're right about that." Which was another reason to trust them. "A sample of my power was taken and bound in a ring. If I escape and try to cast, they can trace my magick." I stopped my pacing and stared into the flames. Unless I did something, fires like these would consume my future. But killing the Tsar had always been my plan on my terms. Trusting to Ocie and Yuri at this point seemed insane. "There must be another option."

"What do you think?"

"When would you remove my manacles?" Maybe the magick wouldn't be ready by Sunday anyway.

"I already began preparing the spell. It'll be ready by Friday morning. No point freeing you until the spell is ready, so I could get you at first light on Friday." He rubbed the scruff on his chin. "And you still haven't answered my question."

"No, I haven't." I pinched the bridge of my nose. As much as I didn't like the idea of relying on someone else for my future... I didn't exactly have a better plan. "I'll try more spells with that scarab."

"I would expect no less."

"In that case, I can meet you at the back gate on Friday at dawn. We're supposed to get deliveries that day, so the gate will be open starting at sunup. Plus, I've been working in the storehouse so it won't draw suspicion to visit the gate." I sighed. "If nothing else, the scarab can let you know when I'm ready at the gate. You don't want to stand around and raise suspicion."

"Dawn on Friday, then," said Rowan. Something I couldn't name gleamed in his eyes. Happiness, maybe?

"Yes. It's agreed."

With that, my dream faded into darkness.

14

I sat in my regular seat in the feasting hall, right beside Nan and Ada. My scarab beetle crawled stealthily under the bench. I kept worrying that someone would see the little thing and stomp on it, but it had an uncanny sense of when to fly away. So instead of discussing rogue insects, the young Novices chattered happily away about the initiation ceremony.

"Tonight, we'll become real Sisters," said one.

"I bet the Tsar will choose me in the Examination," added another.

"Maybe I'll be chosen to join the Tsar's entourage," said a third.

There were so many things wrong with these statements. To begin with, the poor girls hadn't been trained. It was unfair to tell them they'd be real Sisters, let alone give them a mark. And the Examination? That was for the Tsar to decide who ended up drained and dead. I clenched my left hand. What I wouldn't give to be able to cast a thousand fireball spells right now. I'd love to bring down this entire cloister.

Patience. Wait for Sunday.

Ada frowned into her bowl. "I won't be made a Sister. Mother Superior told me no."

It was on the tip of my tongue to say that was a good thing. I thought better of it, though. If Sophia hadn't told her the truth, then I'd respect that.

"Why do you want to be a Sister?" asked Nan.

Ada sniffed. "Everyone else is."

I gave her an encouraging smile. "I'm not. And I'll stay with you in the dormitory. We can grab all the best cots and blankets."

Ada chewed her thumbnail for a moment. "I suppose."

"And don't forget Wulf," I said. "He's staying with us, too. With the three of us, it will be fun."

"Are you going to watch the ceremony?" asked Ada.

"I don't know. I don't think so." I sighed and looked to Nan. I hated the idea of her going through that ceremony alone, but there was nothing I could do about it. Nan caught me looking.

"I'll be fine," she said.

A dozen worries ran through my mind at once. What if the mark changed Nan? What if she ended up in constant pain or worse? Would she be forced to share our secrets? I fidgeted on my bench.

"It's like this," added Nan in a solemn tone. "I've been in tough places before. The key is not to panic. Keep your eyes open for opportunity."

"Is that how you avoided the noose?" I asked.

Ada's eyes widened. She wasn't worrying about the ceremony any more, so that was something good. "They were going to hang you?"

Nan leaned back and folded her arms over her chest. I was quickly learning that this was her storytelling mode. Nan could weave quite a tale. "There I was, the night before my hanging."

"No! What did you do?" asked Ada.

"I got caught taking a necklace from a countess while she was in bed with her lov—" Nan cleared her throat. "While she was playing with a friend."

"But we shouldn't take things that aren't ours."

I shot Nan a worried glance, not sure this was the best story for a six-year-old.

"That's true," said Nan smoothly. "Unless you know for a fact that the person who has the necklace stole it in the first place. Then, it's fair game."

"Oh, that makes sense." Ada turned to the empty spot beside her. "Wulf agrees, too."

"So, there I was, trapped in my cell. Everything looked bleak. And then, the fire broke out."

"What kind of fire?" asked Ada.

"Some baker forgot to close his ovens and the whole town went up in smoke. Gave me time and cover to pick the lock and escape. Coughed up soot for a week, though." Nan gently tapped her temple with her spoon. "Smarts and opportunity. That's all it takes." Nan shot me a meaningful look. "If you work yourself up into a worry, you miss your chance." Nan didn't need to say it, but I knew she wasn't afraid for the initiation ceremony.

"You're a tough girl," I said.

"We're all tough when it's called for." Nan looked over to Veronique. "Or, everyone at this table is."

Marlene swept into the room and headed straight for us. The rest of the feasting hall fell silent. Suddenly, my marrow pudding looked even less appetizing.

Marlene paused at the head of the table. That predatory gleam was back in her eyes. "Hello, Ada."

I gripped my spoon so hard, the metal bent. Wasn't it enough for Marlene to kill Ada's Sister? Did she have to come here and gloat as well?

Ada bowed her head. "Greetings, Mother."

"I've come to take you to the dormitory." Marlene licked her lips. "Such a shame you won't be made a Sister. Again."

Ada's bottom lip quivered. "Yes, Mother."

Marlene looked down her nose at me. "And you're to be passed over as well."

"As you wish." I pushed my bowl away. "I'm not hungry anymore. I'll go with you, Ada."

"Why ever would you do that?" asked Marlene.

"You said I'm not getting a mark tonight, right?"

"You're still going to the ceremony, my dear. I want you to fully understand the requirements of Sisterhood." A small smile rounded Marlene's thin lips. "And I'm sure you'll want to be there to cheer on your friends."

Meaning she'd enjoy watching my pain. I wanted to say something to cut her down to size, but I couldn't attract any more of her attention. I worked hard to keep my features neutral. "How kind of you."

"Not at all," Marlene said sweetly. "And first thing tomorrow morning, I wish you to visit my study. There's something very important we need to discuss."

Long seconds passed as I thought through this request. Marlene was asking me to visit right when Rowan would try to free me. Did she know what we had planned? Viktor did his experiments in his study. Was Marlene planning to do the same thing?

"Is something wrong?" asked Marlene.

"No," I said smoothly. "Thank you for the honor of a private visit."

Marlene's eyes glistened with satisfaction. "I'll see you at the ceremony." She waved Ada to her side. Together, they stepped off to the dormitory.

Enjoy this while you can. Marlene. When I'm through with the Tsar, I'm coming after you.

~

Church bells tolled as Sophia led me and the other Novices through a labyrinth of passages. Sentinel Spirits hurried along beside us. I was so used to them lurking in shadows or pacing with worry, it was odd to see so many moving with purpose. I'd seen this happen hundreds of times as the Zelle. Sentinel Spirits always joined our ceremonies—it was one of the few times their voices could be heard. At the Zelle, they'd float along and smile. These spirits didn't look happy.

We reached the end of yet another hallway and a pair of great silver doors. Sophia pressed them open. Despite everything, I couldn't help but gasp in awe. I'd never been inside a real basilica before. It was beautiful.

The space was a long and soaring and every inch was colored blue. The walls were lined with tall columns and stained-glass windows. Low pews covered the floor. Every seat was filled with Sentinel Spirits. They turned to us in unison, their white eyes heavy-lidded with sadness. The sight made my heart crack with sorrow.

As we stepped down the basilica's main aisle, the ghostly Sisters began to chant. The sound wasn't the lighthearted harmony that I heard at the Zelle.

Their song was discordant with grief and rage. The cacophony made my skin crawl.

The guards marched into the basilica and stood along the back wall. There must have been fifty of them. Two for each Novice about to be initiated.

Sophia walked us up the central aisle. I was first in the long line of Novices with Nan behind me. We all stopped at the front of the basilica.

The main aisle ended with the towering nave. It was a tall semicircle whose curved back wall should have held a mural of the Sire of Souls, the patron god of our order. Instead, it held the image of the Tsar in his black robes. I'd seen so many pictures of him over the years. This was one I considered his fatherly pose. He was all elegant cheekbones and coiffed black hair as he stared benevolently over the crowd.

I couldn't wait to kill him.

Under the painting, the base of the nave was a circular platform divided in two. The back half sat against the curved wall and mural, while the front was surrounded by a semicircle of prayer benches. There were two-dozen benches, one for each Novice. When we reached the platform, Sophia gestured for us to kneel at the benches. Veronique went first, followed by her ladies and the other girls. Nan and I were last. As I knelt down, my body screamed to run.

I gripped the edge of the prayer bench. The touch of solid wood centered me. A door swung open at the base of the mural. Marlene stepped out, followed by the other initiated Sisters of the Midnight Cloister. There were less than fifty of them. All were old and stooped in their black Necromancer robes. None but Marlene wore robes above the Apprentice level. The sight left a foul taste in my mouth. How many of these were actually young girls like Sophia? The Sisters formed neat rows behind Marlene. And there they were—all that was left of the Midnight Cloister.

Only fifty Sisters remained out of the thousands.

Sophia stepped onto the platform and took her place beside Marlene. Her frail shoulders were shaking. We'd never discussed this outright, but I'd no doubt that Marlene planned to kill her publicly. Much more pain to enjoy that way. I stifled the urge to grab Sophia's hand and run.

Marlene gestured toward the basilica's back wall. "Guards, come forward." The warriors stomped down the center aisle. Their boot falls boomed like cannons over the harsh music. Two guards stood behind every Novice. All wore their full body armor and had their faces covered by helms. The ghostly chanting took on an angrier note. Warriors had no place in a church, let alone by the altar.

Beside me, the other Novices started to fidget on their benches, casting nervous glances at the guards behind them. It took an effort not to look at the pair who lurked behind me. I'd never be able to hide my rage if I glanced their way.

Marlene's eyes brightened with a predatory light. "Greetings, Novices. Most of you are about to be awarded the honor of becoming Sisters of the Midnight Cloisters. Your life's energy will now be tied to the Tsar and me."

The Novices exchanged confused looks. What a shame. My initiation had been one of the sweetest days of my life. And here, it was about ruin these innocent girls.

"Let us begin." Marlene closed her eyes and began whispering a familiar incantation. It was the same one the Zelle Sisters had sung for me. The words were about the Sire of Souls and the joy of eternity. What a disgrace to use that song in this sham. As if in response, the ghostly choir only chanted more loudly. The angry note in their voices set my teeth on edge.

Marlene stepped up to the front of the platform, pausing only a few yards away from me. She folded her arms across her chest while scanning the basilica with a greedy stare. Bit by bit, she raised her arms and began the incantation for soul smoke.

Every inch of my body prickled with awareness. Soul smoke was a terrible spell, only used on your worst enemies. It killed you not only in this life, but in the next as well. It was the worst thing you could do to another living being, and Marlene was doing this to innocent girls?

More than that. A small smile rounded Marlene's lips as she spoke the incantation. This woman was enjoying it.

It took everything I had not to scream. Instead, I gripped the prayer bench so tightly, it creaked under my hold.

The spell took shape. Soon, a sphere of blue light appeared before every Novice except me. The other girls stopped wriggling on their prayer benches and began watching the play of brightness with wide eyes. Some of them smiled. They didn't even know what spell they were staring at.

Grinning at soul smoke. What an outrage.

Bile crawled up my throat. This was so wrong. No doubt, that haze was there to seal their innocent souls to the tiny creatures that would soon become their marks. The spell would kill them for all eternity.

Marlene snapped her fingers. "Guards, hold them."

There were two guards for each Novice. Now, it was clear why. One guard held each Novice in place, while the other pressed the girl's hands against the prayer bench.

The smiles instantly faded from the Novices' faces. One by one, Marlene stepped up to them and whispered a spell. The manacles on their wrists fell to the floor with a clang. My guards loomed closer to me, as if warning me not to move or help. I knew there was nothing I could do. Not yet, in any case.

"Guards, expose their shoulders." The girls exchanged worried glances. Marlene looked down on them indulgently. "It's all right, girls. This is all part of the ceremony. You must take on the mark of the Tsar and this cloister. You'll all become mine."

Mine. She was planning to leech off their life force and enjoy doing it. I wanted to kill her now.

The guards tore open the fabric on the Novices' shoulders. It was shameful to touch a Necromancer anywhere, but in a basilica? I grabbed the top of my prayer bench harder, afraid of what I'd do if my hands were free.

Marlene raised her left arm and whispered more of the incantation for soul smoke. Every word seemed to singe my ears. If only there were some way I could stop this tragedy.

The bones in Marlene's left hand glowed blue. Before her on

the platform, two skeletons appeared, both of them shining with sapphires. "Fetch the vessel," said Marlene.

The skeletons nodded and vanished. A moment later, they reappeared, holding a massive golden bowl between them.

Marlene stepped over to the vessel. "Behold the gifts of the Tsar, Viktor the Great." She reached inside the bowl and scooped up something in her hands. I looked over and winced.

Centipedes.

Only, I'd never seen ones so large, and we had all kinds of insects back on the farm. Marlene dropped the wriggling creatures back into the bowl and approached the first Novice in line, Veronique.

"What are you doing with that?" Veronique struggled with her guards, trying to break free. "I'm a Royal!"

"Keep quiet, or I'll make this really hurt." Marlene smiled. "Let me show you." She pulled one of the centipedes out of the bowl, and tickled its belly. Long antennae sprung out of its legs and head. A few of the Novices shrieked. I blinked hard, not sure that what I was seeing was real.

Those couldn't be bone crawlers, could they?

I knew all about bone crawlers, they were the stuff of nightmares. If you took a centipede, gave it a crusty spine and long spindly legs... That would be a bone crawler. They burrowed inside your skin while their legs dug into your organs. These monsters had carried the first plague. Necromancers across the continent had teamed up to wipe them out. I'd no idea any still existed. And these bone crawlers were glowing red. That was a sign of Caster magick. What had the Tsar done to them?

I tried to swallow past the knot of fear in my throat. Who would have thought the Tsar would use bone crawlers? I looked over to Nan. All the blood had drained from her face. This was too terrible.

Closing her eyes, Marlene whispered the final verses of the

incantation for soul smoke. One by one, the bone crawlers levitated out of the golden bowl, their glowing red spines and long tendrils writhing in the air as they entered the bright blue spheres that still hovered before each Novice.

The bone crawlers soaked up the blue light until their bodies became indigo dark. My heart beat so hard I thought it might break free from my rib cage. The creatures stopped squirming, and somehow that was more frightening than when they were wriggling away.

And this could be my fate, too.

Even if I somehow lived past Sunday, this was what Viktor did to anyone with Necromancer power. I scratched at my shoulder, imagining the antennae under my skin.

"Hold them!" At Marlene's order, all the guards gripped the Novices tighter. "Now, become as one." The creatures bolted forward, burrowing into the throats of the girls and digging under their skin. Within seconds, they'd taken the form of a V on every shoulder blade. Nan's chin quivered as tears rolled down her cheeks. My poor friend.

Marlene raised her arms. "Congratulations. You are now tied to the Tsar, the Midnight Cloister, and most of all, to me. You will follow our rules or the penalty will be severe. Sophia, it is time."

My gaze snapped to Sophia. I'd been so concerned with Nan, I'd forgotten that Sophia was here. Like Tristan, I feared another friend die was about to die before my eyes. I wasn't sure my heart could take it.

Sophia's shoulders shook as she tried to stay upright. I'd never seen anyone look more frail and frightened. My heart lurched as Sophia knelt down.

Marlene raised her voice to address the basilica. "Know this. Sophia has decided to gift me the rest of her life energy through our connection via the mark. This has all been sealed in magick."

Marlene gently rested her fingertips beneath Sophia's chin. "Shall we?"

Sophia's back stiffened. The creature in her shoulder glowed blue under her dark robes. Its insect body twisted and writhed. Sophia's gentle face contorted with pain and fear as her frail skin lightened until it became almost translucent. Clumps of snowy white hair fell out of her scalp. She collapsed onto the stage. Her gentle features disappeared as her body withered away. Within seconds, there was nothing left of her but skin and bones. I couldn't stop crying.

Marlene smiled benevolently, and in that moment, I never loathed anyone more. "This ends the ceremony. You are now Sisters of the Midnight Cloisters. Know this. Any time you break a rule, you pay with your life energy... Just like Sophia. The other Sisters can instruct you."

Nan caught my eye. Her proud face was twitching with fear. Something inside my soul cracked.

"My congratulations," announced Marlene. "Guards, escort the new Sisters to the initiates wing." She gestured to me. "And take that one back to the Novices' dormitory." She stalked up to me, an evil grin stretching across her mouth. "I'll see you in my study tomorrow." She arched her brow, waiting for my reply.

"Yes, Mother." My voice came out choked and hoarse. I hated that she knew how deeply she'd hurt me.

"Good." Turning on her heel, Marlene stalked out through the door behind the altar. It swung shut behind her with a clang. The ghostly choir disappeared. A guard yanked me away from my prayer bench and hustled me out the back of the basilica. I forced myself to focus on the one bright spot in this dark moment.

I still had a chance to claim revenge for everything that had happened here today. The odds weren't great, but there weren't gone, either.

The guards shoved me into the Novices' Dormitory. Moonlight peeped through the single window-hole. My footsteps echoed across the stone floor as I lumbered toward my cot. The place felt quiet as a tomb. There were no more young girls giggling, gossiping, or mumbling in their sleep. Ada was curled up in the bed beside mine. She fluttered her eyes open. "Are they all Sisters now?" she asked through a yawn.

"Yes." I was proud that my voice didn't break.

"Why aren't you with them?"

"Mother Superior wants me to stay with you, remember?"

Ada blinked sleepily. "Does Sophia know?"

"She does." I swallowed past the knot of grief in my throat. "She made it happen." I stepped to Ada's side and tucked her blanket under her chin. "Sleep now." Ada yawned again, smacked her lips, and drifted off to rest. Her tiny shoulders rose and fell with each breath. She seemed so tiny and alone in this huge room. And after tomorrow, I might not even be here to keep her company.

I'll come back for you, Ada. I promise.

15

The guard pounded on the dormitory door, waking me with a start. "Get up, you lot."

I rubbed my eyes and looked around. The Novices' dorm was still dark. *How strange.* The guards never work us up before dawn.

Ada softly snored on the cot near mine. Like always, she'd looped all her pillows and blankets around her, reminding me of a baby chick in a nest. A peaceful smile rounded her small mouth. My shoulders drooped.

Ada didn't know about Sophia yet.

The door whipped open. Marlene stepped through, her eyes glimmering with smug excitement. I remembered her promise to take me to her study this morning. Was that why Marlene seemed so pleased with herself? Nan stepped in behind her. My friend looked pasty and ill. I had the sudden urge to hug her. After that, I had even stronger desire to kill Marlene with a bone melter spell.

That damned mark was already draining Nan.

Swinging my legs over my bedside, I turned to Ada. "Wake up, little one."

Ada stayed asleep while my scarab beetle fluttered into view. "Not you," I said. "You better hide until everyone is gone." Whenever I had a moment and a quiet spot, I'd been trying out new spells to activate the little bug. Nothing had worked, but there was no time to worry about it now.

I leaned in closer. "Come on, sleepyhead."

Ada's eyes half opened. "Morning, Elea." She gave me a sleepy smile. Poor girl. Her world was about to turn upside down again.

I gently tapped her shoulder. "We have company."

Marlene walked into view. I half stood, ready for her to order me off to her study. But Marlene's hungry gaze locked on Ada. I froze. *Marlene showed up to break the news about Sophia.* That was why she'd arrived early. Rage sped through my bloodstream.

Ada's gaze flickered between Marlene and Nan. Her sweet face paled. "Where is Sophia?"

I reached forward and pulled Ada onto my lap. She curled into my shoulder and her thin frame trembled. I glared at Marlene. "I'll tell you all about Sophia later, Ada."

Marlene arched her right brow. "I'm Mother Superior here. We discuss things on my schedule, not yours."

Ada shook more violently. A jolt of protective energy shot through me. "The Midnight Cloister is almost empty now. Isn't that enough for you? Do you have to prey on the few who are left?"

"No, it wasn't enough, as a matter of fact." Marlene casually flicked imaginary dust from the skirts of her black robes. "All Necromancer power belongs to the Tsar. Until every mage bears his mark, our work isn't done."

I couldn't believe what I was hearing. She thinks this is some kind of crusade to help Viktor.

Ada whimpered against my shoulder, jostling me out of my thoughts. I held the child more closely and shot Marlene a frustrated look. "You're scaring her."

"She should be frightened, and if you had any sense, you would be, too. I can make life unpleasant for you both, even without a mark. Do we understand each other?"

The question hung in the air for a moment. There was only one answer. "We do."

For now. Come Sunday, it should be another conversation entirely.

"Excellent. Ada..." Marlene tapped Ada's cheek. "You need to look at me when I'm talking to you."

Ada peeped out from under my shoulder. "Yes?"

Marlene gestured around the empty room. "Do you know where everyone is, Ada?"

"They all became Sisters." Ada's face drooped with disappointment.

"And you know that Sophia was sick."

"We can't talk about that," Ada said quickly.

"Oh, now we can." Marlene motioned Nan to her side. "Tell her, Nan."

"Sophia's gone, Ada."

Ada's brows drew together. "Where is she?"

Marlene exhaled a dramatic sigh. "That wasn't a clear statement, Nan. Let me explain it more succinctly. Sophia's dead."

Ada's lower lip wobbled. "Like Mom and Dad?"

"Just so. And Elea and Nan will take care of you." Marlene turned to Nan. "Isn't that right?"

"We'll be a right proper team."

"Sophia was fine for a time. She wasn't very fun toward the end, though." Marlene waved her hand dismissively. "Elea and Nan will be far more entertaining."

Nan and I locked gazes. *We're her next choice to torture for fun.* And if I escaped, I was leaving Nan alone to endure it. Already, everything about my friend seemed gray and hollowed out. What would more time do to her?

Ada turned to Nan. "Will you get sick, too?"

Nan shrugged casually, but I couldn't miss that nervous tic by her eye. "Looks like."

"You mustn't ask Nan to break too many rules, Ada. You wouldn't want her to be in trouble." As she said the word 'trouble,' Marlene positively beamed. How I loathed that woman.

"I'll try, Mother," said Ada.

"That's all I ask," said Marlene. "Now that I've so few Sisters in my collection, I must watch them all very, very carefully." She tapped her chin. "I have an idea. Ada, how about spending the day in the storehouse with Elea and Nan? You always had such fun there with Sophia."

At the mention of Sophia, Ada's bottom lip quivered. "Yes, Mother."

"Ah, ah, ah." Marlene flicked her pointer finger from side to side. "Good Necromancers control their emotions, Ada. Watch out or you'll never be made a full Sister."

Ada's eyes lined with tears. "Yes, Mother."

Nan took Ada's hand and guided her off my lap. "Time to get going. We'll visit the storehouse right after breakfast."

Ada looked so small and helpless as she clung onto Nan's hand. I rose to stand beside them. "I'll go with you, too."

"You can see them later," said Marlene. "You're off to my study now."

That's right, Marlene wanted to meet with me. My pulse kicked up speed. What did she want to talk about, anyway? Could she know my true plans?

I forced my face to be calm. "Yes, Mother."

Marlene motioned to the door. "Fall in." Four guards stepped into the dormitory. "Ada, Nan, I'd like you to meet your new personal guard. They'll be keeping a close eye on you. We wouldn't want anything to happen, would we?" Marlene stalked to the door and paused. "How about a show of gratitude, eh?"

"Thank you, Mother," said Ada.

Marlene glared at Nan and me. "And you?"

"Thank you," we said in unison. The words felt like poison on my tongue.

"Come along, Elea." Marlene swept out the door, her long gossamer robes fluttering behind her.

Nan and I shared a long look. Overnight, fresh lines of misery had dug in around Nan's eyes and mouth. What would happen when I was gone?

"Don't fuss over me," Nan whispered, guessing my thoughts were about her. She shot a wary look at the guards. "The Sisters explained the rules last night. What we can and can't do." She patted Ada's head. "And we can't wait around here. We need to get to our marrow pudding and breakfast."

Marlene stood framed in the doorway. "When I say come along, that means now."

I gave Ada a quick hug. When I embraced Nan, I spoke quietly in her ear. "Whatever happens, I'm coming back for you and Ada. Remember that."

"We'll be waiting." Some of the old fire lit up in Nan's eyes.

"Good."

"Elea! I'm out of patience." The ice in Marlene's voice made me flinch. Turning on my heel, I raced off to follow Marlene. Whatever she had planned for me in her study, I was certain that it wouldn't be pleasant.

16

Marlene whipped open the simple wooden door to her study. I followed her inside, expecting the place to be something like Petra's study back at the Zelle. My old Mother Superior worked in a small room that held only a table and two chairs. Simple, controlled, and spare.

That wasn't what I found here.

Marlene's study was a gaudy collection of jewels, tapestries, and chests that would make a pirate proud. Colorful armoires lined the walls, their doors overflowing with furs and silks. Wooden trunks were stuffed with gold coins and silver figurines. I shook my head in disbelief. No Necromancer should hoard valuables like this.

An odd chill crept over my skull. Treasure wasn't the only thing Marlene hoarded. The woman collected pain, too.

Which is no doubt why I'm here.

Marlene slid into a throne-like chair made of gold. "What do you think of my study?"

I paused before her and let my mouth hang open. It was

important that I continue to play the country bumpkin. "It's very pretty."

"How dull of you to say." Marlene drummed her nails on the armrest. "You've heard we're having guests this weekend... The Tsar, the Vicomte, and even Genesis Rex."

I slapped on my best 'simple farm girl' grin. "Does that mean we'll eat something other than marrow pudding?"

With any luck, it means I'll get my chance at revenge.

Marlene pursed her lips. "That's all you have to tell me?"

"What else do you want me to say?"

"Something that doesn't sound brainless. Sophia was many things, but she was no fool, especially when it came to Ada. If she left her little pet with you, then the two of you must have plotted together for the child's welfare."

So, that's what this is all about. Marlene wanted to know if Sophia and I planned to help Ada escape. Gods-damn it. Marlene knew Sophia too well, and wasn't that fine of a liar. How will I convince Marlene that I have no escape plans, especially when Rowan is waiting outside the back gate right now?

I straightened my shoulders. "Sophia asked me to look out for Ada. I agreed. That's all there is to it."

"You're lying." Marlene held up her hand. "Don't bother to deny it. You're trouble."

The room seemed to heat up by ten degrees. *I'm trouble?* I blinked my eyes innocently. "I don't understand."

"I should give you a mark. Then, you'd have to tell me or die."

Her words sent a pang of panic through me. "No. You entered into a magickal pact with Sophia. You can't give me a mark until next season." *At least, I hope that's how it works.*

Marlene's brown eyes shone with rage. "Don't tell me what I can't do. I'm a Grand Mistress Necromancer. I can break magickal agreements like that." She snapped her fingers.

Sweat broke out along my forehead. Could Marlene have given me the mark all along, yet held out to watch me suffer?

Every bone in my body felt heavy with dread. Leading me along only to give me the mark anyway... That was precisely the kind of game Marlene would play. I worked hard to keep my features unreadable. "I'll say it once more. Sophia asked me to watch out for the child and I agreed. It was a gesture of kindness and nothing else. There are no further plans."

Marlene leaned back in her chair. "Do I have your word on that?"

"Absolutely." My legs turned wobbly beneath me. I needed to get out of here and to the back gate. "Is there anything else you require? I'm due in the storehouse today."

"No, you may go."

I'd never been happier to leave a place in my life. I turned on my heel and sped toward the door.

"Stop there," said Marlene slowly.

That icy feeling returned to my skull. I paused mid-step. *And I was so close to the door.*

"Come to think of it," said Marlene. "I do have one more item for you."

I returned to my place before her throne. Although it wasn't far away, it still felt like one of the longest walks in my life. "Yes, Mother?"

"I've changed my mind. You're far smarter than you let on... And clever girls always have plans. Let's see if we can't find some way to share it, eh?" A low moan sounded from behind one of the cabinet doors. My breath caught.

"Who's in there? One of the Sisters?"

A nasty smile rounded Marlene's lips. "No, that's is something else entirely." Marlene snapped her fingers. "Guards!"

The main door flung open. Four warriors in black armor marched into the study. My mind sped through options. I could run and maybe meet Rowan, but the chances of getting through the cloister without being captured were slim.

The boot falls of the guards thundered in my ears. Their hulking bodies fell upon me. One man yanked my arms behind my back with such force his metal armor tore through my robes and skin. Pain shot across my shoulders. Two others knelt on either side of me, gripping my ankles to hold me in place. The fourth one grasped my chin and held my gaze toward one of the cabinets. That moan sounded again, and it was definitely coming from the bureau right before me. What was in there?

Marlene slowly eyed me from head to toe. "You're afraid." She licked her lips. "That's what I like to see."

By the gods. She's toying with me.

"Shall we bring out someone to talk to?" Marlene stepped forward and unlocked the cabinet. Another moan sounded from inside.

Oh, no.

Marlene grinned. "Last night, you became acquainted with the creatures that turn Novices into Sisters. You're about to meet their maker." She let out a low whistle. "He's very good at causing pain."

I wriggled in the guard's grasp, but couldn't move. Every cell in my body wanted to flee.

"Sophia and I have no plans," I said quickly. "I'm telling you the truth."

"And I don't believe you."

My vision clouded over with panic. What kind of monster gives birth to bone creepers?

The cabinet door slowly swung open. Little by little, a man in ragged Caster leathers crawled out. With jerky movements, he rose to stand before me. Every muscle in my body froze. *This can't be happening.* The man's left arm had been torn off and replaced by a single great centipede.

He's a Changed One.

It was just as Rowan said. The Tsar had kidnapped this poor Caster and attached part of his familiar to his body. Horrible. And now, this tortured soul was going to change me as well.

That can't happen. I must escape and end my curse.

"Don't do this," I said, panting. "You'll break your magickal vow with Sophia and for what? Nothing. I don't know much about Necromancy. There must be some kind of price you'd pay for that, though. The Tsar arrives in three days. Can you afford for your powers to be weakened?"

"So Sophia told you about our little deal, eh? What else did she babble about, I wonder?" Marlene pointed to the Caster. "Slave, give this Sister my mark."

"Don't do this, Mother." Rowan was outside. I was so close.

The Caster stared at me with vacant eyes. His face was covered in stubble, dirt, and scars. Words burned on my tongue. I couldn't say any of them.

I'm your ally.

I'm here to kill the Tsar.

Set me loose or I'll suffer in fire.

But I couldn't speak any of that. Instead, I tried to put all my fear and promise into a single request. "Please."

If the Caster heard me, he didn't show it. His blue eyes were soulless and empty as his long arm slithered across the floor toward me. I've seen my share of insects on a farm. Nothing compared to this. The Caster's limb was a line of gelatinous goo with red organs pulsing under the clear skin. Hundreds of tiny legs click-clacked against the wooden planks as the limb closed in on me. My chest felt so tight I couldn't breathe.

Bit by bit, the arm wound its way up my leg. I groaned and thrashed as the tiny insect pincers bit into my skin as it crawled up my torso. The guard held my chin still as the insect's face stared directly into mine. It was gooey with all-white eyes and needle-sharp teeth. Cold breath brushed my mouth. I choked back a scream.

No, this isn't happening. No.

Little by little, the creature opened its jaws and a bone crawler appeared. The tiny centipede wriggled inside the larger insect mouth like a tongue.

"See that?" asked Mother Superior. "How would you like that deep within you?"

I thrashed in terror as the bone crawler squirmed closer. "Make it stop!"

"You want it to stop? Then tell me. What do you really have planned?"

"Nothing! You're insane!"

Marlene tapped her lips in a casual motion. "I suppose... I believe you." She snapped her fingers. "Enough, Slave. Take it back."

Both the bone crawler and the centipede slid back to its master. I slumped in the guard's hold, barely able to stay upright.

"There now." Marlene checked her nails. "I'm glad we cleared that up." She waved to the Caster. "We're through with you. Go."

The Caster slunk back into the cabinet, his insect arm dragging behind him. I watched him leave and sobbed. Everything here was impossible. This poor Caster's life. My escape. What had I been thinking to start this journey in the first place?

Marlene sneered at me. "Sniveling little fool." She waved at the door. "Guards, take her to the storehouse. This one must work for her keep."

As the guards dragged me away, I began to regain my focus. The haze of terror faded into a new realization. I was going to the storehouse by the back gate.

There was still a chance.

～

It was late morning by the time I stumbled into the storehouse. Two thoughts echoed through my mind.

Rowan. Escape.

With any luck, Rowan was waiting for me right now. We'd had already agreed that my scarab would signal him to meet me at the gate. As long as that back door was open, my escape should be pretty easy. I could simply walk out with Rowan. That Caster was a powerful mage and could easily handle things from there. All I needed was an opened door.

But what if it were closed? I pictured the massive wall that surrounded the Cloister. I hadn't seen it since I first left the wagon. I knew what it looked like, though.

Tall. Heavy. Lined with guards.

I swallowed hard. The gate had better be opened. My worries had me so distracted, I barely noticed Nan rushing over.

"Are you all right, Elea?"

"Fine." My voice sounded dreamy and strange, even to me. My morning with Marlene had left me all jittery. What other Changed Ones were hidden around here? For that matter, what else did Marlene have planned for us?

Escape and you won't have to find out.

The four guards who'd been following me all morning leaned against a nearby wall, right alongside the four Marlene had already sent off with Nan and Ada. I'd hoped the extra warriors might move on with their day, but no such luck. Now, we had eight guards to keep an eye on only three of us. That wasn't going to make my escape easier.

Nan stepped closer. "There's been trouble at the gate, Elea. One trader or another has been complaining all morning."

Thank the Sire. That was probably Rowan. "Is it still open?"

Nan nodded. "Sure, it's always open on delivery days. There are piles of packages out there for you to bring in. Better get going."

I glanced around, looking for Ada. I didn't want to leave without saying goodbye. "Where's the little one?"

"Busy, just like you should be." Nan tossed her head, making her long braids shake. She poked me in the center of my rib cage. "Enough slacking off. You think because you get special time with Marlene you can shirk your work? Ada and me's been dealing with them traders all morning." If I hadn't been watching, I might have missed her wink. "Get moving. Now."

That wink told me all I needed to know. Nan realized that I was up to something. Clever thief. I decided to play along with her act, since it was the perfect way to throw off the guards. "Stop complaining." I wagged my finger at her. "If you'd had the morning I did, you wouldn't be rushing out into more trouble, either."

Nan sniffed. "Just get to work."

I hesitated for a moment. It felt wrong to leave without any goodbye, but a teary farewell would only alert the guards. "Fine. I'll go." Turning on my heel, I stomped out the door.

*a*s the crow flew, it was a short walk to the back gate. It didn't feel that way, though. Every step seemed to take longer than the last. Plus, Marlene's four guards stayed right behind me. That was a concern.

I opened my mouth, ready to summon my scarab to alert Rowan to be waiting. I couldn't very well walk through the gate and stand around like a fool. And Rowan couldn't loiter waiting for me without attracting attention.

I closed my lips and fast. If I summoned the scarab now, what would the guards think? It wasn't worth making them suspicious. Scarabs weren't native to this part of the desert.

Gods-damn it. I'd hoped to summon the scarab while I was walking alone. Instead, it looked like I needed an alternative plan, which would require me to play-act and lie. Both of those were skills they'd discouraged in the Zelle. Amazing how often I used them now that I'd left.

At last, I reached the gate. Another worry got added to the pile.

The door was closed.

Three more guards stood in front of the locked wooden door. I spied two warriors and their captain. While the other guards wore black armor, their leader's chest plate was imprinted with a pattern of white bones. A half dozen more fighters paced along the top of the wall. It was just like when I'd arrived at the cloister, only this time, there were more guards and a closed gate.

I paused a few yards away and tried to look bored. "Greetings."

"Greetings," said the Captain. Around him, the other guards paced the wall or talked casually in low tones.

"I'm here to get a delivery."

"Gate's closed."

"I can see that. When will you open it?"

"Not sure. There's been trouble on the other side all morning. You'll have to wait it out."

I sucked in a shaky breath and started up my act. "Look here, I'm not staying by this gate one moment longer than I have to. I heard all about the plague sign out here."

At the mention of 'plague sign,' everyone froze. The Captain even whipped off his helm. He was gray-haired and dark-skinned with long jowls and steely eyes. "What are you talking about?"

None of these guards had magick. And if there was one Necromancer skill that the Forgotten valued, it was our ability to spot a plague. My kind had trapped the first bone crawlers centuries ago. Since then, we'd killed every other insect that had spread the disease.

"Plague sign." I looked at him as if he were insane. "Beetles. They've infested the sands back here. Everyone's talking about it."

The Captain's jowls shook slightly. "I haven't gotten any reports."

I coughed into my hand to hide my command. "Now."

My beetle burrowed up from under the sands, unfurled its tiny wings, and fluttered toward the sky. I thought they'd watch with mild concern. After all, these warriors always acted pretty tough.

The guards went berserk. Everyone scrambled toward the front gate.

I worried my lower lip with my teeth. I'd wanted to distract the guards, not make them lose their minds. I laced my fingers behind my neck and groaned. With this much fuss, Marlene would be alerted sooner rather than later.

The Captain started barking out orders to his men. "Get back to your posts! There's no plague here." I couldn't help but notice the warble in his voice, though.

Some of the guards turned back to the gate, while others shoved their way in the opposite direction. A few fights broke out, along with lots of shouting. Things were quickly spiraling out of control.

Then I heard Rowan's deep voice rumbling from the other side of the wall. The air thickened with magick. My skin prickled with awareness. My gaze locked on the Captain. Did he even realize what was going on?

If the Captain noticed the spellwork, he didn't show it. He paced the base of the wall, shaking his fist and threatening his men.

Rowan's voice grew louder. I stared at the locked wooden door. For a moment, it rattled on its hinges.

Then it burst.

A wave of termites spilled onto the sand. They spread out, eating through any splinter of wood that remained from what was once the back gate.

Some guards saw it as an attack. Others believed the plague was definitely upon them. More fighting broke out. Someone tackled the Captain. This was my chance. I dodged the battling warriors and slipped toward the gate.

Rowan stood framed in the doorway. I wasn't the type to sing for joy. Still, at this moment, I was considering it. *Thank the Sire.* He wore a long black cloak with the hood pulled low. He began another incantation. There was too much yelling to pick out the words, though. My limbs felt charged with excitement. I raced toward Rowan with all my strength, reaching him just as he finished his latest spell. "Rowan!"

He glared at me from under his hood. "I said *dawn*, Elea."

My mouth fell open. "I may hate you right now."

After that, things began happening so quickly, I could hardly keep track.

The Captain rolled over, spat sand from his mouth, and glared right at me. That wasn't a good sign. My distraction had run out, it seemed. "Lock down the cloister," he cried. "Summon Marlene." He gestured toward me. "And kill her."

The guards organized again and began moving at double speed. Some raced back to the cloister. Others notched arrows into their bows. More rushed toward Rowan and me, their longswords out and ready to fight. The excitement in my body switched to an all-out panic. I grabbed Rowan's hand. "Run!"

Suddenly, the sky darkened. I looked up to see birds and not just any fowl… Crimson falcons. *More of Rowan's spellwork.* The man could be grouchy, but he did know his magick. The falcons swooped in and attacked the guards.

Rowan whistled and a cart careened around the side of the wall. It was an open affair with a flat bed, just like the ones that were used for deliveries. Clever. It wouldn't have drawn suspicion from the guards, unless they looked too closely at the pair of fierce gray stallions at the bit. Those two animals were built for racing, not pulling loads. The horses galloped to us and then stopped so quickly the wagon tipped up its back wheels before settling down with a thud.

I climbed onto the wagon's bed, careful to press as much of my body against the sides as I could. That would provide some cover from the arrows. Rowan leaped onto the driver's bench and grabbed the reins. "Hyah!"

The wagon took off with a lurch. Elation and terror battled it out inside me. I was escaping. It was really happening. The falcons kept the guards busy as we raced away from the cloister at top speed. Maybe things would be easy from here on out. I slumped against the wooden floor of the wagon and sighed.

Then Marlene's voice echoed through the air. My stomach fell to my toes. Blue flashes lit the sky. The ground shook with a roll of thunder.

I thought through the Grand Mistress canon of spells. There were a handful that would be deadly against a fast-moving target. I risked a peep over the edge of the wagon as it lurched along. *Please, don't let her call skull seekers.*

Blurry shapes shot out from the gate. The specters were made of blue light, with skulls for faces and bodies that looked like blurs of sapphire-colored mist.

There were skull seekers, all right. Poisonous teeth and all.

I lay back on the wagon's floor, stared up at the blue sky, and let out an inarticulate 'argh.' All my Necromancer control evaporated. "This was supposed to be a simple escape." Part of me knew I was ranting, but I couldn't stop. "Walk through the gate. Rowan knows magick and—poof—I'd be gone."

Rowan called over his shoulder. "You're wearing enchanted manacles. I was never going to poof you anywhere."

"That's not what I meant." I couldn't believe I was about to say this. "Skull seekers are coming."

"What?" Rowan looked behind us. All the color drained from his face. "Lady, give me strength." He faced forward, raised his right arm, and started a fresh round of incantations. The horses took off at a supernatural pace. It was a good idea, yet I'd cast quite a few skull seekers myself. Speed alone wouldn't be enough.

"You need to—" I wanted to explain more. I couldn't say a word. My entire body with agony as the magick on my manacles took hold. Knives of pain stabbed up my arms and sliced through my chest. I forced one more word through my gritted teeth. "Rowan."

"I know the manacles are hurting you," Rowan called over his shoulder. "Once we get somewhere safe, I'll cast a spell to break them."

I could hear the eerie, chattering laughter of the skull seekers as they drew in closer. The way things stood, we'd be torn apart in an instant. "No." I panted through the pain. "Protection... Skin." It was all I could get past my lips. Hopefully, Rowan would understand.

"I'll cast it." Rowan launched into a fresh incantation. The veins in his right hand glowed red as thousands of crimson snake scales appeared over the surface of the cart and horses. I could feel my enchanted manacles repelling the magick from me, but at least, the protective skin materialized inside the back of the wagon. The leathery coating radiated raw power. I exhaled.

We had a chance at surviving.

The specters slammed skull-first into the wheels. My body smashed against the wagon's side and the impact felt harsh as a hammer. I'd sent skull seekers into the side of a mountain, where they sent wall-sized chunks tumbling to the ground. How long could we hope to hold out?

The cart teetered onto its left wheels, ready to fall over and take the horses with it. Fresh pain from my manacles stabbed straight through my abdomen. I curled forward and moaned.

Focus past the hurt. Stay in control.

The cart rode on two wheels for what felt like ages. If it

tipped, we'd be easy prey. And worse, since Marlene's power came from the Tsar, I wasn't sure my manacles would repel the skull seekers the same way they repelled Rowan's protective skin.

I needed to get us back on four wheels.

At last, I started thinking past the pain. Shifting my weight, I lunged to the right side of the wagon, hoping my shift would help steady the cart. The wagon landed back on all wheels again.

The seekers whirled around for another attack. Their cackling laughter turned piercingly loud. I braced myself for another impact. Despite the protective skin, the wagon was already cracked in some places. Some floorboards had even split in two. I wasn't sure we could handle another assault.

On this pass, the seekers went after the horses, crashing into their flanks and biting at their faces. The pitiful neighs tore at my heart. The animals bucked in terror. I pulled at my irons. *What I wouldn't give to rip these off right now.*

The cart rumbled over uneven ground. A loud snap sounded and my heart sank. I'd heard noises like that before. One of the horses just broke a leg. I looked up to see the two animals lose their footing and topple to the ground. The wagon flipped.

Sire, protect me.

Everything blurred into a jumble of pain and movement. The cart toppled over and shattered. My leg got skewered on the shaft of a wagon wheel. One thought broke through the chaos.

So this is how I die.

Seekers closed in on me. Razor-sharp teeth latched onto my limbs. Each bite burned like acid. I flailed at the seekers, trying to swat them with my manacles. The irons barely made them flinch.

"Stop!" I howled. Their hollow blue eyes and cackling laughter were everywhere. It was something out of a nightmare. I kept trying to hit them, but my movements turned sluggish and weak. A sickly taste filled my mouth, and I knew it was the seekers' poison taking hold.

It's already started. I'm dying.

A burst of red light filled the sky. Rowan's voice echoed over the desert.

Don't let them get him, too.

The seekers broke away. Rowan stood over me, the hood of his cloak pulled away. His rugged features were tight with rage.

Every inch of my body ached. The manacles burned my wrists. The seekers' bites were already pulsing with poison and hurt. "What happened?"

"I cast some sun spheres. Those burn away seekers."

Those were the bursts of light that I'd seen. *Well done.* I slumped onto the sand, every last bit of energy seemed drained from my body. I lay on my back and stared up into the blue expanse of sky. The seekers were gone and I'd escaped. It was tempting to rest. Things weren't safe this close to the Midnight Cloister, though. "We must get—"

Something pulled on my ankle, and it took a huge amount of energy to lift my head and check it out. A guard was crouched beneath my feet and had grabbed my foot. I tried to break free from his grip, but the poison was muddling my head. My body wouldn't even twitch on command, let alone kick the man away.

Rowan was on the guard in a heartbeat. With a single swoop of his arm, he pounded the man's head. The warrior's helm crushed inward from the force of the blow. I'd never seen anything like it. The warrior slumped to the ground, dead. Blood oozed from his helmet onto the sand.

One guard was down. How many more were out there?

We needed to get moving. There had to be more guards coming. I struggled to sit up. My body wouldn't shift.

Someone scooped me into his arms and ran. I stared at the firm jawline and green eyes. *Rowan.* I wanted to ask a question. *What about the guards?* No matter how I tried, my mouth wouldn't form the words. It took everything I had to hoist up my head and look over Rowan's arm to the desert behind us.

What a sight. Great red scorpions burst out of the sand, grabbing the guards in their claws and dragging them back underground. Termites, falcons, a sun sphere, and now scorpions… I'd never imagined Casters had this kind of power.

Rowan curled me closer to his chest. "Don't worry. I've taken care of the guards. There's a place not far from here where I've set up everything to get those manacles off you. It's warded so they won't find us. Do you understand me, Elea?"

I did, but I couldn't get the word 'yes' past my lips. I jiggled my head in a kind of nod. It was the best I could do past the pain. The bites on my limbs, the pain shooting from my wrists, the stabbing hurt in my thigh… It all meshed together in overwhelming agony.

"We're almost there." I was dimly aware that we'd stopped at a circle of darkened sand. "This leads to underground caves. I enchanted the entrance to look like sand and warded off the entire area. I'm taking you down now. Don't worry if it gets dark."

I wanted to nod. Sadly, I was past that ability. Rowan rushed forward and I had the illusion that we were walking through the earth. Soon, we appeared inside a network of underground caves made of red stone. Although the air was fine, I was finding it harder and harder to breathe. My body was breaking down.

Rowan hurried through the passageways and into a side chamber. He set me down on a blanket. "We're here." The cave was tall and narrow with a small opening to the sky. Some small jars were lined up on the floor. Rowan waved his arm and a campfire appeared in the center of the room. The flickering light gave me another glimpse at the bite marks on my arms. Angry purple lines covered my skin. Black pus oozed from the sores. The sight made my pain worse, somehow.

Rowan grabbed a jar. The image of the sun and moon was pained on the side. "This is what Ocie and Yuri gave me to break the manacles. Once they're off, I'll heal you."

Somehow, I forced out one word. "Good." Nausea and pain whipped through me. I arched my back and moaned.

Please don't let me die here.

18

I wasn't sure how long I lay there while Rowan poured different powders into stone cups. With each passing minute, I felt my heart struggle harder in my chest. The poison burned deeper on my seeker bites, making it feel like a thousand knives were digging into my skin at once. I was being sliced apart, over and over.

As last, Rowan knelt beside me. "It is ready." He scooped paste from the cup onto his fingers and brushed it on the skin beneath my irons. The substance felt cool and soothing. For a moment, I almost forgot the rest of my injuries.

"My Lady, your servant calls to you." When he spoke again, Rowan's voice resonated with power and magic.

Give me lion's strength, viper's speed,
Break through these bonds, set your servant free.

Rowan lifted his right hand; the veins inside his skin shone with crimson brightness. Crackling energy filled the cave. The dust motes in the air glistened with power.

Time lost all meaning. It felt as if my life had always been this agony, and would stay that way forever. Some dark part of me knew that was true. Come Sunday, I would surely burn. Days, weeks, hours… It was only pain. It would always last.

I became aware of Rowan gently brushing his fingertips across my brow. "Do you wish me to go on?" His eyes were filled with sympathy. "It's almost dawn."

I forced one word past my lips. "Dawn?"

"You've been here all night."

My breaths came in rough wheezes. This was it; I was dying. Tears streamed down my cheeks. For the first time, I noticed the deep circles under Rowan's eyes. He couldn't keep this up much longer.

"If I stop trying to break your irons, then you can pass on to the Eternal Lands." The rugged lines of Rowan's face softened. "You've been at death's door for hours, Elea. I don't know how you've held on." He sighed. "There's no shame in wanting it to end."

"No," I rasped. "Curse."

"I'll find a way to free you. I swear it."

For a moment, I let go my will to live. Maybe Rowan was right. *It's only a matter of days before I die anyway.* And Rowan had promised to free me from my curse. An image appeared through the haze of hurt in my mind. I saw Rowan at the oasis, pleading with me to give him my totem rings. And I'd found him in my dream. I reached out, grabbed Rowan's hand, and tapped my chest weakly. "Lady." Somehow, I managed to flick my hand toward Rowan. "Sire."

Rowan frowned. "I don't understand."

There was so much I wanted to tell Rowan. I didn't have the strength to say the words, though. I wanted to ask the Lady of Creation for strength.

Maybe I was half dead and fully insane, but suddenly it

seemed the only thing left to do. I gestured lamely to the dishes of herbs. "Hy...brid."

Rowan's eyes widened with understanding. "You want to know how to call upon the power of the Lady. Try hybrid magick with me as your guide."

I closed my eyes. It was the closest I could get to a nod.

"That's a brilliant idea." He gently brushed some stray hairs away from my forehead. The motion was comforting. At last, he understood what I wanted to try.

"Have you tried to summon Caster magick?"

"Scarab." My voice was barely a whisper.

"That's right, you found the beetle and were trying to break the manacles that way."

I nodded as icy fingers of cold dug into my skin and organs. My entire body began to tremble.

Rowan shook his head. "You're freezing." He scooped me into his arms and set me across his lap. He rubbed my arms and legs. "Better?"

Warmth flowed through my limbs. For the first time since leaving the cloister, I truly felt something other than pain. "Yes." My voice came out clear and strong.

Rowan kept up his steady touch. My heartbeat steadied. Huge gulps of air finally made their way into my lungs. I leaned into Rowan's shoulder. I couldn't remember anything that felt more soothing.

"Caster power comes from the Lady of Creation. The first thing we teach young Casters is to picture her. After that, you ask her for what you need, just like I did in my incantation."

The cobwebs in my head started to clear. I understood exactly what he was saying. "Go on."

"The Lady is tall and lithe with golden hair that hangs in waves to her waist. Her home is a garden of green trees, sparkling brooks, and mossy stones. Every beast imaginable roams there, free and at peace." Once again, Rowan brushed the back of his fingers against my cheek. More warmth flowed into me. His touch was its own kind of magick. "Can you see it?"

I closed my eyes. An image of rolling green hills filled my mind. My muscles loosened. Pain sliced through me, but the cuts weren't as deep. "Yes."

"Good. The Lady wears a crown of daisies. Tiny bluebells are woven through her hair. Can you picture her?"

My mind cleared entirely. I could see the Lady standing on the hill, her loose yellow dress fluttering around her legs. She had tanned skin, long golden hair, and strong cheekbones. "I can see her."

Rowan spread a line of paste on the skin on my wrists. "Ask her what you need."

I kept the image of the Lady bright in my mind. "Heal me."

A trickle of magick wrapped my wrist, right where Rowan had rubbed Ocie and Yuri's paste. The pain inside my skull lessened. Purple light began to glow under the manacles.

Rowan's eyes brightened as he pressed the paste onto my lips. It tasted of berries and spice. "Keep fighting, Elea. Allow her power to move through you."

The image of the Lady seemed closer now. I could see the strong line of her chin and a sprinkling of freckles across her nose. Her gaze locked with mine.

All of a sudden, gusts of ethereal power drove through my soul. My body felt weightless. A loud cracking sound filled the air. My manacles tumbled to the floor. The biting pain around my wrists vanished.

The irons are gone. I'm free.

Still, bite marks burned my skin, and my leg ached where it had been skewered. I'd gotten rid of some hurt. So much more remained, though.

"Don't worry," said Rowan "I can heal you." He rubbed my

back in soothing strokes as he began another incantation. Soon his healing energy flowed through me. While the Lady's power felt like a gust of air, Rowan's energy was all solidity, warmth, and comfort.

I wasn't sure how long I sat, soaking up his healing strength. Some part of me never wanted to leave. At last, I remembered Petra's warnings about emotion and control. I started to move away. Rowan's hold tightened.

"I should let you get up," I said.

"You need more healing. A few more minutes."

I relaxed into his hold and rubbed my wrists, not believing the manacles were gone. "We did it."

Rowan rested his chin on the top of my head. "Yes, we did." I could hear the smile in his voice.

More of his warm power flowed through me. Suddenly, I couldn't remember my eyelids ever feeling so heavy. Maybe I'd doze off for a second or two.

I wanted to ask Rowan a question, but it came out as, "Must... Sleep..."

"That's all right. Rest now. I'll finish your healing."

I drifted off into the deepest slumber I'd had in years.

hen I opened my eyes again, I was curled up on a pile of furs and wrapped in soft blankets. On the other side of the cave, Rowan lay on his side, fast asleep. It felt wrong for him to be uncovered when I'd been so carefully tucked in.

Rowan opened his right eye. "You're staring at me."

I shrugged. "You gave me all the blankets. I feel guilty."

He grinned one of his crooked smiles. "All part of my master plan."

"I always suspected that you had one, you know." I rolled onto my back and looked up through the hole in the cave's ceiling. A full moon shone in the night sky. *Oh, no.* I sat bolt upright. "How long have I been asleep?"

"Only a few hours."

I exhaled. "Good."

Rowan sat up slowly. "How do you feel?"

"Better." My wrists and thigh still stung, but I supposed that was to be expected. Beside me, the campfire's flames crackled and flared. An ember landed on my ankle, setting off a tiny burst of pain that quickly disappeared. It was nothing like the agony that awaited me on Sunday. That was eternal. I shivered. "What day is it?"

"Saturday. Barely."

"The Tsar arrives tomorrow. How far away are Ocie and Yuri?"

"A day's walk away from here."

Might as well be a month, with the way I was feeling. "I wish I were strong enough to cast a transport spell." I sighed. "Or any spell, really. Mother Superior still has some of my magick. If I cast at all, she'll find me in a heartbeat."

"I can transport there and then cast another spell to bring you to me."

"That means you cast two transport spells to go to the fair, and two more to return." Casting one transport spell had exhausted me, let alone four. "Since I can't cast, you'll need to do spellwork for both of us. You can't waste your energy on transport. We'll just have to secure another way to get there. Perhaps we can find a new wagon?"

"Something like that. I have a few ideas. Not to worry."

I didn't worry about Rowan finding us a wagon, but I didn't like the way he was staring into the fire. His entire expression was darkening.

"What's wrong?" I asked.

Rowan huffed out a long breath. "I have some news."

The dark note in his voice set me on edge. "What kind of news?"

"It's about your friend, Tristan. Jakob turned some things up."

I scrubbed my hands over my face. More bad news? I'd been thinking through Jakob's last news. It was entirely possible that Tristan had traded my life for Quinn's. The idea made me ill. "Whatever he heard, I don't want to know. I've put it all out of my mind to focus on Sunday and that's where my thoughts need to stay for now."

"I understand. The offer is there when you're ready."

"Thank you." I shifted my weight, trying to find a better way to sit. My thigh felt like it was getting worse. That might be a trick of my mind, though. In any case, didn't want Rowan poking around it right now. We needed to get to Ocie and Yuri. "You said you had some ideas about how to get to the Sanctuary Fair?"

"Yes." Rowan stood up and stretched. "I know exactly what to do about transportation."

I rolled onto my side and winced. I wished I could sleep for a year. "Horses?" As long as it was a short ride, I might be fine.

"No. Snow tigers. Remember my familiars?"

"Right." He'd mentioned them at the oasis.

Rowan set his fingers in his mouth and let out a loud whistle. Two white tigers stalked into the cave. I'd never seen anything like them. Their heads came up to Rowan's shoulders. They had great green eyes and red swirls were painted on their pristine white coats. Long fangs poked from their mouths. "Elea, I'd like you to meet Radi and Umeme, my snow tigers."

"Aren't you lovely?" Seeing them made me miss the presence of my little beetle, though. "I have a familiar, too." I looked around. "You can come out now." My tiny scarab didn't appear. I nibbled my lower lip with my teeth. "I hope he's all right."

"An insect familiar?" Rowan shrugged. "He's fine, I'm sure. Those things could live through the end of the world."

I stood and realized that the tigers were almost as tall as I was. I eyed them warily. "How does this work?"

With the two tigers in the cave, the place felt positively cramped. Rowan scratched one behind the ears. "This is Umeme. She wants you to ride her."

"Ride her?" I rubbed at my inner thigh, which still burned from my injury. The wound had only partially healed.

"They're much more comfortable than a horse, I can assure you. Although, if you'd rather find a wagon—"

"No, I'd rather ride." It was Saturday already, for the Sire's sake. I had precious little time left before my curse struck. A queasy feeling crawled up my throat. I'd just spent a few hours in excruciating pain. What would an eternity of that do to my soul? "The Tsar arrives tomorrow. We have to get to Ocie and Yuri as soon as we can."

"Agreed. If we leave at first light, we'll arrive at the fair by noon."

"Are you sure we can't leave now?"

"Positive. Besides, this will give you time to eat and wash up."

"I suppose so." I tried to run my fingers through my hair. It was too tangled to get far. I didn't even want to sniff my robes. "I suppose it wouldn't do to meet the mightiest mages in the realm looking like this."

"Everyone feels better after food and a bath." Rowan grabbed a small basket from against the wall. "What do you think of hardtack?"

"That's a block of dried bread, right?" Tristan used to keep some on his ships. He said it was only for emergencies since it tasted so foul.

"That's the stuff." He tossed me a small bar and I nibbled carefully at one corner. A delicious, nutty flavor filled my mouth. I stuffed in a huge bite. "This is good."

"Glad you approve. Once you're done, I'll show you to where you can wash. There's an underground spring in one of the caves." He looked up at the moon. "We've a few more hours until dawn. That should give us plenty of time to heal that leg of yours."

I made a great show of scanning my arms and legs. "The bite marks from the seekers are almost gone. There's nothing to heal."

"You know that's not what I meant. I was talking about your inner thigh. It could use a little more magick."

"No, it's fine."

"And you're still a terrible liar."

He was right. I should let him heal me, even if the injury was pretty high up on my leg. But last night was a one-time situation. I'd been out of my mind with pain and Rowan had helped me. It was a special circumstance that should never happen again.

So from here on out, I was healing on my own terms. "It's not perfect. Even so, it'll get better soon." I gave him a sly look. "My body can heal without any magick involved, you know."

Rowan chuckled. "I'll try to remember that."

I stuffed the last bite of tack into my mouth. Now that I'd eaten, I couldn't wait to wash up. "Where is that underground spring?"

"The pool is just down the passage. You'll find baskets with soap and fresh clothes. I'm going to look into some things with Radi and Umeme. We'll be back by dawn."

One word popped out at me. "Things? What kind of things?"

"I want to scope out the roads and I'm going to cast a few contact spells too. I may be able to get some maps at the sanctuary fair. Depends on who's there."

"Maps of the Midnight Cloister?" I knew a handful of places, but there was much the guards hadn't let us see.

He nodded. "Exceptionally accurate ones, too."

"That could help." Rowan walked toward the outer passage. His huge frame seemed to dominate the entire cave, even with two snow tigers at his side. I cupped my hand by my mouth. "And thanks."

"Nothing to thank." He glanced over his shoulder. "We're a team, right?"

"Right." My heart began to beat double-time. Last night, Rowan's touch had felt so warm and right.

Watch your emotions, Elea.

This was exactly the kind of emotion that could blow a Necromancer's focus. Of course, I'd have odd feelings about the man. He'd saved my life. But I had much bigger things to worry about than being held. If I didn't figure out a way to kill the Tsar, I was in for an eternity of pain. I needed to get my mental control back and fast.

20

I leaned forward on Umeme's back as we scaled another sand dune. Her white fur felt lush and cool under me, which was a nice difference from the baking sun overhead.

If I lived through this quest, I was visiting the woods. In the wintertime. For an entire year.

"I can cast one for you, if you like," said Rowan.

His deep voice startled me. We hadn't spoken much since leaving for the sanctuary fair. I looked to my left. Somewhere along the line, Rowan had snuck up beside me on Radi. The man could be positively stealthy.

"Cast what?" I asked.

"A cooling spell. I put one on Umeme, and I know you can't do any spellwork right now."

I wiped my forehead with my sleeve. I'd changed back into a Commoner's dress before we left the cave and already, the fabric was sticking to me. Rowan didn't have so much as a drop of sweat on his skin. The man had obviously cast a cooling spell on himself already. I fanned myself with my hand. "Is it that obvious?"

His mouth slowly wound into a crooked smile. "Maybe." I had the urge to brush my fingertip along the dimple in his cheek. *The sun must be getting to me.* Rowan was nothing more than a useful ally.

"I'd like that," I said.

"Won't take long." Rowan reached toward me. The veins in his right hand glowed red as he whispered an incantation. The air thickened with magick. His palm flared with crimson light and then, the perfect amount of cool air wrapped around me. Rowan knew his spellwork, that was for certain.

I sighed. "Thank you."

"Anything else troubling you?" Rowan shot a pointed look at my thigh. It ached. I was sure that it would heal in time, though. I was having enough odd feelings just looking at his dimple. This week was doing strange things to my brain.

"No, thank you. I'm fine."

Rowan raised his right brow in a movement that said 'you're a terrible liar.' He opened his mouth, ready to push the point about my injury. Fortunately, I remembered a key piece of information that I'd forgotten to share. "In all the excitement, I didn't tell you something."

"Really." His flat tone said that he knew I was avoiding my leg.

Maybe I was changing the subject, but that didn't alter the fact that I had some genuine information to share. "I met a Changed One at the cloister."

Rowan's full mouth tightened into a thin line. "What did they look like?"

"When you said your people had familiars, could those be huge insects?"

"Easily. Insects are some of the most powerful forces in nature."

Like my scarab beetle. My tiny friend was still missing, unfortunately. I feared that he'd done his job in alerting Rowan and now, I'd never see him again. Such a shame. "Marlene is holding the Changed One in her study."

Rowan's face paled. "His familiar was an insect?"

"He had a centipede arm." My next bit of news was huge for Rowan and I wished I knew a gentle way to break it. I looked around the desert, like the right words would be written in the sand. I guessed the best way was not to delay. "The arm spat out bone crawlers. They burrow under the skin to become the Tsar's mark. That's the hybrid magick Viktor created."

Rowan frowned. "What do you mean?"

"Viktor's mark is made by bone crawlers. Or at least, it is in the Midnight Cloister. The creature connects Necromancers to the Mother Superior. In turn, she's linked to the Tsar."

Rowan leaned in, his face growing more intense by the second. I was beginning to worry that he might fall off Radi. "Why would Viktor do that? What do you think he's planning?"

I could see how upset Rowan was getting, and I hated to be the one to give him more bad news. There was no avoiding it, though. "The Tsar's using Caster magick to pull Necromancer power into himself. Once Viktor has enough, he'll be able to control all the Changed Ones."

"I see." Rowan stared the horizon for a long time. I didn't push him to say anything else. When he spoke again his voice was so low I almost didn't hear him. "Centipedes and bone crawlers. The Alfajiri clan uses them for familiars. They were the first group Viktor targeted." Rowan shook his head. "They're all but wiped out now."

A whole tribe was gone. I could only imagine the pain of Rowan and his people. "That's terrible, Rowan."

"What did this man look like?"

"Tall, thin, and raggedy." I pictured his blank eyes and empty voice. "He wasn't in his right mind. I suspect he's been tortured into following Viktor."

"Did you notice anything about the man?"

"He still wore Caster leathers. I could make out part of a large red swirl on the back of the jacket."

"Linden."

"You know who that was?" How could Rowan identify him so quickly? I hadn't seen much, only a walking skeleton in a scrap of fabric.

Rowan ran his fingers down the line of swirls on his jacket. "These symbols may look the same to you. Each one is unique to a Caster. It's a secret code we share. I wear all the symbols because I'm from the Imperial family. First sons wear them large and on their backs. Linden was the first son of the Alfajiri clan."

I hadn't known about the symbols, but I'd heard that the title 'first son' was like being a prince. The realization left me feeling hollow inside. Viktor had taken a leader and turned him into a slave. *Was there anything that man wouldn't stoop to?* "I know where they keep Linden. When we leave the cloister, he'll come with us."

"We'll get him if we can. If not, I'll return later."

"What do you mean?"

"If we kill Viktor and there's time to rescue Linden, then fine. But once this is over, you're my first priority." His gaze locked with mine. "I'm not risking your safety."

I straightened my shoulders. "I can take care of myself."

"I know. You're the strongest independent Necromancer left. But you aren't immortal. We lose you, Elea, we lose everything."

Memories of Linden's vacant eyes haunted me. "That man was the last of his kind, too. You said yourself that tribe has no more princes." Right now, Petra would tell me I was working myself into an emotional state for nothing. She was wrong. "We'll figure out a way to rescue Linden, and that's all there is to it." His gaze turned so intense, it made me squirm. "What is it?"

Rowan stared at me for a long time. "You. You're not at all what I expected."

"What do you mean?"

"Necromancers are all about control."

"Oh." A blush crawled up my cheek. *He had me there.* "Yes, I'm what we call *zuchtlos*."

"And that is?"

"Another way of saying I'm impulsive. My Mother Superior worked on it with me constantly. Controlling emotion is the key to Necromancy."

"Why do they fill your head with such things?" Rowan shook his head. "You're one of the best mages I've ever met. I'd say *zuchtlos* works fine for you."

My mouth fell open. "That's not possible."

His gaze searched my face. "Why, Elea?" The question had become larger in a way I couldn't define. "Tell me."

"I…" I needed to change the subject. Things were deepening between Rowan and me. The words fell from my lips on their own. "I'd rather you told me about Tristan."

"Are you certain of this?"

In truth, I actually was. It was time to talk about what had happened. As of tomorrow, I might be spending eternity with the man. If Rowan knew something useful, I'd better find out. "I'm positive."

"It must seem impossible to you that your friend cursed you."

"It does." My voice was rough with pain. "Can I ask you one thing?"

"Anything."

"Did you test the betrothal ring?"

"I did."

I tried to swallow past the knot of sadness in my throat. "And did you find the same thing that Jakob did?" For some reason, I couldn't some out and say 'did you find the layered spell that proved my friend got me cursed.'

Rowan kept his gaze steady with mine, which somehow made things worse. "I did."

The words hit me like a slap. It's true. "Tristan betrayed me."

"Jakob found out about the other person. The one who the curse originally targeted."

"You mean Quinn?"

"Yes, he was Tristan's Brother."

"I know. They were in the same monastery."

"No. His blood brother."

"Oh." I hugged my elbows. All of a sudden, Rowan's cooling spell made me feel downright freezing. "I didn't know." Tristan had never told me, but then, it seemed he'd left out a lot of facts. "That does make sense. Tristan would want to protect his own blood, and the curse would go after whoever he loved the most."

"I thought you'd want to know."

Right. Just in case my curse comes to pass.

My eyes stung with held-in tears. Even if he was trying to save Quinn, how could Tristan do that to me? Just the last time I'd seen him Tristan had lied, saying he had no choice about the curse. I straightened my spine and pulled on my Necromancer training.

Emotion is the enemy. Focus on the mission.

Rowan kept watching me carefully. "I hope it wasn't the wrong decision to tell you."

"No," I said calmly. "I had a right to know."

Our snow tigers paused and Radi let out a growl. It wasn't an angry noise, more of something to get Rowan's attention. Lucy used to make the same sound when she was hungry.

Rowan patted the tiger's side. "What's wrong, Radi? You smell people?" The tiger growled again and Rowan slipped off its back. "We're getting closer to the sanctuary fair. We'll need to travel the rest of the way on foot. We need to keep a low profile and showing up on tigers won't help."

I gingerly dismounted from Umeme. "You're sure Ocie and Yuri will be here?" They were seeming more real over time. Still, I had my doubts. Those children's stories were hard to forget.

"That's what they told Jakob."

Umeme nuzzled into my hair. *So sweet.* I wrapped my arms around her neck. "See you soon." She slunk off into the desert with Radi at her side. "Will they be all right?"

"Don't worry about those two. They can cast a little magick if they run into trouble."

I pursed my lips, interested. "How much of your power have you given them?"

"Not too much. I've only been working on them for five years." He rubbed his chin. "I think I want to make a phoenix next."

"Phoenix? How many familiars does a Caster have?"

"Depends on the Caster. Some have one. Others have a whole zoo full of them. I'm more the zoo type, myself."

I tried to picture Rowan with a menagerie of animals. What had he created so far? "I'd like to see that someday."

"If we make it past this mission, I'll take you."

I grinned. After all the doom and gloom of eternal fires, the thought of visiting Rowan's familiars was a welcome distraction.

Rowan and I finished hiking up a particularly tall dune. At the crest, a long stretch of flatland opened up before us. Striped tents stood everywhere, all of them in some combination of gray and black. A few curled low to the ground. Others soared with pennants flapping from their many peaks. A great crowd of Forgotten milled around them, Commoners mostly.

"It seems we've arrived." Rowan focused his attention on me. "Have you been to one of these before?"

"Never. I've heard they aren't very safe."

"True enough. Let's stay close."

Rowan and I stepped off toward the growing crowd and towering tents. The scent of burned meat and sweat filled the air. Bodies jostled around us and pressed in closer. Voices muttered, moaned, and squawked at me, all at once. I'd thought the oasis was bad. This was far worse. Sometimes the swell of the crowd got so tight, I could have lifted my feet off the ground and not fallen down. All the walking didn't help my leg injury, either.

Oh, well. It would heal on its own.

After an eternity of shoving our way forward, we entered one of the main aisles through the tents. All the bodies were making me anxious. "Where are they supposed to meet us?"

"They said they'd find us. That was all."

Well, that was quite mysterious of them. It didn't bode well for this being anything other than a waste of time. We pushed our way through mob after mob. It was a good thing Rowan was a head taller than me. At least, we could see where we were going.

Hours ticked by and I started to lose my temper. Precious little time remained before I could kill the Tsar. Were Ocie and Yuri some kind of prank? What kind of people posed as mythical mages? I opened my mouth, ready to suggest that we discuss other options.

That was when I saw them in the crowd.

Ocie and Yuri. The mages of legend. They looked just like the pictures I'd seen in books.

Both were cloaked in purple robes with the hoods drawn low. Even so, there was no missing the golden light dancing across the fabric in the image of the sun and moon. Everywhere, the crowd bumped and jostled through narrow walkways, but Ocie and Yuri stood still as statues. Yuri was taller with broad shoulders and Ocie's golden belt highlighted her curvy form.

I glanced at Rowan. "Do you see them?"

"I do."

"You've come for our help." I still couldn't see their faces under their hoods, but I could tell the voice was Ocien's. She had a velvety smooth tone with an accent I couldn't quite place.

"Yes," I said.

"Go to the purple tent." Yuri spoke this time, and his voice was deep and gravelly.

I frowned. There were only gray and black tents. What did they mean? All of a sudden, one of the tents shimmered as its color transformed from black to purple. Rowan and I headed toward the entrance flap.

Ocie held up her hand. "Only Elea."

This wasn't a surprise, considering the two had insisted that they speak to me directly.

"No," said Rowan. "I'm going with her."

I appreciated his concern. That said, I could take care of myself. "I'll be all right."

"You can't cast."

"And even if we both could, what good would it do us, if they are who they say?"

"But we don't know who they are."

I frowned. This was true.

"She'll be safe," said Yuri.

I took his hand in mine. That sweet jolt of connection rolled over my skin. I knew it was weak of me to rely on touch, but I considered this an extreme situation. "Trust me."

Rowan stepped between the mages and me. "I know she will be. Because we're a team and we don't go dangerous places without each other." His thumb rubbed a soothing arc on the back of my hand. It surprised me how much strength I drew from that.

"No harm will come to her by our hands," said Ocie.

"I don't—" Rowan froze in place. The rest of the crowd poured around us, oblivious to anything except their own business. My eyes widened. They'd placed a spell on Rowan. How powerful were these two?

"Into the tent," said Yuri.

I started at Rowan for a long moment. His rugged features were fierce with protective rage. I didn't want to leave him like this. I didn't want to leave him, period. He was right. We were a team.

"The tent," repeated Ocie. Her words carried the power of magick. "You know what's at stake."

"Right." *My eternal life.* I slowly untwined my fingers from Rowan's. It hurt to lose the warmth and security of his touch. There was no other way through this than to move forward, though. The Tsar arrived at the Midnight Cloister tomorrow. We couldn't defeat him without some kind of hybrid magick.

"You're doing right by your people and yourself," said Ocie in her smooth voice.

"I hope so." I walked forward, took a deep breath, and slipped in through the open tent flap.

21

*O*nce inside the tent, total darkness enveloped me. The sound of my own breathing echoed deafeningly loud. Magick filled the air around me, the ethereal energy tickling my skin.

A pool of white light formed a few yards in front of me. Ocie and Yuri stepped into the brightness. The hoods of their purple robes were still drawn low.

"You desire protection from the Tsar," said Yuri.

"Protection? No. I want a weapon that will kill him." The pair flinched at the word 'kill.' *How strange.* I couldn't imagine mages like these being squeamish when it came to destroying someone like Viktor. Perhaps they didn't expect me to be so blunt about my purpose. "Does that surprise you?"

"Somewhat," said Ocie in her silky voice.

I wasn't sure what kind of Necromancers they usually met. They'd better get used to me. I wasn't going to sugar-coat my purpose here. "Can you help me?"

"We can," they said together.

Those were two simple words, but they lifted a boulder-sized weight from my shoulders. *At last.* I may actually get the power to kill Viktor, break my curse, and avoid an eternity of pain. The relief was so intense my legs felt rubbery beneath me. "How?"

"It's called a leveling spell," said Ocie.

Leveling spell? The words echoed in my mind.

"I've never heard of such a thing." And I knew every Necromancer spell that existed.

"That's because we created it for you," said Yuri. "It will place you and your Caster at the same level of hybrid power as Viktor. Except, the magick will only last for a short period of time."

There was a dismissive tone in the way he said 'your Caster.' It roused my protective side. "He has a name. Rowan. And what does he have to do with this?"

"We will empower you both to cast at the same level as Viktor," said Yuri. "It serves a purpose. You will be better matched against him."

Serves a purpose. I didn't like how Ocie and Yuri randomly pulled Rowan in and out of their plans.

"You wouldn't let Rowan into the tent, yet you want to involve him?" I was surprised at the angry edge to my voice. *Get back in control, Necromancer.* I cleared my throat and organized my thoughts. "If you want Rowan to help, then you should allow him in. Now."

Yuri let out a long breath, and even his sighs had a gravelly rumble inside them. "You are in no position to make demands. If you want our help, then it must be on our terms."

My hands balled into fists, and I had the overwhelming desire to pummel them both. I held back, though. Yuri was right. My curse would strike me down tomorrow. The two of them were strange. Still, they were also very powerful. If I were to live through this, then I needed their help.

That said, I wouldn't agree to any terms without understanding precisely what they intended. "Let's say I share power with Rowan. How would that work?"

"As a rule, the Tsar's hybrid weapons are unstoppable," said Ocie. "His knives can slice through any armor. But when you wield the magick of both Necromancer and Caster, hybrid weapons return to being ordinary."

"So if someone tried to strike Rowan with a hybrid dagger, it wouldn't slice through his armor anymore."

"Precisely," said Ocie. "But that would only be in effect with you and Rowan, and only for as long as our spell lasts."

"From dawn until dusk on a single day," added Yuri.

A spark of hope lit in my chest. "And what about Viktor's magick?"

"Yes," said Yuri. "There's no way to block or counter Viktor's magick. But for one day with our spell, you and Rowan will cast on an even level with him."

Another boulder-sized weight tumbled from my back. I pictured all the guards and mages who followed Viktor, especially Marlene. "Will your spell make me as strong as Viktor against any other enemies?"

"Not at this time," said Yuri slowly.

That was an interesting way to put it. Maybe this was something Rowan and I could practice. "So this is a skill I could gain someday?"

"Perhaps," said Ocie. "But you must survive this encounter first."

The way Ocie said the word 'survive,' it was as if she had already planned my funeral. "I'm well aware that my task won't be easy." This time, I didn't bother to control the bitter edge in my voice. "But I hope to do more than survive. My plan is to rid the realm of a great evil, too. Viktor dies tomorrow."

Ocie and Yuri exchanged another long look. Something about

my wanting to kill the Tsar alarmed them. "Don't forget," said
Ocie. "There are conditions for our help."

I wouldn't expect these two to help without getting something out of it. I could only hope the price wasn't too steep.
"Go on."

"You must spare Viktor," said Ocie.

I looked her over from head to toe. Purple robes, curvy body,
and golden sash... Ocie looked the same as she had when I first
saw her, so how had she transformed into a mad woman? "You
can't be serious."

"We forbid you from killing the Tsar," said Ocie. "You must
not even begin to do so. We only wish for you to transport him
into this tent."

I staggered a step backward. "Transport him. To this tent."

"So we may talk to him," said Ocie.

My head was spinning. This was ridiculous. "You want to talk.
To Viktor. The man who killed thousands of Sisters in the
Midnight Cloister alone? The man who turns peaceful Casters
into killers? You can't be serious."

"These are our rules," said Yuri. "No murdering Viktor. Not
even an attempt. You must open a portal and push him through."

"We exist on a magickal plane," explained Ocie. "Once he's
here, we will contain him in safety."

Sure, you can. These two may be powerful, but I wasn't
convinced they weren't semi insane. After everything Viktor had
done, I doubted that anyone could hold him captive, even Ocie
and Yuri. "That doesn't help me with Viktor's curse. Come
tomorrow, I'll start an eternity in flames. The only way I avoid
that is by killing the man."

"No," said Yuri, and his voice took on its roughest note yet. "If
you transport Viktor here—directly here—then your curse will
be broken. We can do this for you. But if you should try to injure

the Tsar in any way, then your curse will activate no matter what befalls Viktor."

Some of my excitement began to wane. What they were talking about flew in the face of all magickal logic. Kill the mage, kill the spell. It was the oldest rule around. How could sparing Viktor end my curse?

And their ideas made no sense in the realm of regular logic. Some people deserved to be brought to justice. Viktor was one of them. I glanced around the darkness, wondering if there was an easy way out of this tent.

Not yet. You've come this far. Hear them out.

No matter how insane these two might seem, they were powerful mages and I believed they could give me the spell to defeat Viktor. "Is that all of your conditions?"

"The leveling spell is an extraordinary amount of power," said Yuri. "You must also pass a test so we can ensure you will use it wisely."

"A test." This bargain was looking worse by the second. I couldn't kill Viktor and I still had to pass a test? Perhaps there was a way to bypass all this nonsense. "So you two can break my curse. Can you end it now?"

"We operate on a different plane of magick," explained Ocie. "The rules for us are... Strange."

"Strange." Like the pair of you.

"Ending your curse now is simply not possible," said Yuri. "Even our power has limits."

I laced my fingers behind my neck, stared up into the darkness, and tried to think things though. I simply had too many questions about this pair. "I'm sorry to have wasted your time. If you'll excuse me—"

"We know this appears suspicious," said Ocie.

"You must believe us," added Yuri.

I raised my arms to shoulder level, palms forward. "All I want to do is leave."

"We'll have to show her," said Ocie.

"Agreed," said Yuri.

The two of them slowly lowered their hoods. I froze in shock. I'd seen Ocie's face before.

When Rowan had helped me imagine the Lady of Creation. Ocie didn't just look like the Lady, she *was* the Lady.

And Yuri... there was no mistaking the elegant lines of his pale face. He was none other than the Sire of Souls. Now that they were both uncloaked, the pair radiated a singular power and presence. Light and energy danced across their skin.

I just sassed off to a god and goddess. What have I done?

I grasped my hands in supplication, just like I'd learned at the Zelle. "Forgive me. I had no idea who you were. It's an honor that you wish to help me." Petra would lose her mind if she knew how I'd acted.

"So, you won't kill Viktor?" asked Ocie.

"I won't. You have my word." Who refused a god and goddess? They must have their reasons.

"And you'll take our test?" asked Yuri.

"Of course."

The Sire and Lady raised their arms. Although they didn't speak any incantations, the air around me thickened with energy. White clouds appeared, obscuring my view. When the mists settled again, Ocie and Yuri were gone.

Tristan stood in the pool of light. As shocked as I'd been to see the Sire and Lady, I was almost as surprised to see him. The man I'd thought was my best friend, who'd actually sold me out for Quinn. Tristan looked whole and healthy in his captain's uniform. For the first time, I missed the fire. "Hello, Elea." He shifted his weight and gave me an awkward smile. "I'm your test."

"You!" I got so angry, I couldn't see straight. "You tricked me into taking on this curse to spare Quinn. What could I possibly have to say to you?" I craned my neck to yell into the darkness above. "This test is ridiculous. Do you hear me?"

Tristan stepped closer. "You have to listen, Elea. Everything I've done, it was only to protect and help you. If there were any other way, I'd have chosen that path. I meant it when I said I loved you." His expression turned haunted. "I have burned, day and night, these last five years, and all of it for you."

"You could have taken the Tsar's mark. I'd have been fine."

"Think, Elea. You've learned things at the Midnight Cloister, I bet. Do you know what those marks really are? I saw Viktor give out the first ones and… I simply can't speak of them."

I looked at him out of the corner of my eye. "Can't or won't?"

"Can't. I'm under a magickal aegis." Tristan's voice turned pleading. "Tell me you know what the mark truly does."

"Yes. I know. Viktor uses it to drain Necromancers and kill them."

"And what would have happened to you if you hadn't gone to the Zelle?"

I hated to admit it, but he was right. Everyone in the shire knew I was a Necromancer. If they were paying people for good Necromancers, Wyatt would have sold me out in a heartbeat. There was no doubt. I'd have been tracked down and abducted, sooner or later. "You should have told me."

"I couldn't. The aegis wouldn't let me. Even now, I can't speak the words about what really happens." He moved closer until he only stood an arm's breadth away. "I won't lie. When Viktor took power, I was tempted to take his mark. I'd have been accepted into Viktor's entourage. Do you know what that means?"

A sick feeling crept into my stomach. "Power."

"Without training, you'd never have been allowed to join the entourage with me."

"I'd have been drained." And died, both body and soul.

"That's why I chose the curse and I meant what I said. I've burned for you, and I'd do it again to give you a chance to live."

His words were so sincere, I felt myself faltering. Besides, this was my Tristan. He could be a fool sometimes, but he always had good intentions. "You shouldn't have done that. I might have gotten trained without the curse."

"Even if I could have told you everything, would you ever have left Braddock Farm? Be honest with me. Be honest with yourself. Nothing except the curse would have forced you to seek training. Today, you have a chance and more than that, everyone else in the realm does, too." He raked his hand through his long black hair. "You're the only one with the power to stand up to him."

His words inspired and frightened me in equal measure. "It can't come down to me. No one else has the magick to face Viktor? That doesn't make sense."

Tristan shook his head. "My sweet Elea. There's still so much you don't understand... So much I can't tell you. You need to trust me. I did what I had to do, and now, you need to play your part as well. Listen to the Sire and Lady. Remove Viktor from the land. Can you do that? Can you trust us?" He stepped up and gently cupped my face in his hands. It was one of the most intimate touches we'd shared. "Trust me one last time. Please?"

Part of me wanted to believe him. More of me couldn't get past the fact that I was cursed to burn for eternity. "You lied to me, Tristan. You were my only friend and you cursed me."

Tristan kept up his gentle touch. "I did what I had to."

I gripped his wrists and held them hard. "You can't ask me to trust you on blind faith. That's not who I am. I take things in my own two hands and get them done."

"You're right. That's always been you." He gave me a sad smile. "Welcome to the heart of the test."

Which is what this is all about. Trust and teamwork. Rowan had talked about this as well, back when we first spoke at the oasis. I gave Tristan's wrists a gentle squeeze. At some point, I had to choose my allies. "All right." I lifted my chin and spoke in a steady voice. "I'll trust you, Tristan. I can't say that I'll ever forgive you for putting me under a curse without my consent. Even so, I do believe that you had my best interests at heart."

"Good." Tristan stepped back, breaking our connection. "You passed the test."

A haunted look returned to his eyes, and I knew that my friend was headed back to the flames. "I'll find a way to free you, Tristan."

"And I'll be waiting."

White smoke rolled between us, covering my view of Tristan. My heart sickened to think of the pain he was now going through. When the mists disappeared, the Sire and Lady stood in front of me once more.

"You called Tristan out from the flames, didn't you?" They nodded. "You wanted to see if I'd trust your judgment and follow your edicts. You want me to spare Viktor."

"Yes," said the Lady. "Will you?"

They were my god and goddess. "I already gave you my word." I couldn't imagine why they'd want to save Viktor, apart from the fact that they lived on a different plane. Perhaps it made sense to them.

The Sire and Lady shared a long look, and then stepped into the darkness. In their place, appeared a small box covered in amber lacquer. A spell box. These often held the ingredients for a spell, but with the Sire and Lady, who knew what this one really contained?

I scooped the box from the floor and sped out of the tent.

I found myself in a thin alley between two tall lines of tents. Based on the long shadows around me, I must have been inside for hours. It was late afternoon by now. Bodies pressed in around me as they rushed through the fair. My thoughts were rushed, too. For someone who'd lived the last five years in a quiet cloister, today had been a lot to process.

I just met the Sire of Souls and the Lady of Creation.

And they'd given me magick to help defeat the Tsar.

I held in my hands the means to end Viktor's curse, both for Tristan and myself. The key to my future. I gripped the lacquer box more tightly. Now, I just needed to find Rowan.

Falling into the flow of the crowd, I began my search. The fair was a sprawling mess of thin passageways. It felt like miles of hiking to reach any place. The ache in my thigh started to flare and fatigue began to play on my mind. Everything looked the same to me. I could have sworn I walked by the same fortune-telling tent three times. Even so, I didn't see anyone who resembled a Caster.

Had Rowan left without me? What if something happened to

him? I wandered through the maze of makeshift streets until the flow of the mob led me into the largest tent of all. Wooden barrels were stacked up along the walls while long tables covered the floor. Patrons held huge steins. Clearly, I'd reached the ale tent.

I hugged the wall and kept an eye out for Caster leathers. The crowd was too dense to be sure. At last, a man with tanned skin caught my eye.

"Rowan!" I shoved through the mob and grabbed the man's shoulder. Jakob spun around to face me. My stomach sank.

"Greetings," said Jakob. The word was so drawn out that I got a good whiff of his breath. *Foul.* I winced. The man was drunk again. What a disgrace.

"Where's Rowan?" I asked.

Jakob plunked onto a nearby bench. "Oh, he's nearby. My man got worried when you didn't reappear after a few hours, so he summoned me to help search. I cast a transport spell, so I needed a little pick-me-up before I started looking for you." He scooped a mug of ale from the table and took a deep gulp. "And lo, you're here."

It was one thing to be drunk, and another to be completely useless. "That didn't answer my question. I'll find Rowan myself."

Jakob grabbed my wrist and yanked me closer. "Stop casting your spells on that man."

Speaking of casting spells. It would definitely bring the Mother Superior down on my head, but I'd love to drop a kill spell on Jakob. "Watch your mouth," I said. "You've no idea what I'm capable of."

Rowan appeared beside us. Finally.

Jakob immediately dropped my wrist.

"Rowan," I said cautiously. I'd seen crazed bulls that were less enraged than Rowan was right now.

"Elea." Rowan glared at Jakob. The drunken man seemed to shrink into his bench.

"Greetings," said Jakob.

"I summoned you here to help." Rowan's words were a low growl.

Jakob shrugged. The drunken movement came off more as a twitch. "And I *was* helping her."

Rowan rounded on me. "Is this true?"

I appreciated Rowan stepping in with Jakob, but I had the situation under control. "Jakob was not helping, which was why I—"

Before I got a chance to finish, Rowan slammed his fist directly into Jakob's face. A nasty crunch sounded. I winced. *That's a bone breaking.* Rowan gripped Jakob by his jacket. "When I say help Elea, you help Elea. Do we understand each other?"

My mouth was still hanging open from where I'd been caught mid-sentence. Necromancers discouraged physical fighting. It was considered an uncontrolled display of emotion. But seeing this punch? Rowan appeared to be in complete control. I wondered if Necromancy could make exceptions. Plus, I'd be lying if I didn't say that part of me enjoyed watching Jakob get some just desserts.

Jakob cupped his hands over his face. "You broke my nose."

"I said, do we understand each other... Or do I have to smash something you can't mend with a spell?"

Jakob stared sulkily at the ground. "I understand you."

"Good. Sleep it off. I expect you back in camp at dawn."

"Yes, Rowan." Jakob rose from the bench and staggered away. I almost felt sorry for him. Almost, yet not quite.

Rowan turned to me and gently rested his hands on my shoulders. "Are you all right? You were gone for hours."

"I'm fine." I stepped away from his grip. One way or another, there'd been a lot of touching with Rowan lately. I needed to be careful. "I spoke to—" I stopped myself from saying the Sire of Souls and the Lady of Creation. "Ocie and Yuri. Time just flew by." There was no quick way to explain that I'd been pulled onto an alternate plane of existence by a god and goddess. At least, not in a crowded tent. The story would have to wait until I could ease into the truth.

"Did they help as they promised?"

I raised the box in my hands. "That they did."

"Excellent work." His praise made me feel light as air. "Have you opened it?"

"Not yet."

Rowan scratched his cheek. The look in his eyes said he wasn't eager about waiting. "Don't you think we should check?"

"Oh, I'm positive this holds what we need." A god and goddess had given me the box, after all. "But we should get away from here before we open it."

"If that's what you suggest." Rowan patted his top pocket. "I succeeded in my task as well."

My brows lifted. That means Rowan got us maps of the cloister. "Excellent work, yourself."

"My team did all the hard bits before I got here. I don't mind taking credit, though."

I smiled. It sounded like there was quite a story behind those maps. Even so, I knew it was nothing we could discuss in the open. "Do you know a safe place nearby? We need to set up our plan."

"Genesis Rex and his people aren't far and their camp is well warded. Radi and Umeme can get us there in an hour or so."

I frowned. *An hour.* I hated to wait that long. We couldn't risk exposure. "All right."

"You don't seem happy. Is your leg still hurting?"

In truth, my thigh did ache. It wasn't the injury that made me frown, though. "Every time I think I've finally found a way to finish this mission, something happens to make matters worse than ever." I tapped the lid of the box. "Until we open this and reset our plans, I'm holding off on any sense of happy."

"I understand completely."

"Thank you." It was a relief that Rowan didn't think my logic strange. Because in about an hour, there was a whole lot of insanity that I needed to talk him through. How would I tell him that I spoke to not just one deity, but two?

I'd have to find a way. Right now, my mission hinged on Rowan's trust in me.

And mine in him.

*R*owan and I rode our tigers across the darkened desert. Moonlight shimmered on the sand, making it look like burnished silver. Overhead, the sky wheeled with more stars than I'd ever thought possible. We soon closed in on the Caster encampment. A dozen tents surrounded an open fire. All the structures had arched poles in their framework, giving the tents a swirled look.

"Which one belongs to the King?" I asked. When the Tsar traveled, his yurt was made of golden cloth.

"There." Rowan pointed to the far side of the fire, where a pair of guards in red leathers stood outside the largest tent. Their bodies bristled with weapons. Full helms covered their faces. Rowan pulled a heavy scrap of leather from his pocket and unfolded it into a padded helm.

If Rowan was pulling that out, then there was only one place he planned to go. "Do you need to speak with Rex?"

"Yes. Right after I get you settled." He glanced at me over his shoulder. "Unless you have need of me."

"No, I'll be fine." In all honesty, I was looking forward to sitting down for a while. Despite the softness of Umeme's fur, my thigh was hurting worse than ever.

As we closed in on the camp, a small group of Casters rose to greet us. Soon, Rowan and Radi were surrounded by a half dozen men and women. Once again, I was struck by the differences in their bodies. The men were all broad and tall, while the women were petite and lithe. Rowan slipped off Radi's back and embraced each person in turn.

I dismounted from Umeme and watched the scene with wide eyes. The times Rowan's fingers had brushed mine or he'd held me close had been burned in my memory.

Suddenly, those embraces seemed stilted and half-hearted compared to what Casters shared. My cheeks reddened as I looked away.

"Elea?" Rowan stepped closer. "Is something wrong?"

"No." I forced a smile.

"Come, join the circle." He set his hand on the base of my back and guided me toward the Casters. "You remember Laurel and the others from the oasis." Their helms contoured to their faces, covering everything above the chin. Even so, it was easy to recognize Laurel's smiling eyes. The man she was holding hands with had to be Orion.

I forced another grin. "Hail and well met." Silence fell. Everyone focused on me. Something wasn't right here.

Orion stepped forward and bowed at his waist. "Thank you."

"You thank me?" I paused. *This made no sense.* "What have I done?"

"You've given us the chance to save our brethren who've been transformed into Changed Ones." They all nodded their agreement. "Their bodies are forever changed, but the Tsar wishes to control their minds. Now, we can keep them free."

All the attention made me squirm. "Defeating the Tsar will protect both our peoples."

The group chattered their agreement until silence fell again. Jakob had stepped into the circle.

I steeled my shoulders, preparing for a verbal battle. If Jakob wanted to go at it, I was more than ready.

Jakob turned to me. His leathers were no longer covered in mud, but his left eye was swollen shut. "I won't say hail and well met. I'm certain that you don't wish to see me again." He shifted his weight from foot to foot. "I came to apologize for how I acted at the fair." Jakob looked to Rowan. "Am I dismissed now?"

Rowan shook his head. *Apparently not.*

Jakob huffed out a long breath. "My actions were terrible. I left Necromancer lands because I was betrayed by a woman. That's my history. I shouldn't have applied it to you." He stared at his hands. "You've brought us closer to our aim than ever before. The Casters owe you a debt."

"The Tsar isn't defeated yet," I said. "But I appreciate the sentiment all the same."

"Can you accept my apology?" asked Jakob.

I pursed my lips and considered. I'd no doubt that if I asked for a more thorough punishment, Rowan would deliver it. Still, Jakob looked sincere. That kind of behavior should be encouraged. "You're forgiven."

Jakob looked to Rowan once more. "May I return to preparations for tomorrow?" This time, Rowan nodded. Jakob bowed at the waist and left.

Once Jakob was gone, Rowan rubbed his palms, which was his way of saying the subject was closed. He scanned all the Casters in turn. "How fares the King?"

"He is well and resting," said Orion. "Rex would like to speak with you after you've eaten, if that's agreeable." It struck me how casual the Casters were about their ruler. Even Tsar Dmitri had been treated as a mini-god.

"And he will." Rowan turned to me. "Would you like a warm meal?"

My mouth watered at the thought of the roasted meat I'd eaten at the oasis. "Very much so." One advantage of Caster society was the lack of marrow pudding.

The Caster group began to break up. Rowan and I approached the campfire, where spits of meats were roasting. The scent was delicious.

I accepted a few skewers of rabbit meat and tried to enjoy my meal. My thigh was still troubling, and I kept shifting in my seat, searching for a comfortable spot. Once I finished eating, I turned to Rowan. "I'd like to wash up before we start planning. Do you have a bathing tent here?"

"That we do." The moonlight cast pale shadows on his sharp jawline and messy brown hair.

"After you've eaten, can you show me the way?"

"I will… Once I've healed your leg."

"My leg is fine. It only needs to be cleaned. Just as all of me does," I added swiftly.

"You've been favoring it ever since we escaped. My guess is that some bit of wagon got lodged in you during the crash. If the protective skin of my spell got inside, it won't heal without my aid."

I searched my memory, trying to find some reason, any reason, why that was impossible and Rowan should not do anything that remotely involved my bare thigh. Unfortunately, everything I knew about magick told me he was right. "Where would you cast?"

"Follow me."

My heart hammered against my ribs as Rowan and I stepped away from the fire and into one of the spiraling tents. Inside was neat and snug. Heavy rugs covered the floor and small baskets lined the round wall. Rowan fished through the containers, pulling out herbs. I sat on the most comfortable-looking rugs, careful to favor my bad leg.

Rowan opened one of the jars. "This is the one."

My heart pounded so hard, I thought it might burst. "What should I do?"

"Hike up your skirt. I need to see your thigh."

He said the words casually, but my palms turned slick with sweat as I pulled up the black fabric. I kept my legs firmly together.

Rowan knelt in front of me. "You have nothing to worry about, Elea. I've healed many women."

"Oh." That thought gave me more to worry about, though. How many women had he touched this way? And why would I care if he had?

"I can't heal you like this."

"Right." I parted my legs and he leaned in closer. This was now the most embarrassing thing that had ever happened to me. It was even worse then when I'd fallen in the pigsty before Tristan came to visit.

Rowan shook his head. "As I suspected. You've a bad infection." He chanted over his cup of herbs until they flared into a paste. He scooped some onto his fingers and began to paint long lines down my inner thigh.

I hissed in a pained breath as the paste burned my skin. Rowan continued his incantation and the hurt dissolved into a much nicer sensation. For the first time since leaving the cloister, my leg didn't hurt.

Rowan met my gaze. "Better?"

"Much. Thank you."

"I'll send Laurel to take you to the bathing tent. Meet back here in an hour?"

"Agreed."

As Rowan left, I kept replaying the feel of his fingers on my thigh.

Watch it, Elea.

If I was gong to live past tomorrow, I needed to stick to my training. No emotions. Otherwise, the fires would surely claim me.

*a*n hour later, I had bathed and changed into a set of Caster leathers. They were the most comfortable clothes imaginable. I swore that if I actually lived through this, I'd wear nothing but leathers ever again.

If I survive past Sunday, that is.

Tomorrow at sunset, my curse would officially start. I shivered as images of my afterlife appeared. Flesh melting away from bone. Smoke, pain, and death… Only to be restored and burned once more. An endless cycle through eternity, and it could be my fate in a matter of hours.

Rowan stepped into the tent, interrupting my dismal thoughts. "What's troubling you?"

There was no point in pretending. "My curse."

Rowan sat down beside me. "We'll fight it, Elea. With this new power to use against Viktor, I'm sure we'll win."

Perhaps he's right. After all, the magick came from none other than the Sire of Souls and the Lady of Creation. I set the box onto the rug. "This holds what they called a leveling spell."

"I've never heard of it."

"I hadn't either."

Rowan frowned. "Is that why still haven't opened it? Don't you know what the spell will entail? I've seen spell boxes like these before. Mages usually place herbs inside them."

"Ocie and Yuri aren't typical mages." I couldn't believe I was saying this without the benefit of heavy drink in my body. "They're deities, Rowan. Ocie and Yuri are the Lady of Creation and the Sire of Souls." I was pleased with how sane I sounded when I said that.

Rowan stared at me, his green eyes darkening. It felt like a life age passed before he spoke again. "I'd say you were teasing. Necromancers aren't known for their practical jokes, though."

Here it comes. Rowan was certain to think I'd snapped and gone insane. Not that I blamed him. Some small part of me was hoping that I had. Being insane would certainly be easier than capturing the Tsar.

"Are you sure it wasn't an illusion spell?" asked Rowan.

"Positive. There's no doubt in my mind that I met the god and goddess."

"I see." Rowan's rugged face stayed maddeningly unreadable.

"And I saw their powers before the sanctuary fair. Ocie and Yuri—I mean, the Lady and Sire—have been intervening in my life for some time now."

"How?"

As if on cue, my scarab beetle flittered into view. I couldn't stop my smile. "There you are. I haven't seen you since the Midnight Cloister." The scarab began crawling around the spell box. "This is the beetle I told you about. It should never have gotten past Viktor's wards and into the storehouse. That's one example of their handiwork."

Rowan leaned in for a closer look. His features still didn't give me a clue what he was thinking. Would Rowan back out of our partnership?

"Plus, consider how your spell brought me to the desert in the first place. You said you thought the Sire had a hand in it."

Rowan examined the spell box carefully, but didn't reply. He wasn't leaving, at least. I took that as a good sign.

"In any case," I continued. "I wanted you to understand who they really are before opening their box. I don't think there's anything dangerous inside. That said, who knows what's possible with deities? Besides, Rex is nearby. I wouldn't want to risk his safety without your consent."

Rowan set the spell box down and glared at it as if it would evaporate under the strength of his gaze. I worried my lower lip with my teeth. This was where everything could fall apart. And in all honesty, that might be best for Rowan. *I'm the one who's running out of time, after all.*

"I realize how this all sounds," I said. "If you want to back out of our partnership, I understand."

"Listen to me carefully, Elea." Rowan's deep voice reverberated through me. "We've been after the Tsar for years. Nothing worked until you joined our circle. If you say they're the Sire and Lady, then that's who they were. If you tell me this spell box is safe, then it's safe." He folded his arms over his chest. "Open that container whenever you wish. I'm staying right here."

My heart swelled. Rowan trusted my judgment. Together, maybe we *could* handle whatever came next.

With steady hands, I pried the wooden lid off the container. Its contents left me speechless.

Two rings sat inside. Both had prongs for holding a stone. A second beetle crawled between them. This scarab was the perfect match to mine. I had trouble pulling in my next breath.

This couldn't be possible.

Those look like mating rings.

The new scarab fluttered over to rest on Rowan's shoulder. The man's features were back to being unreadable again. Damn.

I worked hard to keep my face calm as well. The Sire and Lady had said this spell was for both Rowan and me.

What exactly did that mean? Did they expect me to marry Rowan?

Suddenly, I found it impossible to meet Rowan's gaze. "I don't know what to say. This looks like something your people do. Not mine."

More awkward silence followed. The air inside the tent felt thick with tension. At last, Rowan spoke. "Did they mention a time limit for this spell?"

Excellent question. Being married might not be so bad, so long as it was temporary. "They said the magick would last from sunrise to sunset on a single day. During that time, our weapons and spells will be equal to the Tsar's." I shifted uncomfortably on the rug. "Is that how bonding rings are supposed to work? Laurel said hers didn't have any magick."

"Laurel and Orion are warriors, so their rings are more symbolic. It's different with mages."

"They're not mages? But you call them Casters."

"Among my people, everyone is a Caster and each person carries their own kind of magick." Rowan set his scarab on his palm. "This is definitely a bonding animal."

I wasn't sure I liked that name. "How does that part work?"

Rowan lifted his brows. "You really don't know?"

My insides squirmed at the look of disbelief on his face. What I didn't know about relationships was a lot. "Mating rituals never really came up at the cloister."

"Fair enough." The edges of Rowan's mouth curled up into a gentle smile. The knots of worry in my shoulders loosened a little. "When two Casters are ready to be mated, their bonding animals simply find them."

"Let me guess. Those animals then turn into stones for the rings."

"Correct. It's part of the ceremony."

As in marriage ceremony. My pulse kicked up speed. I was doing this. I was considering some kind of mating ritual with Rowan.

"And this bonding can happen between a Caster and Necromancer?"

"Oh, yes. It's the magick of the Caster people as a whole that makes the ritual work. We've never had a Caster-Necromancer mating that resulted in hybrid magick, though." He picked up one of the bands and examined it. "There are many layers of spells on these rings. The deeper tiers must contain the leveling spell."

"So, we go through a ceremony to get married for a day. That's it." *I can do that. I think.*

Rowan rubbed the edge of the ring with his thumb. "We'll say a few words and trade rings. That's all. We should hold the ceremony at dawn, so the magick lasts the day." He gave me a sly look. "Or were you thinking of doing something else?"

The memory of Rowan holding me appeared. Damn. I really was going crazy.

"No, not at all." I said quickly. I scooped up the spell box and set it aside. "Now that you know what the magick can do, we need to work on our plan."

And no more thoughts of cuddling.

"Sounds like you have a strategy or two in your head," said Rowan.

"The first priority is regaining my ability to cast without alerting the Mother Superior where I am. To do that, I need you to destroy a snake ring."

"That has your magick in it?"

"Yes. It has to go or they'll be able to track me forever."

"If the leveling spell works, then I can destroy that snake ring easily enough. What else?"

"Once we activate the leveling spell, we'll both need invisibility spells to get into the cloister."

"Makes sense," said Rowan. "The question is, what will my people be doing during all this?" Rowan leaned over, popped his head out the tent flap, and whistled.

"What is it, Rowan?" asked a woman.

"Can you send Rex over when he's free? We need to talk things through for tomorrow."

"I'll bring him straight away."

Rowan closed the flap, leaned back on his elbows, and kicked his long legs out in front of him. He didn't seem particularly concerned that his king was stopping by. "My uncle is a master schemer. He'll have some useful insights for us."

My body felt like it had been dipped in ice. "Rex is coming here. To this tent. Right now."

Rowan leaned fully back and laced his fingers behind his head. "Is that a problem?"

I couldn't believe he had to ask that question. "I've never met a king before."

"Well, you're about to meet a Tsar, and that doesn't seem to bother you in the slightest."

"Mostly because I plan on sending him into exile versus having an actual conversation with the man."

Rowan sat right back up. "Exile? When did that plan change?"

I needed a memory spell to keep track of everything, it was happening so quickly. "It was one of the conditions of the Sire and Lady's help. I must transport Viktor to them and they'll keep him on their plane."

"And you believe they can actually do that?"

"I didn't when I thought they were Ocie and Yuri. But when they revealed themselves to be divine, I changed my mind. Viktor's just a person. They're two deities. I'm sure they can keep him secured." *At least, I'm fairly certain.*

Rowan drummed his fingers on his knees. "It doesn't matter, I suppose. Either way, it frees my people from the Tsar's control."

"You've said something like that before. Why don't you want Viktor dead?"

"Whether Viktor's alive or dead, my Changed Ones will stay transformed. The process was physical as well as magickal. Right now, I'm more worried about your curse. What happens to you if Viktor's sent away?"

"The Sire and Lady will free me from the curse."

"And if you kill Viktor instead?"

"It must be exile. If I even try to kill Viktor, then I'll be sent into the flames." The words felt like acid on my tongue.

Rowan scratched at the scruff on his jawline. "I don't like this."

"There was no other way to secure their help." I didn't add this, but the pair seemed oddly protective of someone as evil as Viktor.

"Don't misunderstand," said Rowan. "I realize you had no other options. It doesn't mean I have to like it, though. I don't care if they are deities, the Sire and Lady should have tried to protect you more and Viktor less." The way he spoke, I sounded like the most precious Necromancer in the realm. I liked that more than I should have.

The tent flap opened and a man in Caster leathers stepped inside. He had the same rugged body shape as Rowan. *Genesis Rex.* My mouth hung open for a few seconds before I caught myself.

Rex limped over to embrace Rowan. "Hail and well met, Nephew."

"And also to you, Uncle."

Rex turned to me. "And you must be Elea."

"Your Majesty."

"Call me Uncle R." He began to unbuckle his helm. "I hope you don't mind if I take this damned thing off. It itches like crazy, and my nephew assures me you're not an assassin." He gave me a smile that was so dazzling his teeth might actually have sparkled.

"I don't mind at all." My voice was far breathier than I meant it to be.

Rowan turned to me. "My esteemed uncle is a terrible flirt. Consider yourself warned."

Rex removed his helm, revealing an older version of Rowan. He had a strong jawline and rugged features. His once-brown hair was now mixed with gray. He limped to my side and sat down. Rowan had said that Rex survived an assassination attempt, but ended up with a leg injury. I hoped it didn't hurt too badly.

Rex rubbed his palms together. "I take it we're here to plan a murder."

"We've downgraded it to a permanent exile, Uncle."

"Whatever for?"

"That was my doing," I explained. "It was the only way to get the magick we needed." I watched Rex carefully, wondering if he was the kind of person who'd lose his temper over a change of plans.

"Well, whatever stops that bastard Viktor from trying to control my people, that's all that matters."

I shook my head in disbelief. While Rowan was intense, his uncle was incredibly easy going.

Rex gestured to Rowan. "Where are those plans you found? I'd like to get a lay of the land before tomorrow."

Rowan reached into his leathers, pulled out some folded sheets of parchment, and carefully unrolled them onto the rug. "These are maps of the Midnight Cloister." He pointed to different areas as he spoke. "It has a square layout. Guarded wall. Four towers, one on each corner."

Rex nodded as he looked things over. "And the main entrance?"

I pointed to the appropriate spot on the map. "You'll come in through the gate here. It's right beside the basilica."

Rex rubbed his chin in an endearing movement that reminded me of Rowan. "We'll start the day at the main gate. The Examination will be held in the basilica."

My shoulders bunched. That was when the Tsar planned to drain Nan and the other new Sisters. "You know that ceremony is a sham, right? If you go into the basilica, chances are you won't leave alive."

"Oh, we're well aware," said Rex. "We're happy to get a chance at him in any venue. We've spent years trying to pinpoint when Viktor would be at a certain place. Must have sent him a hundred requests for an audience. All of them were refused. Finally, my clever nephew here got to work."

It seemed odd for Rex to be praising Rowan so openly, but then again, I wasn't used to praise at all from Petra. Perhaps it was common for Casters to be this way.

"It wasn't that much," said Rowan.

"What are you saying? You cast a finding spell that figured out when Viktor would be at the Midnight Cloister."

Just like I did. I caught Rowan's gaze. "When did you cast yours?"

His face softened with a gentle smile. "About a week before we met."

Warmth bloomed across my chest. "Same here. Maybe our spells crossed before."

"Maybe."

"And that was just for starters!" Rex was quite a talker. His face positively lit up as he went on. "Rowan found you found you to help us as well. A Grand Mistress Necromancer." He leaned back on his elbows and kicked his legs out in front of him. "We'll be set now. Tomorrow will be smooth sailing, mark my words."

I shook my head. "I'm not so sure about that. The examination is dangerous. Why risk it?"

"Viktor respects one thing," said Rex. "Power. He didn't want to meet with us because he didn't think we had enough magickal ability to find him. Well, imagine his surprise when we tracked him down. I sent a request for a meeting on a particular date and time." He bobbed his gray eyebrows.

"And then, what happened?" I asked.

"You should have seen the letter Viktor wrote back. The man was enraged that we tracked him down. No doubt, he accepted the request for an audience just so he could find out how and then kill us. In that order." Rex started to pick something out of his back teeth. What a character.

Rowan met my gaze and half rolled his eyes. It was like teasing the king was our little secret.

"Back to the map," said Rex. "The basilica is a death trap. Our people can't go in there. I say we attack while everyone is here." He pointed to the courtyard between the main gate and the basilica. "Lots of room for attack animals."

I didn't know much about Caster animals. That said, I did know about the various levels of mages. Casters had a similar system to Necromancers. "What level mages are you sending?"

"We aren't sending any at all, outside of myself," said Rowan. "Viktor's killed them off. We're trying to train new ones. Unfortunately, it will be years until they're ready."

"And we're training women, too," huffed Rex.

Here was that strange belief that Caster women couldn't be mages. I leveled Rex with a withering glare. "Afraid of some competition?"

The king stared at me, open-mouthed. "Well, you see... I..."

Rowan gave me a sideways glance. "I knew you wouldn't let his title get to you."

I met his sideways glance with one of my own. "It's a little frightening that you know me so well already." Our stare held a little too long, so I went back to examining the map. "Moving on. We attack in the courtyard, right?"

"Yes," said Rowan. "All the Casters there will be warriors. No mages."

Rex frowned. "Surely there should be one mage." Based on the pouty expression on his face, he had a pretty good idea who that mage should be.

"No, Uncle. I'm the only mage who's going. You're staying here."

I couldn't believe Rowan was so forward with his Uncle. They were like any other family. At least, the little I remembered from when I had one myself. Rosie had always complained that I told her what to do.

"But this is our first chance to strike back at that bastard." Rex pounded his fist onto the palm of his hand. "You know how many of my friends I've seen tortured and turned into Changed Ones. I want vengeance."

"You're too valuable," said Rowan simply. "It's out of the question."

This conversation had the sing-song tone of one that they'd shared many times before. I wanted to get back to the plan to send the Tsar into exile. "And what about the Royals? Do we need to worry about them?"

"I wouldn't give them a second thought," said Rex. "Gaspard has no magick. With Viktor gone, the Vicomte will run at the first sign of danger."

"In that case, I say Rowan and I transport in here." I pointed to the basilica. "The guards never patrol the roof and it's covered with skeleton statues. They'll provide some nice cover for us."

"I like that idea," said Rowan. "We'll attack Viktor once he reaches the courtyard. Elea sends Viktor into the care of the Sire and Lady, and we're done."

Rex narrowed his eyes. "What plans do you have for Linden, eh?" I was pleased that he was concerned for the imprisoned Caster.

"He's in Mother Superior's study." I pointed to spot. "Once we're rid of the Tsar, we'll go directly to get him out."

"Agreed," said Rowan.

"What do you think?" I asked the King.

"I like the plan," said Rex. "But I'd rather be there in person." Rowan opened his mouth while Rex waved him off. "I know, I know. I'll take care to be seen leaving for the cloister. But this is our first encounter with the Tsar. I don't like the idea of a double in my place." He glared at Rowan.

"Forget it, Uncle." Rowan didn't look up from examining his maps.

Their easy manner made me feel right at home. It wasn't so hard talking to a king after all. As we continued to plan, a bubble of excitement formed in my chest. *This could really work.* I almost forgot that I might die a horrible death in a matter of hours.

Almost, but not quite.

The sky was starting to lighten by the time I left the tent. Rowan, Rex, and I had spent the entire night planning. I knew I should feel exhausted. Today was too important for me to be anything but buzzing with anticipation. After so many years of hard work, the time had finally come. I would either defeat the Tsar... Or suffer forever in fire. I rubbed my arms, imagining the flames licking my skin.

A matter of hours would decide my fate.

Rowan gently touched my shoulder, making me jump.

"I didn't mean to startle you," he said.

I forced myself to look calm. "I'm a little restless."

Rowan leaned in closer and lowered his voice. "I am, too." His grin was all things open, honest, and encouraging. It helped me relax a little.

"Will Rex come to see us off?" I no longer thought of him as a ruler. Instead, he seemed like a smiling man who overflowed with positive energy. I could use some of that this morning.

"No, he's being forced to stay in his tent."

The way Rowan said 'forced,' I got the idea there was more to the tale. "Don't tell me you put an armed guard on your king?"

A mischievous glint shone in Rowan's eyes. "I most certainly did. I've sent a double to the cloister in his place. Now Rex is pouting like a six-year-old who must miss out on his own birthday party."

I smiled at the image of Rex in a party hat. "We need to get moving. Dawn will be here soon."

Rowan scanned the sky. "Agreed."

My pulse quickened at the thought of leaving for the cloister. I reached into my pocket and grabbed the ring from the Sire and Lady. We'd spent most of the night discussing battle tactics. I still wasn't sure how the ring ceremony worked. "Do I just put this on?"

"Not yet." Rowan reached into his own pocket and pulled out something that glittered. *My totem rings.* The silver bands shone like stars in the pre-dawn light. Since I'd left the Midnight Cloister, my life had moved at a non-stop pace. In all the excitement, I'd forgotten about my rings. Now that I saw them, my fingers positively itched to have them back. As long as I didn't use them, the Mother Superior wouldn't be able to find me. And if all went well with the leveling spell, I could use them very soon without fear.

"Here's where they belong." Rowan set the bands onto my palm. Wherever his fingers touched me, a charge of heat drew across my skin.

Be careful, Elea.

My control over my emotions was already paper thin, and we hadn't even broken into the cloister yet.

I stepped back and quickly slipped the rings on. It felt like a limb had been returned to me. "Thank you, Rowan."

"You're welcome. I almost forgot about them."

"Same here." *And I spent five years making them.* It had been quite the week.

Rowan pulled out his band from the Sire and Lady. "Now, we come to these."

At those words, two tiny mounds of sand appeared on the ground between Rowan and me. The scarab beetles peeped out from the tops. It was a little unsettling for them to show up now. Still, I supposed it was all part of the magick.

Rowan lifted his ring. "The ceremony is pretty simple. You set your ring onto my right hand and say the following spell."

My bond, my life, my one.

"That's it?" I asked. "You Casters have very short incantations."

"True." The rugged lines of Rowan's face softened. "Do you want to start?"

"Yes." I gripped the ring tightly. I knew this wasn't a real bonding. Even so, it felt huge to me. I'd never kissed a man, and here I was, going through a marriage ceremony. "Have you... Have you ever done anything like this before?"

"No." Rowan's answer was immediate and firm. It made me feel better that this was a first for him, too. I reached out and wrapped my fingers around the palm of Rowan's right hand. His skin was so warm, firm, and distracting. I centered myself with a deep breath.

This isn't real, Elea. Stay focused. It's just to finish your quest.

I spoke the incantation.

My bond, my life, my one.

My voice was firm, but my hand was unsteady as I set the band onto Rowan's finger. Nothing happened. "Did I do it right?"

"You did. The magick shouldn't begin until both rings are on."
Rowan took my right hand in his. His green eyes met mine as he
slid on the ring.

My bond, my life, my one.

This time, everything changed.

The desert disappeared. The world became nothing except
Rowan and me surrounded by white light. Every aspect of him
was brighter and wrought with more detail. I could sense the
weight of his muscles as he heaved in every breath. How the
warmth of his body built out from his chest. And a dozen
different shades of green glittered in his eyes. It was too much to
take in, and not enough, all at once.

The scarab beetles flew onto our bands and hardened into
tiny stones. Our mating bands were complete.

Colored lights glimmered beneath Rowan's skin, lighting him
up from the inside. With every fiber of my being, I knew I was
witnessing the man's soul. I saw the red of passion, gray shades of
determination, and deep amber hues of pain and loss.

It was so beautiful I found it hard to breathe.

I looked down. My skin shone with the same colors. What did
that mean? Was it some side effect of the spell?

The illusion disappeared. Rowan and I were back in the
desert once more, standing near the Caster encampment. A long
moment passed before I could speak.

"So that placed our magick on the same level as Viktor? I
raised my left arm and pulled some Necromancer energy into
me. "My powers don't feel any different."

Rowan raised his right hand and did the same. "Mine don't
either."

"Is that... Is that how a typical bonding works?"

"Not that I've ever heard of. Normally, the rings empower you to cast major spells beside your partner without any worry that your magick will interfere." His gaze locked with mine. "That was extraordinary, Elea."

There were a thousand things to talk about. How did the leveling spell work? What were the Sire and Lady really up to? Would this change our friendship? Only one topic really mattered, though.

Whatever stops me from burning alive.

"We need to try and cast some spells," I said. "Test out our magick before we go against Viktor's."

"Right." Rowan shook his head, like he was waking up from a dream. I supposed we both were, a little. "Which one do you want to start with?"

"I'd like to destroy the snake ring Sophia created when I entered the cloister. The one that tracks my magick." I twitched my fingers, anxious to pull power into them. I hadn't been able to cast since leaving the cloister. All my spells would alert Marlene where I was. She'd be able to track me down with a transport spell in seconds.

"I'll do it. You need your magick again." Raising his arm, Rowan quickly cast an incantation. His veins glowed red and faded as the spell ran its course. "You're free. Go ahead and cast."

Rowan didn't need to say that twice. Although it had only been a week, it felt like years had passed since I'd last used my magick. Using my senses, I reached out to the Necromancer power all around me. This desert had once been a mighty ocean, and the echoes of long-dead sea creatures surrounded my soul. I pulled that energy into my body, concentrated it into my left hand, and spoke the words for an invisibility spell. Meanwhile, Rowan cast a counter spell to void Viktor's wards on the cloister.

When we finished, Rowan and I looked ghostly to each other, but we couldn't be seen by anyone else. The invisibility extended to our magick—no other mages would feel our castings. *Perfect.*

I shifted my weight from foot to foot. This was my first casting since I'd arrived at the Midnight Cloister. What if Rowan's spell hadn't really broken the snake ring? Marlene would know I'd just cast nearby and someone would appear on the roof within seconds. Every muscle in my body tensed, ready to cast or fight. I counted down the time.

Four.

Three.

Two.

One.

It was only Rowan and me. I exhaled a relieved breath and smiled. "It worked."

He returned my grin. "That it did."

I meant far more than the invisibility spell, though. The leveling spell from the Sire and Lady had come through for us in general. Rowan should never have been able to cast past Viktor's wards and destroy something inside the cloister. Enduring all the tests and conditions had been worth it. I could cast again.

"How are you feeling?" asked Rowan.

"Ready to test the leveling spell some more. Let's see if we can transport." Being able to cast past Viktor's wards was one thing. But physically passing through them to get right inside the basilica? That was another matter entirely. Here was the real test of the leveling spell's power.

"Agreed." He raised his right hand. "See you at the basilica."

My heart pounded in my chest as we began our incantations. Soon, a swirling cloud of red and blue mist surrounded us. When my words were finished, the transport magick began. Darkness instantly enveloped me.

Hybrid magick pressed in all around me, solid as rock. The magickal weight crushed into my body. My transport froze in place. Panic chilled me to the bone.

Could the leveling spell have failed?

I pumped more Necromancer energy into my magick than ever before. Waves of energy shot through my limbs. The heavy press of hybrid magick pushed back at me for a moment before shattering entirely. My transport spell sent me hurtling forward. I could move again. My heart soared.

It's working.

The transport spell only took me a short distance. Even so, it hurt like blazes. Magickal energy pulled at my limbs and yanked the air from my lungs. Seconds later, I reappeared on the flat roof of the basilica, set my hands on my waist, and gasped in huge breaths.

Rowan appeared beside me. Sunbeams reflected through his ghostly body.

We were both still invisible. Good.

I stood up and scanned the roof. Giant skeleton statues were everywhere, each one of them at least three times my height.

We were in. Part of me wanted to wrap my arms around Rowan's neck and cheer, but I needed to control my feelings. We weren't nearly finished. Until the plan was done, my emotions were more dangerous than ever.

Raised voices reached us. A man and a woman were talking somewhere nearby, and it wasn't going well.

"Behind us," whispered Rowan. I was glad he kept his voice low instead of casting spells for privacy or silence. We both needed to save our energy. My limbs were already rubbery from my last casting, and all I'd done was transport here.

Rowan and I stole over to the opposite edge of the roof, leaned against one of the skeleton statues, and peered down. A small courtyard stretched out below us. Veronique stood in her black robes, tugging the sleeve of a lean man who was dressed in a yellow longcoat. Round timepieces dangled from his pockets and his mustache and beard were tinged with gray.

The infamous Vicomte Gaspard. Veronique had cornered him at last.

"I'll scream unless you promise me right now," said Veronique. "Say you'll free me from this thing and send me home." She hissed in a breath and clutched at her left shoulder. To approach Gaspard like this, Veronique must be breaking about a dozen rules.

Gaspard stared at her, his gray eyes as calculating as the time-pieces he wore. "Never. You go where Viktor puts you. And that won't be back in Royal society."

"But I'm your ward."

"You're nothing to me." He sneered. "Less than nothing. I only adopted you into my family because I thought you could help with my work. Turns out, you're one of *them*. Necromancer filth. You disgust me."

Veronique gaped at him for a long moment. "I should have known. Amelia warned me about you. Why didn't I listen?"

"Go." Gaspard pointed to one of the access corridors. "Speak to me again and I'll see you peeled like a pear."

Veronique shuddered and ran off.

Watching them made my blood boil. In truth, I'd never thought the Vicomte would do anything to help Veronique, but the way he treated her was chilling.

Rowan was leaning against one of the statues, his arms crossed and jaw tight. "I underestimated him."

"What do you mean?"

"I thought he was a sniveling toady. I was wrong. That man's scheming to be a power."

A door opened in the courtyard, drawing my attention.

The Tsar himself stepped through.

In the classic Necromancer style, he was tall and broad-shoul-dered with long black hair, pale skin, and high cheekbones. The hood of his black robes was pulled away to reveal a circlet of gold around his head. His hands were loaded with totem rings.

I watched him with morbid fascination. Here was a mass murderer and torturer. Yet nothing about him looked particularly extraordinary. I could easily see a younger of Petra approaching him at a sanctuary fair. He seemed like the typical mage who prayed over the dead and joined in on feast days—not someone who destroyed whole cloisters full of people.

The Tsar stalked toward Gaspard. Instantly, the Vicomte's shoulders slouched forward. "Greetings, my Tsar." His face took on a look that could only be called sniveling.

Viktor eyed Gaspard with the same calculating glance that had just been used on Veronique. "I saw you eyeing the merchandise."

Merchandise. That was how the Tsar saw the Brothers and Sisters he led? I turned to Rowan and mouthed one question. "Now?" I pointed right at Viktor's nose. I didn't want to wait to take this bastard down.

Rowan shook his head. "We can't take down Viktor just and leave Gaspard to become a bigger problem. I've been watching them both for years and have never gotten this close to the truth of their plans." His voice lowered to where I could barely hear him. "I don't know when we'll get another chance."

It took all my control to tamp down my rage. Rowan had a point. The way Gaspard was acting, he was more than a mindless follower. The man had plots of his own, and we needed to know what they were. "Fine, but soon, right?"

"Right."

I turned my attention back to the courtyard as Viktor stepped closer to Gaspard. "Who was the girl?"

"She approached *me*, my Tsar."

Viktor twisted the totem rings on his fingers. The mindless

rhythm of the motion made me think it was something he did when he was scheming. "And is she strong?"

"No, my Tsar." Gaspard forced a fake smile. "She's quite weak, as a matter of fact. What did you think of the other new Sisters?"

"Weaklings, every last one." Viktor's upper lip curled with disgust. "There was one who may be suitable to drain. A slum thief or some trash."

His words shook me to the core. *A thief?* He had to mean Nan. He'd seen my dear friend and wanted to drain her power and life. We needed to stop him first. I glanced at Rowan. "Now?"

"Not yet."

I gritted my teeth and waited.

"So," Gaspard said slowly. "You want only want the one girl." He leaned in closer. "And the rest?"

"The others you may have for your machine."

Rowan's eyes were as wide as mine felt. *Machine?* What was that man up to?

"To be clear," said Gaspard. "I can have any girl I want from this cloister?"

"As I said. Take whatever you wish." Viktor scanned the court-yard with a disgusted look. "Time to close this place. I have other cloisters producing far better stock and it's past time I drained Marlene."

Gaspard bowed rapidly. "Thank you, my Tsar. You're so generous, my Tsar."

How disgusting. I knew Viktor had connected all the Necro-mancers and was gathering their power to him. But to hear him speak of my Brothers and Sisters as if they were no more than cattle?

No, it was far worse than that. I treated the animals on my farm with much more respect. This man was brutal.

Viktor raised his fist, showing off his totem rings. "I'm giving you what you ask for, but mark my words. My patience isn't endless." Viktor's amber eyes gleamed with rage. "I need more Necromancer power. I've drained every decent body I can find and I have nowhere near enough energy to control the Changed Ones. You promised me a machine that would turn someone with barely any Necromancer energy into a fountain of power. You need to deliver."

I shook my head in disbelief. Gaspard was using some kind of machine on my fellow Necromancers... And more than just those at the Midnight Cloister. But if Gaspard had done this to so many, wouldn't I have heard about it? I looked at Gaspard's fancy yellow jacket. If you had enough money and resources, you could hide just about anything.

No question about it. Some of my lost Sisters and Brothers were out there alive. If Gaspard had them, then they might still be freed. It was something to consider tomorrow... If I lived to see that day.

"Patience, my Tsar." Gaspard grabbed one of the timepieces from his pocket. "My work is just like one of these. All the gears and pendulums add up to something greater. I'll get you the power you need. I swear it."

Viktor bared his teeth. "You and your useless inventions. I'll give you one more month. That's all. After that, I drain every last mage and throw your sorry soul into eternal fire." Viktor smiled in a way that was both sickly sweet and evil. "Like the idea of my curse, Gaspard?"

My curse. He'd throw Gaspard into the fire, same as he was doing to me.

Focus, Elea.

"No, my Tsar." Gaspard was visibly shaking. "I'll deliver what you need."

"Good." Viktor steepled his long fingers under his chin. "Tell me. What have you found out about the Caster delegation?"

"The King awaits us in the courtyard." Gaspard kept bobbing

in miniature bows as he spoke. "He genuinely wishes to parlay with you."

"And you believe this is truly Rex, not one of their ridiculous body doubles?"

"Absolutely."

Was he ever wrong. Rex was safe at camp.

"Are there any new mages in his party?" asked Viktor.

"None that I saw."

Viktor paced the courtyard. "You're not looking closely enough. Genesis Rex has someone aiding him. At least one powerful mage."

Rowan and I shared a long look. There was no question who was helping us. *The Sire and Lady.*

Viktor threw up his arms. "The man's tried for years to track me without success, and suddenly he's able to find me? I doubt it. Find out who is supporting that fool and what they want. That's your mission for today."

"But, my Tsar, there isn't time."

"I'll stall things before we process into the basilica."

Did he say stall? The idea of waiting made my stomach squirm. I only had hours remaining.

"With all due respect, I—"

"Get them to talk, Gaspard. All Casters are weak. They'll reveal themselves."

Rowan chuckled soundlessly. I was learning his reactions, and this one meant he didn't think Gaspard had much chance of finding anything out from the Casters.

Gaspard began bowing again. "Yes, my Tsar."

Viktor waved his hand. "Dismissed."

Gaspard headed for an access door at the very fastest he could walk without calling it a run.

I glanced at Rowan. "Now?"

"Now."

Excitement prickled across my skin. This was it. I raised my left hand and felt for the Necromancer power in the air.

Before I'd pulled any to me, Viktor raised his fist. "Transport."

One of his dozen of rings flashed blue and he disappeared.

I couldn't believe it. I'd worked for years on my totem rings, and none of them were carrying a spell as powerful as a transport. An uneasy feeling crept into my chest. How powerful was the Tsar? What chance did we really have?

Rowan stepped to my side. "We have a solid plan. We'll get him."

By the placement of the sun, it was early morning.

There was still time to end my curse. Whatever Viktor could or couldn't do, I had no other option but to attack. "Let's get in position."

Rowan and I moved to the other side of the roof. Viktor and his men would come out before the ceremony and process into the basilica. Then we'd finally strike.

Our attack would work. It had to.

gritted my teeth and waited. Beside me, Rowan casually polished a dagger with a leather scrap. It was amazing how many blades the man had hidden on him. I stopped counting after six. I'd found a skeleton statue that was crouched into a chair-shape, so I'd been sitting on that. There wasn't much to do but wait, watch the courtyard below, and tamp down the occasional wave of panic.

And I had plenty of reason to panic. It was well into the afternoon. Time was running out.

Whenever I closed my eyes, I saw the skin melting off my bones. I even smelled phantom whiffs of charcoal.

Don't think about the flames. The Tsar will arrive any second.

I forced myself to scan the courtyard yet again. The place was mobbed with people. I counted Casters in brown leathers, dark-robed Necromancers, and over-dressed Royals. Based on all the gowns and longcoats, it looked like the Royals were visiting a ballroom, not a cloister. And of course, there were the ever-present guards in dark armor. Hundreds of them. Everyone was waiting for the ceremony to start, just like Rowan and I.

In the center of the courtyard, Gaspard diligently worked the crowd, approaching every Creation Caster and peppering them with questions. All of Rowan's people gave quick, one-word answers. What a sly bunch.

The new Sisters were in the crowd with their elderly counterparts. From time to time, I spotted Nan and Ada in the throng. They were too far away to see much, and I couldn't risk casting a magnifying spell. I'd need every ounce of power for the upcoming battle. Even so, there was no mistaking the sad stoop to Nan's shoulders, or the streaks of gray that wove through her long braids. I only got little glimpses of Ada as she cowered behind Nan's robes. Every time I saw them, something inside my soul tore a little more. These were the first friends I'd ever had, and they were dying before my eyes, body and soul.

How could Nan have changed so quickly in only a matter of days? My imagination ran wild, thinking of the foul things Marlene must have done to her. I couldn't wait to bring an end to both her and the Tsar.

I drummed my fingers on the skeleton's ribs. "Do you think we should—"

"No," said Rowan, his voice flat.

"You didn't even hear what I was going to ask." He could be so prickly sometimes.

"Because you were about to ask if we should seek out the Tsar." He reset his last dagger, pulled out a new one, and slid his leather scrap along the edge. That may have brought the count up to nine.

"Maybe I wasn't."

Rowan paused and looked at me sideways. I was still trying to get used to the ghostly version of him. "What *were* you going to ask?"

I huffed out a breath. "Fine. You were right. I was going to ask if we should seek him out."

"And the answer remains no. From here, we know the terrain, the players, and the plan." He pointed at the courtyard with his dagger. "So do the other Casters. If we go off to find the Tsar, then we'll be on strange ground without informing our people. We need to stay right here."

I shifted in my skeleton chair. "That's a good speech. You give it often, don't you?"

"All the time. My team spends days watching ominous places. The oasis, the Midnight Cloister... It's enough to try anyone's temper. You're not the only one who likes to attack first and ask questions later."

I smiled. It was good to know that I wasn't alone in my impatience. "Let me guess. Orion?"

"No, Laurel. She's downright bloodthirsty when—" Rowan froze. "Something's happening."

I hopped to my feet. The groups were starting to line up in the courtyard. My body hummed with excitement. The ceremony was about to begin.

I raised my left arm and began pulling in Necromancer power. When it came to fighting Viktor, I wouldn't make the same mistake twice. Viktor had all his spells loaded onto totem rings. That made him fast. Rowan and I needed to finish as many incantations as possible right before he reappeared. That way, we could strike quickly, too.

Rowan lifted his right arm, and began drawing in energy as well. My invisibility spell cloaked most of our magick, but even that incantation had its limits. We couldn't discharge too much power into a mist without Viktor detecting it. So, we'd need to keep our energy concentrated in our hands. It would be tough to hold back for long, though. Hopefully, the Tsar would arrive soon.

A torrent of Necromancer magick flowed into my limbs. The

bones in my left hand glowed blue. Excitement tightened up my rib cage. In a matter of seconds, I'd be ready.

Rowan and I had outlined this battle down to the last detail. I'd start off with a bone vault spell that would hold the Tsar in place without killing him. Meanwhile, Rowan would send in some of his creatures to take care of the guards. After the court-yard was safe, we'd team up, transport Viktor into exile, and my curse would be over. Simply picturing it made me want to cheer.

And all that remained was for Viktor to arrive.

So much magick poured inside me, it felt like the power was about to burst through my skin. At last, a courtyard door swung open. I stared at the spot, breathless. *This is the Tsar, I know it.* My left arm ached to release the pent-up magick.

Viktor stepped out onto the sandy ground. *Yes.*

Rowan still looked ghostly, but there was no missing the veins on his right hand that shone with magick.

"Now?" I asked.

"Now." His voice was a deep rumble.

Thank the Sire.

I focused on Viktor and unleashed the energy. Power sped from my hand and congealed into a massive white sphere that hovered above the courtyard. A blue haze shifted lazily around it. If you didn't know Necromancy, the orb looked like a full moon hiding behind a sapphire-colored cloud. In reality, the sphere was made of tiny bones, none larger than a thumbnail. They were a Necromancer's most powerful spell for freezing someone while keeping them alive. Not that I wanted Viktor alive. I wouldn't argue with deities, though.

A handful of people looked up to see my magick sphere, including Viktor. My heart raced, knowing the Tsar would act soon—there wasn't much time. Even so, complex magick always took a while to cast properly. I sped through the rest of my incantation, going as quickly as I dared.

Finally, the spell was complete. With a flick of my wrist, I commanded the bone vault to stream straight at Viktor's head. It exploded onto him, encasing him in a thin sheath of tiny bones. Viktor could breathe, but he couldn't move. My heart swelled with triumph. The Tsar stood still as a statue. He was immobilized. It had worked.

Beside me, Rowan released his power, too. Red mist swirled around his right arm, quickly swelling into a giant crimson cloud that spun around the basilica's roof. Rowan finished his incantation and the red haze dropped to the courtyard below. The billowing mist twisted, solidified, and congealed into six giant tarantulas. Each one could immobilize someone in a silk cocoon within a matter of seconds.

Rowan raised his fist and the spiders took off after the guards, Royals, and Necromancers. The insects made a flurry of red on the golden sand.

After our spells hit, everyone in the courtyard had stood dumbfounded. Once the spiders started to move, people woke up from their shock. Chaos erupted everywhere. A crowd rushed toward the main gate. The spiders picked off their targets, wrapped each one in silk, and then set them onto the sand like cordwood. Some Sisters followed the rush to the gate. Most huddled by the wall. The Casters rounded up as many Sisters as possible and guided them to the safety of a nearby courtyard. Rowan's people were a marvel under pressure, moving in a coordinated dance of action.

I looked at Rowan. Pride and excitement warmed my soul. I couldn't help but smile. "Time for the transport spell."

"Looking forward to it."

I raised my hand and released the rest of the magick I'd built up. Tendrils of blue mist twisted down my arm like so many ribbons. The sapphire bands fell in a great arc onto the courtyard, where they swirled around Viktor's frozen form.

Beside me, Rowan added his power into the mix. The red cords of his energy wound through mine and entwined around the Tsar. Viktor's body began to fade from view as the transport grew stronger. I inhaled a shaky breath.

It was working. I could have cheered with excitement. We were sending the Tsar into exile.

A loud crack sounded from inside the red and blue mist. My body went on alert. I strained to see beyond the haze of our spells. Small bits came into view and what I saw made me stagger back. The bone vault was crumbling around Viktor as his counter spell kicked in. Bits of white cascaded onto the sand. He was escaping.

I pumped every last bit of power I could into the spell. More cords of mist flowed out of me. Rowan did the same. Even so, more of the vault collapsed around the Tsar. I crumpled to my knees as my energy drained to the dregs. I had to send Viktor away before he broke free.

The Tsar disappeared.

I'd seen transport spells at work many times. There was no mistaking the way the Tsar faded from view. He was gone. Off to the tent with the Sire and Lady.

Imprisoned at last.

A little eternity passed as I watched the empty spot where Viktor had stood. I was vaguely aware of what else was happening in the courtyard. The spiders trapping the last of the guards... The younger Sisters running for the gate... The elder ones cowering in the shadow of the cloister wall... And all the Royals loading themselves into their carriages in preparation to run off, just like Rex had predicted they would.

Only one thought held my focus. Viktor was really gone. Exiled. We'd done the impossible with a few hours to spare. I glanced to Rowan's ghostly face. Relief shone in his bright green eyes.

"We did it," I said.

"Yes." He grinned that crooked smile, the one I'd come to treasure.

I leaned back and tried to catch my breath. I was free. No more threat of burning. "We'd better—"

A great boom shook the air. With a flash of violet light, Viktor reappeared on the courtyard floor. I almost fell over with shock. He must have cast a counter spell before the transport was complete. The Tsar raised his left fist and his totem rings glistened in the sun. "Visibility. Harm to creatures. Transport. Disarm. Lock."

This couldn't be happening. One after another his totem rings flared blue as the magick inside them came to life.

Darkness enveloped me as Viktor's transport spell took hold. Vicious energy tore into my arms and legs as I was dragged through magick and space. I reappeared in front of Viktor, with Rowan at my side. We were both visible once more.

Enchanted manacles now encircled my wrists, the same as with Rowan. And my totem rings were gone. I couldn't cast if I wanted to. Sadness pressed around my body, heavy as a shroud.

All my years of work and planning. I'd come so close to breaking the curse, and now this.

Viktor lifted his fist once more. "Awaken!" Another totem ring flashed on his hand. This was the brightest flare yet, and it sent a queasy feeling into the pit of my stomach. A mage always saved their best spell for last.

Ear-splitting cracks sounded from the basilica's roof. A low rumble shook the ground. I blinked hard, trying to clear my vision. What I was seeing couldn't be real.

The skeleton statues were moving.

By the gods. I'd thought that Viktor placed those statues to frighten the Sisters. They were actually a hidden army. The huge creatures scaled down the face of the basilica.

White-hot rage overtook me. I wasn't going down without a fight. Pressing my wrist manacles together, I swung my irons at Viktor's head. I knew this might break my vow to the Sire and Lady, but so much had gone wrong, I couldn't control myself.

"No—Elea!"

Before I could make contact, Rowan heaved Viktor to the ground and launched into a punishing series of jabs. Viktor hadn't been expecting a physical fight and his face quickly became a bloodied mess.

Suddenly, the Tsar's skeleton warriors were everywhere at once. One slammed into my spine, sending me face-first into the sand. Pain exploded through my stomach. As much as my belly hurt, it was more agony to watch the skeletons destroying my hopes. Three restrained Rowan. Others freed the guards, rounded up the Sisters, and killed the spiders. About a dozen of them went after the Casters. Rowan's people fought back at every step. Still, they were soon bound in chains. My soul ached at seeing their leathers covered in blood.

I struggled against the skeletons holding me. It was no use. It was like fighting a mountainside. One hoisted me back onto my feet. Rowan stood nearby, his face bruised and beaten. Blood seeped through fresh slashes on his chest. He kept struggling against his captors, but had no more luck than I did. His gaze snapped to mine. "Are you all right?"

And his first thought is to check on me. Rowan really was extraordinary.

"For now."

Viktor stood in front of us, with Marlene and Gaspard on either side. Beyond them, the army of black skeletons and guards ushered everyone into the basilica. A bitter taste crawled up my throat.

I'd failed. The curse was coming, the ceremony was starting, and all my plans had fallen apart.

Viktor paced in front of us, eyeing us carefully. I felt like a slab of meat in a butcher's window. "I don't know either of you." He held up our mating rings. "But I know who gave you these. Ocie and Yuri have expanded into matchmaking."

Marlene slipped up to his side. "My Tsar, this is the girl I told you about. My best recruit yet." Pride shone in her eyes. Fury sparked in mine. How many innocents had she presented to the Tsar in this way? The woman was evil.

Viktor stepped around me slowly. "She certainly has some power in her. Well worth the effort of draining." He stared down his nose at me.

I wanted to spit in his face.

"Excellent work, Marlene. I look forward to seeing what you bring me next season."

Gaspard almost dropped the timepiece he'd been tinkering with. "But I thought I was to have *all* the Sisters."

"I changed my mind," snapped Viktor. "You may have your choice of the new ones and be thankful for it."

The angry look in Viktor's eyes sent Gaspard bowing. "Yes, my Tsar."

Viktor inspected Rowan next. "What a productive day. I suspected the Casters had extra help and here you are. And I thought I knew every Caster mage who had a lick of magick. However did Rex manage to hide your skills from me, I wonder?" He tapped his chin. "Care to talk about it?"

In reply, Rowan only glared. All the defiance in the world shone in his face. No matter what happened, I was proud to have teamed with a man like him.

"I suppose not," said Viktor. "Once we're done with the ceremony, you and I will spend plenty of time together." Viktor grinned, and a hungry sort of evil lurked in his smile. "In the end, my test subjects tell me everything."

The image of Petra's scars appeared in my mind. I couldn't stand if that happened to Rowan.

Viktor grinned and surveyed the group. "Shall we go in?" Without waiting for a reply, he turned on his heel and stepped off toward the basilica. The sun dipped so low behind the church, it almost touched the horizon.

Panic chilled me to the core. The curse was happening.

The fires awaited me, and there was nothing I could do.

a guard whipped open the tall blue doors of the basilica. Like the rest of the warriors, he wore black armor with his face covered by a full helmet.

"Get in, you." His voice dripped with contempt.

As I stepped past, the man mashed his sword hilt straight between my shoulder blades. *Not again.* Hurt shot down my spine. I schooled my features into careful calm. These guards were brutal with their sword hilts. Showing any reaction or pain only made the next hit worse.

As I stepped across the threshold, the noisy chatter of the crowd washed over me. I'd never seen the basilica so full of people. Once I began walking down the center aisle, everyone fell silent. The quiet was almost a physical thing as it pressed around me, making it hard to breathe.

I'd never been in many crowds. The oasis and sanctuary fair had been overwhelming, even when I was just trying to blend into the mob.

Now, I was the main attraction.

As I stepped toward the stage, all eyes locked onto me. No one said a word. Still, I could sense what was in their heads.

Traitor.

Whore.

Viper.

Liar.

Walking dead.

The worst part of them thinking I was doomed? They had no idea of the real peril. Yes, being drained by the Tsar would rob me of my power. It wouldn't free me from my curse, though. An eternity of flames still waited for me.

There was an audible grinding of metal as the guards craned their armor, all of them turning to stare in my direction. Rage rolled off them in waves. Most of these warriors hadn't seen any real battle until my escape from the cloister. I'd made fools of them with my plague sign act. Today, they wanted revenge and in all likelihood, they'd get it. My back ached from the many bruises I'd gotten already.

I stepped past Royals who were lounging, fanning themselves, and looking bored. Why would anyone wear ball gowns and longcoats to the desert? They gave me curious glances as if I were a dessert tray that had come out with soup instead. Not what they expected, but not something they particularly worried about, either.

As I moved by the elder Sisters, they huddled more closely in their pews. Some fiddled with the ties on their robes. Others found the all-blue windows fascinating. None of them made eye contact with me. Neither did any of the Sentinel Spirits, for that matter. They'd been here long enough to know what Marlene and the Tsar had in store for me. The thought made my insides squirm.

You don't know the half of it.

The new Sisters openly gawked. Once I'd been a Novice, the

same as them. Then, I'd run away and returned in Caster leathers, trying to kill none other than the Tsar. These were the only girls I'd ever spent much time with. Once, they'd called their Sister. Now, they stared at me, slack jawed, as if I were a freak of nature.

I was halfway down the aisle when I spied Ada. She sat curled across Nan's lap and stared at me with miserable, red-rimmed eyes. The happy-go-lucky girl who'd snuck through the cloister on secret adventures with Wulf was gone. Sophia's worst fears had come to pass. I remembered her withered corpse on the basilica stage.

Sophia hadn't wanted this for any of us.

Up close, I could see the changes in Nan as well. Her once-bright eyes were sunken with despair. Where was the girl who'd teased Veronique while riding in a prison wagon?

Nan's old self must still be inside her, somewhere. Ada's as well. Anything else was unthinkable.

At last, I reached the platform at the back. The huge painting of the Tsar glared at me from the curved wall behind the altar. I wanted to chip the thing away with my fingernails. The small door at the base of the wall caught my eye. Ada had told stories about sneaking through there with Wulf. It opened onto a maze secret passages inside the basilica. My spirits lifted a little.

Maybe that was a way to escape.

The guards shoved me onto the right side of the stage. A small troop of them lined up behind my back. I scoped out the distance to the door. It wasn't a long run. If I could find the right moment, I might make it. My manacles had no chains between them, only bands around my wrist to block my magick. I could reach the handle and open it easily enough.

It might work.

The guards hauled Rowan onto the opposite side of the platform, right alongside the other Casters. They were a bruised and bloodied group. Still, there was no missing the defiant gleam in their eyes. Maybe they'd try to escape with me. Other than Rowan, none of them wore enchanted manacles, since they didn't have magick anyway.

We just needed the right moment and the element of surprise...

The door at the base of the mural swung open. The Tsar, Marlene, and Gaspard all stepped onto the stage. I'd be close enough to kill them, if only I had a sword in my hand. I might even find a blade in the passageways beyond the door. A girl could hope.

Viktor stepped forward and raised his arms. "Welcome to the Examination Ceremony for the harvest equinox." Some polite applause followed, mostly from the Royals. I guessed they must have attended these events enough that they knew when to clap.

Yet another reason to hate them.

"New Sisters have been initiated into the Midnight Cloister," continued Viktor. "I am here to select some of them to join in my personal entourage." He paused for dramatic effect, and it made me ill to see the younger girls share excited smiles. Viktor set his hand on Gaspard's shoulder. "Others will be sent off with the Vicomte for further training. This is a great honor."

Gaspard straightened the lapels of his yellow jacket and bowed slightly at the waist. "The honor is all mine."

Conniving bastard.

Viktor turned to Marlene. "And a small number of you will stay to serve this cloister. You'll be blessed to live under Marlene's wise and gentle leadership as Mother Superior." Marlene fluttered her lashes and blushed. I supposed it was an attempt to show her humility, gentleness, or wisdom. I wanted to kick her teeth in.

"And there are unpleasant topics for us, as well." Viktor gestured between Rowan and me. "Here, you see two master assassins. They came to our cloister with murder on their minds and evil in their hearts. Along with them came a league of rogues and thieves, one of whom was posing as the great Genesis Rex." He raised his pointer finger. "And although every last one of these fiends is a bloodthirsty killer, not a single member of my company was killed."

Only because I wanted to be merciful to the guards. Although, knowing what I knew now? I'd have suggested *poisonous* tarantulas.

"As you witnessed, I was able to foil their plans with ease." Viktor stared at me in open contempt. "To atone for their foul actions, the Casters have volunteered to participate in my latest experiments."

My chest tightened. *I can't let that happen.* I stared at the platform door. *It's such a short distance...*

Viktor raised his arms once again. "It is time for the principal announcement of our ceremony. I know how the young Sisters dream of joining my entourage. I have spent time reviewing each of your qualifications. It was a hard decision, but after much deliberation, I have made my selection. Only one girl will be chosen." Viktor paused again. A few new Sisters trembled with excitement. Others held hands, their eyes wide with anticipation. The sight made me want to scream. "This time I choose... Sister Nan."

I'd known he would say her name. That didn't make it any easier to hear, though. It was as if a vise clamped down on my heart.

Viktor pointed to the spot beside him on the stage. "Come forward, Sister."

With that bone crawler inside her, Nan had no choice but to obey. She slowly rose from her pew and shuffled to stand beside the Tsar. The whole time, Ada watched with tears streaming down her cherub-sweet face. I kept reminding myself that Ada was safe here until next season. She had time.

Viktor set his hand on Nan's shoulder and looked down at her indulgently. "I shall accept you into my inner circle. This ceremony is something that very few of my followers have been privileged to witness. Therefore, I invite Vicomte Gaspard to announce the names of those chosen for his training program. After that, the rest of you may leave."

More lies. Viktor just wanted to kill Nan with as few witnesses as possible. I tried to catch her gaze. Nan only stared forward, her features slack with shock. I glanced at the door. *Should I run now?*

Rowan caught my eye. He carefully scanned the distance between him, me, and the doorway to escape. His brow furrowed for a moment before he tilted his head to the side. I knew the movement was his way of asking 'are you planning to run?' In another situation, I might worry about the fact that Rowan and I were guessing each other's thoughts, but at this moment, I was thrilled.

I gave him the barest of nods. Rowan returned the gesture. *He would help me.* My body felt a jolt of hope and energy. With Rowan involved, there was a far better chance of success.

Viktor motioned to Gaspard. "Vicomte, if you're ready."

Gaspard fingered one of the timepieces dangling from his pockets. "This is a remarkable class of initiates. So many fresh faces that—with a little more training—may be suitable to join the Tsar's inner circle. I am happy to say that I have accepted all of you into my training program." The girls actually cooed with excitement. Those poor souls.

Viktor nodded. "You may take them now."

Gaspard waved at the basilica entrance. "Up and out, everyone. Exit through the front door. My people will help guide you to your carriages." The new Sisters rose and strode away. Veronique stood still as a statue in the middle of the group. Her eyes blazed with rage as she glared at

Gaspard. I'd seen her peevish and whiny before, but nothing like this.

Viktor waved his hand absently. "The ghosts may go as well."

My hands curled into fists. *They're called Sentinel Spirits.* These women had dedicated their souls to the cloister. It was nothing like a haunting. For a moment, the Sentinel Spirits looked around with sad eyes and stooped shoulders. After that, they disappeared entirely. What a disgrace to treat them this way.

Viktor stared at the elder Sisters before letting out an exasperated sigh. "Must I spell out everything for your bovine sensibilities? The older Sisters may go. You're no longer needed."

It didn't hurt that the Tsar compared the elder Sisters to cows. What pained me was that they didn't flinch at the words. I was used to older women being treated with respect. Here, they kept their eyes down as they shuffled out a side door. Infuriating.

Suddenly, Ada was racing down the main aisle. "I want to stay with Nan and Elea!" An elder Sister tried to quiet the child, but the damage was already done. Gaspard had noticed.

He pointed directly at Ada. "What about that one?"

On reflex, I shook my head. *Not Ada.*

"She isn't a Sister," said Marlene.

Gaspard shrugged. "I'll take her anyway."

Viktor pursed his lips. "Aren't you concerned about discipline, Gaspard?" *Discipline, my eye.* Ada didn't have the mark, so she might not be harder to control.

"Not at all," said Gaspard. "My training program enforces complete obedience."

Viktor stared at Ada for a long moment. I twisted my hands so hard the manacles drew blood from my wrists. *Please, let her be. Leave her for one more season.*

Viktor waved at the door. "Take her, then. Go."

Mindless rage roared through my soul. Somewhere in the back of my mind, a small voice warned me about acting zuchtlos.

It sounded a lot like Petra. But as Ada raced toward me, she wore a smile of pure joy. The child didn't understand that I was in trouble, only that she could run into my arms for safety. The innocent love in her eyes crushed any thoughts of control.

In that moment, I made my decision. *I'm taking her. Now.*

I glanced over to Rowan, who gave me another nod. Ada raced closer.

Twenty feet…

Ten feet…

Five…

I leaped off the stage and scooped Ada into my arms. Rowan and his people sprang into action as well. They picked up prayer benches and slammed the wooden frames into the guards, clearing our path. Even Nan grabbed a prayer bench and jumped into the battle. A fighting light was back in her eyes. It was beautiful.

With Ada in my arms, I raced to the back of the stage. Guards were everywhere but I only focused on the exit door. Rowan ran at my side. We had to make it.

The three of us sped across the stage. Ada's little hands gripped me tightly around the neck as she buried her head in my shoulder. Rowan pulled daggers from his leathers and whipped them at the guards. His accuracy was deadly despite the manacles weighing down his wrists. Blade after blade embedded directly in the guards' helms. They fell over, dead.

We were almost at the door. Nan tore a dagger from a dead guard's helm and jumped back into the fight. Rowan gripped the handle and whipped the door open.

Almost there.

Something smashed into the base of my spine, heavy as a boulder. I fell forward and landed on my side. Agony seared up my rib cage. All the air was knocked from my lungs as the guards pinned me to the floor. One of them grabbed Ada.

Her small voice cried for me. "Elea!"

"I'm coming for you, Ada!" My voice was a rough wheeze as I struggled to pull any air into my lungs. That vise in my chest pressed tight, I thought my heart would burst with sorrow. I had to get her. With all my strength, I tried to wriggle free from the guards. It was no use. The most I could do was twist my head and watch Ada being dragged away.

Of all people, Veronique walked over to Ada and calmly plucked the child from the guard's arms. The man seemed too stunned to fight back. Veronique comforted Ada with gentle words before hoisting her onto a hip. Then Veronique then turned to me.

I had no illusions about this girl. *What game is she playing?*

Cold determination shone in Veronique's eyes. "Amelia," she said clearly. With that, Veronique carried Ada away, and the other Sisters followed.

Amelia. It was only one name. Even so, it held a world of meaning. Veronique believed I could get out of this alive and when I did, I'd return to save Ada.

There was only one reason why she'd do this. Veronique wanted me to save her favorite person as well... And that would be herself. Watching over Ada was Veronique's best way to ensure her own safety. Still, if it helped Ada, then I'd track this Amelia person down.

At least, I would if I lived to see the morning.

The guards dragged me to the right side of the platform. Rowan and his people were set back on the left. They all looked worse for the wear. Fresh lines of blood dripped down the side of Rowan's handsome face. Nan was hunched over in pain as well. She clutched her shoulder and looked away. So many brave souls, and we'd tried to do the right thing. It simply hadn't worked. My eyes burned with held-in tears.

We were so close.

Viktor rounded on me. "What an amusing display, my little assassin. Do that again and I'll bring the imp back. You'll watch me slice off her fingers and toes, one by one." He stepped closer. "Am I clear?"

How I hated saying this. "Clear."

Next, Viktor turned to Nan. "The same goes for you. No acts of defiance or I'll disembowel both your friends before your eyes."

My mouth fell open. I'd known Viktor to be evil, but pulling out fingers and disemboweling children? Where had this fiend come from?

"Am I understood?" asked Viktor.

Nan kept her gaze steady. I was so proud of her, I could burst. "Clear."

"Then, we come to the most important part of the ceremony," said Viktor. "Sister Nan shall join my entourage."

Nan lifted her chin. "Get on with it, then." Even though our escape plan had failed, I was happy to see my friend's spark had returned.

Viktor grasped Nan's throat in his meaty hand. His grip was so tight, her head flipped back in pain. On reflex, I stepped forward to help. A guard slammed his sword hilt into my tender ribs. A riot of pain broke out over my torso.

"Stand back, little assassin. No more trouble from you."

I barely heard his words. All I could do was focus on how Nan gasped for air while the bone crawler slowly twisted under the skin of her neck. Once the creature was parallel with her throat, it flared a violet hue.

"Stop it!" I cried. "What do you want? I'll do anything."

Viktor ignored me. All his focus was on Nan's writhing throat. "Come out, my pretty." The insect punched a hole through her neck, its body glowing purple as it wrapped itself around Viktor's wrist. A horrible gurgling sound came from the wound.

I screamed. "No!"

The skin on Viktor's arm shone violet-bright as he drained Nan's energy into his body. I'd give anything to spare my friend this horror.

Nan's flesh withered while her hair turned white. Her healthy young body wasted away into an empty cadaver before my eyes.

"You bastard! I'll make you pay!" This was *my* Nan, who'd chased Ada around the storehouse. Who'd told happy tales of avoiding the hangman's noose. Who approached any tragedy like an adventure. Her withered form lay on stage. That light—the sacred brightness that was only Nan—had been taken from the world. We all lived in a darker place. I hated Viktor with all my soul.

The Tsar tossed Nan's limp body to the floor like trash. Her body fell to the side, arms arching over her face. I held in a sob.

A defensive pose, even in death. Her whitened braids fanned out behind her like a halo. *Bastard.*

Viktor stepped up to me. "Your turn." Bands of icy fear tightened around my chest. "But first, I must prepare you." Viktor clenched and unclenched his fingers, making his totem rings glisten in the dying light. "Bonding animal," he said.

One of his totem rings flared blue. A moment later, a bone crawler squirmed on his palm. The slimy beast was just as disgusting as I remembered. My heart pounded so hard, I could hear the blood whoosh in my ears.

Viktor held the wriggling insect right by my face. It smelled of rotting flesh. "Any final words, little assassin?"

The bone crawler's long antennae flicked down my neck. It took all my Necromancer training not to scream. "Elea. My name's Elea."

"Such a proud thing," said Viktor. "I'd like to hear you howl again, but this time in fear. Will you do that for me?"

"No." My voice came out level and even. Petra would

be proud.

"Everyone screams when I do this." He jammed the creature against my shoulder. But the insect didn't burrow into my skin. Instead, a shock of magick smashed into me, solid as a wall. Violet light flashed across my collarbone.

Viktor's eyes narrowed. "What tricks are you playing?"

Suddenly, I knew the truth. I could wield hybrid magick.

When I'd touched Rowan's dagger at the oasis... The day Sophia set the hybrid snake on my palm... And now, this bone crawler. For whatever reason, touching an animal with hybrid magick brought out the same power in me.

Excitement bubbled up in my soul. I glanced at the stained glass windows lining the walls. A few sunbeams shone across the floor. The day hadn't ended yet. There was still time, and there was only one thing to do.

Send Viktor into exile.

I grabbed the bone crawler in my fist, pulled its hybrid magick into me, and began the words of a transport spell. The enchanted manacles around my wrists couldn't stop my hybrid powers. The insect writhed in my hand, its husky shell glowing with purple light. I welcomed its energy and movement. Violet mist appeared around my arms, solidifying into bands of bright energy that whipped off my arms and wrapped around Viktor like a mummy.

The Tsar stared at the spell in utter disbelief. "What are you playing at?"

"This is no game. You are being exiled."

"Exile?" Marlene stepped forward. "Who are you to say such a thing?"

I spoke an incantation of freedom and sent the power toward Rowan. The enchanted manacles fell away from his wrists. His face was bruised and bloody. Still, he gave me his crooked smile. "I was hoping you'd do that."

"You're welcome. Can you get us a little privacy?"

Rowan began a spell of his own. His hand flared brightly as a thousand red doves appeared. They flew around Viktor, Rowan, and me, creating a magickal shield from the rest of the basilica... And Marlene. My thoughts ran to Rowan's people. "Are the Casters—"

I was about to ask if the Casters were protected. I didn't finish my words before Rowan folded his arms over his chest. "Yes."

We were finishing each other's thoughts again, but there was no time to worry about it now. I returned my attention to Viktor. He writhed under the purple coils of power, unable to escape.

"This isn't possible." Viktor eyed me carefully. "Who are you?"

I took in a long breath and held onto the moment.

This is for you, Petra.

"I am Elea de Braddock, a Grand Mistress Necromancer trained by Petra. You know her name?"

Viktor gave me a simpering smile. "Release my bonds and I'll cast a memory spell."

That would never happen.

"Petra was a Novice you kidnapped and experimented on." I remembered the scars that wound around her ribs. "You used bone hooks on her."

Viktor looked annoyed. "I am the Tsar. I experiment on many people."

"Well, Petra has a message for you." I stepped closer, grinned, and spoke very slowly. "Rot in hell."

I finished the rest of the transport incantation. The cords of violet power that encircled Viktor flared more brightly than ever before. A flash of brilliant violet light appeared. The color reflected in beautiful shadows off Rowan's dome of birds.

When the brightness disappeared, Viktor was gone. I looked at the bone crawler in my hand. It was dead. Every sign pointed that the transport spell had worked. That said, Viktor had returned the last time. A little voice in my head reminded me that I hadn't used hybrid magick before. It sounded like Petra.

Minutes ticked by. Rowan stepped closer. "Is he gone?"

"Not sure." I waited for another full minute to pass. All the while, the birds encircled us in flight. There was no sign of Viktor while before, he'd returned within seconds. I focused my attention on Rowan. "Yes, I think he's gone." Excitement prickled over my skin as I thought through what that would really mean.

My curse might be over, too.

On reflex, I looked toward the windows. The cone of birds blocked my view. "Do you think the sun has set?"

"Let's find out." Rowan snapped his fingers and the crimson doves broke formation to fly away. I stared around the basilica. The guards were gone, as were most of the Casters. Only Laurel waited. Her face was bruised and a tooth had been knocked out, but her smile still shone brightly.

"Hail and well met!"

"Where did everyone go?" I asked.

Rowan gave me a sly look. "I cast more tarantulas. Poisonous this time."

I couldn't stop my smile. "I like that about you."

He set his hand on my shoulder and turned me to face the basilica windows. "And there, you see, the sun has set."

I stared at the colored glass, unable to form words. *The sun has set.*

All those years of hard work and fear. Tristan's suffering and sacrifice. Finding the Sire and Lady. It was all worth it. "I'm no longer cursed." Joy bubbled through me. It was as if I could sprout wings and fly among the doves. "Thank you." I leaped to wrap my arms around Rowan's neck. "We did it."

He slid his hand up my spine, leaving a trail of heat behind. "Yes. We did."

Laurel let out a low whistle. "I'll just go see what Orion's doing." She disappeared, leaving us alone.

Let go of him, Elea. Walk away. You're a Necromancer. Take control.

I didn't move a muscle. Neither did Rowan.

"There you are!" Marlene stalked onto the platform. We instantly broke apart to face her.

"You." Marlene pointed directly at me. "You ruined everything. You're an assassin that I took into my home. A viper that I nurtured. And you stole my Tsar away. What am I without him?" She raised her hand and began an incantation.

"I'll say this once, Marlene. I'm a Grand Mistress Necromancer who just took down the Tsar. Do you really want to start a mage's war with me?"

Blue mist swirled around her hand. "You stole everything!"

"No, you took from me." My voice broke. "You robbed me of Nan."

A low hum filled the air, followed by a thwack. *What was that?*

Marlene looked down at her chest and I followed her gaze. Rowan's dagger was embedded in her heart. She turned to Rowan. "Why?"

He stepped to my side. "If you go after Elea, you pick a fight with me." His voice lowered. "Tell that to everyone in hell when you get there."

Marlene stared at both of us, her mouth open in shock. For a long moment, she wobbled on her feet. "This isn't over." Her knees crumpled under her and as she fell over. Marlene was dead. I sighed with relief and sadness.

That was for you, Nan.

The other Casters crowded on the platform around us.

"I told you they were here," said Laurel.

"How are you feeling?" asked Orion.

"Good." *Exhausted.*

Laurel bobbed on the balls of her feet. "You cast hybrid magick. Can you do it again?"

I shrugged. "I don't know." I certainly wasn't about to find another bone crawler to check.

"You look tired," said Rowan.

And my head was feeling fuzzy, too. But we couldn't stop now.

"There's more work to do. Someone needs to track down Gaspard's carriages. The Tsar may have allies still in the cloister. The elder Sisters need someone to take care of them. And Linden must be set free."

And that was just what I could think of off the top of my head. If I weren't feeling so woozy, I could probably come up with a dozen more.

"Which is why it's the perfect time to call in my uncle," said Rowan. "He loves saving the day once the danger is over." He gave me another crooked smile, which only made me feel more unsteady. "Honestly, the man is good, even if he is a king. And you need to rest."

I leaned my head against his shoulder, and felt the deepest sense of calm I'd known since Rowan healed me in the cave. "I'm convinced. Let's get back to camp."

That night, I dreamed that I'd returned to my old kitchen on Braddock Farm. Tristan stood at the hearth, looking better than I'd ever seen. The color had returned to his cheeks. "Elea."

I smiled so hard, my face hurt. "Tristan."

I'd said his name before I went to sleep, but I wasn't sure if I really wanted to see him or not. If he still appeared, it might mean that he remained cursed. Now that he was here and looking so healthy, my hopes were rising.

Tristan walked around the room, something that he'd never done in my dreams before. "I can move now." He returned to stand in front of the hearth, where he stared at the flames. "And the fire isn't coming for me." He smiled. "It's over, Elea. You did it. You broke the curse." His voice cracked. "I knew you could."

My heart soared. "I did, didn't I?"

"I always said it. You're the most powerful Necromancer I ever met."

It was so good to be near him, just like the old days. I wanted more of that. "What happens after this?"

"You'll go back to your realm, and I'll return to mine. We'll keep our secrets for another day."

The realm of the dead. His words sent a chill across my skin.

"What do you mean?" The joy at the breaking our curse gave way to other, darker memories. "You said before that there was much I didn't know. I'd like you to tell me. Can you do that?"

"I'm so sorry. I can't." He sighed. "All I can say is that I love you. On the rest, you'll have to trust me."

On the one hand, Tristan was still—and always would be—my best friend. On the other, he'd broken my trust and was continuing to play games.

I decided to leave his judgment to the Sire and Lady. I didn't think they'd bring him to me if they thought he was a fiend. At least, I hoped they wouldn't.

"I'll try, Tristan."

"That's enough for me." He sadly shook his head. "I have to leave now." He crossed the kitchen and opened the door.

"Good luck." The words stung my throat. It wasn't fair that we had so little time together before we were parted once more.

"Farewell, Elea."

As the door swung shut, I wondered if I'd ever see my best friend again.

28

TWO WEEKS LATER

I stepped up to the campfire and looked over the roasting meats. Laurel was cooking tonight, and that woman could burn rabbit in no time flat. I picked out a decent-looking skewer and took a seat next to her.

"How is it?" Laurel nibbled on her thumbnail. She always did that when she worried.

"I haven't taken a bite yet." I chomped down and got a mouthful of charcoal. The stuff crunched in my teeth like sand. It was an effort to force a swallow. "This is good."

"Are you sure? Orion says I burn it every time."

"Orion's a baby." Laurel beamed with joy, which was worth lying about a mouthful of charcoal any time. "You don't know where the mead is, do you?" My mouth still felt gritty.

Laurel's smile faltered. "It's the meat. You need to wash it down, don't you? It's terrible, isn't it?"

"I said it's good and I meant it. I'll just find the mead now." *Before I'm tempted to wipe my tongue off with my palm.*

I quickly stood and almost walked into Linden. The man was getting stronger every day, but he was still pretty frail. A heavy gust of wind could knock him over, and I had more force than that. "Sorry, Linden."

He stared at me blankly for a moment and then shook his head. "Elea?" He wore a heavy duster to hide the stump of his amputated centipede arm. Some days, I found myself forgetting that he was a Changed One.

"That's right. I'm Elea."

His eyes widened. "Oh, I'm so sorry." Every so often, Linden remembered what had happened in Marlene's office and tried to apologize. "My familiar, I—"

"It's nothing to worry about. Really." I patted him on the shoulder and stepped off before he could launch into his full apology speech. Laurel pulled him toward the fire and food while I made my way to the edge of camp. The view here always took my breath away. Every night, the sky shone with more stars than I'd ever thought possible. I could spend hours staring at the lights and counting shooting stars. Nothing could compare to the desert at night. My shoulders slumped with sadness.

I was going to miss this when I left.

Rowan's familiar step sounded in the sand behind me. It was getting harder and harder for him to sneak up on me. "If you stand out here looking at the stars, you'll miss dinner." He stood beside me with a sly grin on his face. "It's going pretty quickly, I hear."

"I already ate my fill." And I'd be picking charcoal out of my teeth for a week. "How about you?"

"I'm fine." The moonlight outlined his muscular frame. I used to think he towered over me, but now? Standing beside Rowan made me feel safe. "Have you thought about my offer?"

I'd told Rowan stories about Braddock Farm, and he'd volunteered to help me return. He even said that Rex would buy up Wyatt's land, if I wanted. Knowing a king was handy like that.

"I can't go back yet." *Much as I'd love to.*

Rowan rubbed his neck. "And why not? You've done so much already. The Tsar has stayed in exile—"

"For two whole weeks."

"And the Vicomte is a different kind of enemy. This is a diplomatic war. That's Rex's territory, not ours." He set his hand on my shoulder and moved his thumb in soft arcs on my leathers. I'd seen him do this with other Casters. Still, I liked to pretend it meant something else with me.

Control your emotions, Elea.

I bent to pick up a stone from the sand. It gave a believable excuse to break the connection between us. I tossed the rock from hand to hand. "Ada is out there with the Vicomte."

"We're getting closer to tracking where those carriages went."

They were making no headway, and we both knew it. Not that I blamed Rowan's people. The Necromancers had been disappearing with the Vicomte for years with no one noticing. The man was a marvel at hiding things. In the end, the carriages didn't really matter one way or another. Only one thing mattered.

"The Vicomte has Ada and I'm going after her."

"She has an ally in Veronique. They could escape."

I'd hoped that too, once. "It's been weeks. There's been no sign of Veronique, Ada, or anyone else that the Vicomte took. These are my people. I have to do what I can to find them." I tossed the stone out into the desert. "After all, I'm the last Grand Mistress Necromancer." That was what the other Casters were calling me. It wasn't half bad, as names went.

"There are others."

I rolled my eyes. "The last one under ninety, then."

"You have me there." He chuckled and the sounds pulled at my heat. I'd miss his laughter when I left. "Where do you plan to start looking?"

"Amelia. I'm going to try to track her down. She may know

something."

"Sounds very boring. Why don't you go back to the joys of farm life and leave spy work to others?"

"If I didn't know better, I'd think you were trying to hide me away."

"Only a little." He stepped closer. "I like to think of you as safe." His eyes took on that intense look again, and it always made me squirm. That was another reason I needed to go.

"I'll be fine." I kicked at the sand. "How about you?"

"Another mission with my Caster team. We're working on infiltrating the Vicomte's court."

"Maybe we'll cross paths."

"I hope so." A long pause followed. It felt like we both had things to say, but for some reason, neither of us were talking. At last, Rowan broke the silence. "When do you leave?"

"Tonight. I didn't want to make a fuss. I've already stayed far too long."

"Figured you might be planning something like that." He reached into his pocket and pulled out some silver bands.

I smiled from ear to ear. "My totem rings." When the Tsar cast the spell to remove them, I'd thought they were gone forever. I managed to scoop the bands from his palm without brushing his skin, which wasn't an easy thing to do.

Touching Rowan was one of the main reasons I'd been staying at camp instead of looking for Ada. That wasn't right and I couldn't afford the distraction any longer. "Thank you. I thought they were lost at the cloister."

"Rex turned them up."

I slipped them back onto my fingers. They were more lovely than I remembered. "I'll have to load new spells now."

"There was something else as well." Rowan held up my mating band. My breath caught. The scarab stone glimmered in the moonlight, lovely as a star. I never thought I'd see that ring again.

Rowan shifted his weight from foot to foot. "I didn't know if you'd want this one. There isn't any magick left in it."

"I'd like to have it."

"Good." Rowan touched my elbow, and then slid his fingers down the inside of my arm. His skin was just the right mix of roughness and warmth. I shivered as Rowan lifted my hand and slid the mating band back on my finger. Even though I'd only worn it for half a day, my hand had felt empty without it.

"Thank you." It felt right to have the ring back. Rowan and I stayed like that for a while, standing in the moonlight with our fingers entwined. I didn't want it to end.

It had to, though.

Rowan slowly raised my arm toward him. My body froze with anticipation as bit by bit, he gently brushed his lips across the back of my hand. "Be safe, Elea."

I opened my mouth, ready to share a dozen things at once. That fact that I'd learned so much from him. How I'd come to respect and rely on his presence. The way I could still count every time he'd touched me. Nothing came out, though.

Eventually, Rowan dropped my hand and strode back to the camp.

Once he was out of earshot, I finally knew exactly what to say. "I'll see you in the Vicomte's court."

As I spoke the words, a shooting star streaked across the night sky. It was the first one I'd counted tonight.

I took it as a very good sign, indeed.

—*The End*—

~

The adventure continues with CONCEALED, Book 2 in the Beholder series. Read on for a sample chapter!

ALSO BY CHRISTINA BAUER

CONCEALED

Elea's adventure continues with CONCEALED … find out more at Bauersbooks.com!

ANGELBOUND

The kick-ass paranormal romance with more than 1 million copies sold ... more at Bauersbooks.com!

FAIRY TALES OF THE MAGICORUM

Modern fairy tales that *USA Today* calls a 'must-read!' More at Bauersbooks.com!

DIMENSION DRIFT

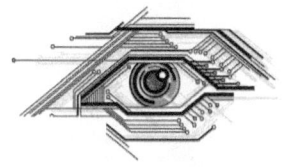

DIVERGENT meets OCEAN'S EIGHT in this dystopian adventure … more at Bauersbooks.com!

*W*ith a sigh, I rode deeper into the old forest. Here was a scene fit for a fairy tale. My elegant horse. Woods in the summertime. And me, a girl with pale skin, dark hair, and a flowing white gown: the innocent young maiden.

What a lie.

In truth, I was one of the realm's most deadly Necromancers. Mages like me wielded powerful magick over spirit and bone. Most people were terrified of us and for good reason. Necromancers were known for summoning ghosts and reanimating the dead. Not that I dabbled in that kind of thing personally. Ghosts whined for ages before doing even the smallest task. And decaying bodies? When reanimated, they became just as petulant as any ghost, only they smelled something awful. *Not worth the effort of casting, in my opinion.* There were other spells that I preferred.

My horse let out a high-pitched whinny. *My poor Smoke.* She so wanted to gallop. As did I, for that matter. But my plan called for me to ride slowly while looking innocent. The reason? I sought out sensitive information from the brigands who hid in these woods. Of course, I could just lure them to me with a spell.

However, that meant projecting magick over long distances. Not too clever. That kind of casting could easily be detected by my enemies and used to track me down. I needed to be careful.

No, the scum of the forest had to approach me of their own free will. And that could only happen if I looked harmless.

Please, let me look harmless.

A weight of worry settled on my shoulders. I needed information and badly. My Sister mages from the Midnight Cloister were still missing. The desire to find them constricted my heart, tight as a vise.

As did my need for Rowan, if I allowed myself to think about him.

Suddenly, the tree branches rustled with extra force. I tilted my head, every sense in my body going on alert. Was someone finally approaching?

Seconds passed. No one appeared. I tried to hide my disappointment and kept riding along at an inching pace. *Clip-clop. Clip-clop.* The monotony made me wish to pull my hair out.

Images flickered through my mind. I pictured the Necromancer girls that I'd met in the Midnight Cloister. My Sisters. They'd all looked so wide-eyed and innocent as the evil Vicomte led them off to his secret prison. And these were no ordinary dungeons either. The Vicomte had a mysterious device that siphoned off Necromancer power. I shivered at the thought. My Sisters would writhe in agony as their magick was removed. And once their powers were fully drained, my young friends would transform into withered husks of skin. *Dead.* The thought made my stomach churn.

Sadly, the treachery against my people didn't end with my Sisters. Over the past five years, thousands of Necromancers had been imprisoned and marked for death. It was the Tsar who began all the abductions. Three months ago, I put that villain into exile, trapping him on a random magickal plane. Afterward, I assumed that our worries were over. How foolish of me. The moment the Tsar was gone, one of his main followers, the Vicomte, took up the heinous plans against my people.

Since then, things have only become worse.

The Vicomte has expanded the Tsar's program of abduction and murder, killing far more Necromancers than the Tsar ever did. No one has found any bodies, though.

By the Sire, please let that mean some of my people are still alive.

I could only hope that when I found my lost Sisters, I would discover some trained Necromancers along with them. So few of us remained. My Cloister, the Zelle, was the last of its kind, and it now held less than a dozen expert Necromancers. All were over ninety and could no longer cast any serious spells.

Footsteps rustled in a nearby thicket. *Someone's close.* My heart thrummed in my rib cage. Only certain travelers stole through the shrubbery.

Thieves. How perfect.

A hulking brute of a man lurched out from the trees and grasped my horse's reins with his meaty fist. Any other lady would have screamed. I could have cheered for joy.

"Afternoon, my lovely. I'm Bartley." His voice had the deep rasp of someone who enjoyed far too much whiskey. Like the other thieves I'd met, Bartley wore a mishmash of whatever clothing he'd claimed from his latest kills. In this case, Bartley donned a gentleman's longcoat over ragged pants and a patched-up shirt. He rubbed his thick hand over his bald head, a movement that showed off his small black eyes.

A warm sense of satisfaction bloomed through my chest. Someone this evil looking was certain to have good information. "Hello. I'm Elea."

"Call me Bartley. Are you alone?"

"Yes. And you?"

Bartley didn't say a word. The barest rustling in the trees

answered for him. More thieves waited nearby, not that I cared. At close range, I could use certain spells without attracting attention. And since I was a Grand Mistress Necromancer, I didn't have to bother with reanimating the dead or calling on ghosts. Satisfaction warmed my blood. With any luck, I would cast my favorite spell today.

Ah, the joy of conjuring skeletons from stone.

After all, rock contained the concentrated remains of what had once been part of a living thing. It was an advanced form of cadaver, if you will. A Grand Mistress Necromancer could reform that raw material into a new skeleton.

I really loved casting these.

My skeletal servants had no personalities unless you counted mindless obedience. They smelled only of chalk if they had a scent at all. Best of all, a good Necromancer could give her skeletons some flair. I often covered mine with glittering gemstones. My teachers had frowned on this, but I was a girl, and we girls needed sparkly things.

Bartley took a half step closer. "Hand over your gold, and we'll let you go easy." He stared at my chest. "Yes, easy."

I stifled the urge to roll my eyes. Thieves always stared at my breasts and threatened my virtue. It was getting rather tedious. "I'll gladly pay you for information. Will you answer my questions?"

This was a rule of mine. *Always give the thieves an honest way out.* Not that any of them had taken it.

"By the Lady of Creation, you're a feisty one." Bartley grinned, showing a mouth full of yellow teeth. "Now, you've got me curious. Go on. Ask your questions."

"I'm searching for a child." My voice cracked as I pictured six-year-old Ada. She was a tiny wisp with a huge smile and an invisible friend named Wulf. "The Vicomte Gaspard took her."

Bartley's eye twitched, which came as no surprise. With the Tsar was gone, the Vicomte was the most feared man in the realm. "Never heard nothing 'bout the Vicomte kidnapping Necromancers."

Of course, he hadn't.

"I didn't say she was a Necromancer." My voice dripped with venom. "*You* did." Bartley knew something about my people—I could tell that without even casting a truth spell. "One last chance. Talk to me."

"I already did, wench." His thin mouth twisted into a snarl. He wouldn't answer any more questions voluntarily.

Let's see what magick can do.

Raising my left hand, I pulled Necromancer energy into my body. The power was everywhere, if you knew what to look for. Thousands of travelers had passed along this very road, their hearts filled with joy, dreams, and despair. That force was still in the ether, waiting for a Necromancer to transform it. I pulled the energy into my soul.

Magick rushed through me, energizing my body like a breath of fresh air. I focused it into my left arm. My bones there glowed blue as I whispered an incantation.

Bones born in night
Honed by magick's light
Heed my call
Rise up for the fall

The thief's piggy eyes narrowed. "You don't look like no Fantome."

Hope sparked in my chest. Fantomes were trained Necromancers who served the Vicomte. If Bartley knew about them, then he might be even more valuable. "I'm not a Fantome."

"Well, you can't be no free Necromancer. They're hardly none left." His mouth set into a determined line. "Is this some kind of trick?"

"No, it's more of a trap." I slipped off Smoke and stepped to the side. Pushing the power out of my hand, I set my spell loose. Blue mist appeared about Bartley's feet just as he lunged straight for me.

The man didn't get far. In fact, his feet stayed rooted to the spot.

Bartley shifted his weight, trying to break himself free. "What did you do?"

"Me? Nothing." I gestured toward the ground. Bartley couldn't know it, but more of my magick had whirled beneath the soil, shifting the stones into new forms. "The skeleton I conjured, though…"

Bit by bit, Bartley tipped his head down to peer at his worn leather boots. Skeletal hands had pushed through the earth and were now wrapped around his ankles. The white granite bones contrasted against the dark soil.

"You bitch!" Bartley reached under his longcoat. No doubt, he was searching for a weapon.

This wasn't my first battle, however. I still had plenty of ambient energy left to conjure more skeletal servants.

With a flick of my fingers, another set of bony arms burst through the ground nearby, followed by a third. Two new skeletons wiggled their way out of the soil and stood at attention. They were magnificent—seven feet tall with amber bones and glowing blue gems in their eye sockets. What a sight.

Bartley gasped and yanked a knife out from under his coat.

With a wave of my hand, I summoned more blue mist around me as Bartley tossed his blade at my head. My enchanted shield shattered his weapon before it got anywhere near. Metal shards burst in the air and fell in a glittering cascade to the forest floor.

Necromancers weren't supposed to show emotion, but I allowed myself a small smile.

Four more thieves leapt out of the forest, a mixture of men and women in raggedy dress. While howling in unison, they all rushed toward me. Unfortunately for them, they hadn't counted on my skeletons. It was a common enough mistake. Most conjured skeletons were clumsy things that lumbered toward their enemies. Not mine. All my castings were whip-fast and deadly. The moment my skeletons saw I was under attack, they wrapped their bony arms around the thieves' throats, snapping their necks in quick succession. All except one.

Bartley gasped. "Who are you?"

"Someone who deserves answers." I rubbed my palms together. For extra effect, I allowed a small puff of blue mist to whirl about my hands. "Let's try again. What do you know about the Vicomte Gaspard?"

He lifted his chin. "Nothing. I swear."

"I see." This one wouldn't be easy to intimidate into talking. *He must be hiding something really important.*

I waved my left arm, and two more skeletons wiggled out of the ground. This time, I cast them to look extra frightening. Both were eight feet tall with opal-black bones and pointed teeth. Blue light shone about their bony hands, which meant they could not only fight, but cast spells as well. The pair loomed over Bartley, their jaws clacking with silent laughter. A wet spot appeared on his pants. *Excellent.*

"Tell me what you know, Bartley. If you don't, I'll be forced to ask them to cast a truth spell. You've heard about those? The skeletons squeeze information from your head. I'm told it's very painful."

"I can't tell you nothing." Little bits of spittle flew from Bartley's mouth as he spoke. "The Vicomte—"

"He's not here and I am." I snapped my fingers, and the two

dark skeletons went to work. One held Bartley's head still while the other pointed its bony finger right above his eyeball. "Perhaps we'll work up to a truth spell. There are other ways to injure your skull, you know."

"No!" Bartley stared cross-eyed at the skeletal hand. "He's got Necromancers hidden away."

"Where?"

"On Royal lands."

"I've checked every inch of that man's estate." Or cast spells on his servants to do it for me. "My Sisters aren't there."

"I said Royal lands, didn't I? It's one of the nobility that has them."

My heart sank. I was afraid of that. There were hundreds of noble families. Searching all their lands could take years, even if I dared to use magick. "Which noble is hiding the Necromancers?"

"I don't know." Bartley was visibly shaking now. I believed he was telling the truth—the man didn't know anything more about where my people were being held. Still, I needed other kinds of information. "There's a machine that drains magick from my kind. Have you seen it?"

"I can't tell you 'bout that. He'll find out. He'll kill me."

"He *might* kill you." I snapped my fingers, and the skeleton twisted its wrist, bringing the pointed bone of its fingertip even closer to Bartley's eye. "But I definitely will."

Bartley howled with fright. "He's got a device. A small thing, no bigger than a skipping stone. I never got to see it close up, but it's made of metal. Them Fantomes put it on the prisoners. That's what drains 'em till they're dead."

I pictured little Ada, six years old and subjected to some kind of evil contraption. The thought made me ill. "Who made this device? How does it work?"

Tears streamed down his dirty cheeks. "I don't know. I swear."

I thought back to the single clue I had from Veronique, one

of my Sisters from the Midnight Cloister. As she was dragged away, Veronique spoke the name of a Royal. I'd been searching for that girl ever since. "What do you know of a Royal named Amelia?"

"You mean the Lady Amelia Masson?"

My pulse sped. I was hoping that Veronique was referring to the Lady Amelia Masson. Mostly because I'd already checked another dozen Lady Amelias already and had come up empty. "What do you know of Amelia Masson?"

"Lady Amelia lives near here. She's crazy. Locked herself up for years."

Worry weighed on my shoulders. I hadn't considered that one of the Amelias wouldn't be sane enough to answer my questions. "And that's all you know about her?"

"Bandits broke into her mansion a few months back. Took some silver and ran for the forest. After that, they all disappeared. No one knows what happened to them, but I'm guessing it wasn't good."

"Why do you say that?" I happened to know for a fact that those bandits were dead. I'd found the bodies myself, after I uncloaked the magick that concealed them. They lay in the forest not far from here.

"Lady Amelia is under the Vicomte's protection. One of his adopted children, you know?"

"I've heard." Amelia Masson was also said to be a genius with mechanics, not that I was about to volunteer that information.

"Well, them bandits had no business breaking into her house. Everyone knows what happens when you attack what the Vicomte sees as his property."

"Indeed." The Fantomes had tortured those bandits for days before they finally killed them. My chest tightened with rage. The bodies had been twisted and flayed almost beyond recognition.

Bartley was shaking more violently now. "That's all I know. I swear."

I believed him. Still, I needed to be sure. I nodded to the skeleton holding Bartley. "Test him."

All the blood drained from Bartley's face. "You said you wouldn't cast no truth spells."

"Forcing you to speak is different from testing whether you just lied. This one won't hurt."

The skeleton gripped the thief's head while blue light flared more brightly around its bony hands. "He's telling the truth, Grand Mistress."

"Fine." I couldn't hide the note of disappointment in my voice. "Erase his memory and set him loose."

"As you command."

The skeleton's hands flared blue once again. Bartley's eyes rolled back into his head, and he collapsed onto the ground. He'd sleep for an hour and wake up with a headache. Not to mention a lot of work to do if he chose to bury his friends.

One of the opal skeletons turned to me. "Will you need anything more?"

"No, you all may go." I waved my hand, and the skeletal servants settled back into the earth. Once they were gone, I tapped my cheek and thought through Bartley's news. There were two kinds of people on my continent. First, there were Necromancers, who had magick. Second, there were the Forgotten Ones, who had none. Of course, Forgotten Ones would say they had learning and machines, which were superior to mage craft. Personally, I'd rather have magick any day.

In turn, the Forgotten were divided up into Royals—like the Vicomte—or Commoners such as Bartley. Bartley just told me the lost Necromancers were on Royal lands. No matter how I turned over that information, it didn't narrow things down much. I shook my head. There was nothing to do but move forward. Crazy or not, perhaps the Lady Amelia Masson would have more insights for me.

I hoisted myself into the saddle and patted Smoke's neck. "Let's keep going, girl." I sat up straight, scanned the road ahead, and saw the man who'd haunted my thoughts for weeks.

Rowan.

My breath caught. Rowan and I had teamed together once. He helped me send the Tsar into exile. Afterward, we'd parted ways. I thought I'd forget him. That hadn't happened. Instead, every day I found myself listing the many reasons why Rowan could never be more than my friend.

It was a long list.

To begin with, Rowan was from a different continent than mine. Visiting each other meant casting transport spells, which wasn't easy to do. Plus, Rowan only visited my continent because he served his King as a master spy. Not exactly the kind of man you built a life with.

Then, there came the fact that Rowan was a kind of mage called a Creation Caster. That made him the exact opposite of a Necromancer in almost every way. His magick came from life and nature. Necromancers pulled from death. Casters were known for open displays of affection. Necromancers were schooled to control every feeling. So, although we'd successfully teamed in battle, chances were that Rowan and I weren't compatible in other ways.

To make matters worse, Rowan wasn't just any Caster. His uncle was their ruler, Genesis Rex. Everyone knew that the Imperial family only married for political gain. Meanwhile, I was a lone Necromancer who only owned a small farm.

Not exactly the ideal for an Imperial marriage.

On reflex, my fingers brushed the mating band that Rowan had given to me. I wore it on a chain that hung around my neck and under my clothes. It wasn't a real symbol of genuine affection, only something we'd been forced to exchange in order to fight the Tsar. Even so, I wore it every day.

It was a silly thing to do, but I couldn't help it.

"Hail and well met, Elea." Rowan gave me one of his crooked grins. Warmth spread down to my toes. He was leaning against an oak tree, wearing the loose green leathers, hooded cloak, and longbow of a Forgotten One and a hunter. Some kind of disguise, obviously. When Rowan had helped me fight the Tsar, he'd worn fitted Caster leathers.

Other than the hunting gear, Rowan looked as he always had: tall and strong-limbed with broad shoulders and tousled brown hair. A day's growth of beard rounded his chin. His green eyes seemed to pull me closer, and his full mouth looked delicious.

A delicious mouth? I needed to stop thinking this way about Rowan and quickly. Straightening my spine, I gave him a proper greeting, the way any Creation Caster would. "Hail and well met."

"I should say so." Rowan scanned the corpses. "Excellent work with the Band of Eight, by they way. Those are some of the most fearsome thieves around."

"Band of Eight? I only ran across five of them."

Rowan's smile broadened. "I might have helped a bit. Someone has to keep an eye on you."

A warm feeling spread through my chest. *Rowan watches over me.* "You didn't need to do that."

"I know." He nodded toward Bartley. "How long before he wakes up?"

"An hour."

Rowan offered me his hand. "Come down and walk with me. We need to talk."

Panic tightened up my spine. Touching Rowan was a bad idea. It always made me lose focus. "I'm fine up here."

"If you insist." Rowan raised his right hand, closed his eyes, and began an incantation. This man was the most powerful mage

I'd ever seen. While Necromancers like me pulled their energy from the remains of the past, Casters like Rowan pulled in living power to make magickal animals.

A red mist hovered around the ground at Rowan's feet. Within seconds, the haze solidified into a massive black horse with a red saddle. That could only mean one thing.

Rowan plans to ride alongside me. The thought made me giddy.

"Nicely done," I said. "But where are your snow tigers?" Normally, Rowan rode either Radi or Umeme.

"I'm trying to keep a low profile." He winked. "You should try it sometime." He effortlessly hoisted himself onto the horse's back.

"What do you mean?" I had a fairly good idea, though.

"Your spells. I saw flashes of ethereal light from a league away."

I shrugged. "A girl has to cast sometimes. It may have been bright, but the power levels were low and at close range. No Fantomes would have detected anything."

His full mouth thinned to a determined line. "I still don't like it. The Fantomes are dangerous."

"I'm aware." At one time, the Fantomes had been the personal entourage of the Tsar. Now, they followed the Vicomte. For months, these mages had been scouring the continent and arresting anyone with Necromancer ability.

Mostly, they wanted to find me.

Officially, the Vicomte announced that he desired an audience with the brave Necromancer who sent the Tsar off into exile. I didn't believe that nonsense for a second. What the Vicomte really wanted was another Necromancer to drain.

No, thank you.

"Be careful, Elea. That's all I ask."

I gave him a sly grin of my own. "I suppose I'm not an expert at sneaking about, unlike some people."

"No, you're not." Rowan's gaze suddenly locked with mine. Once again, I felt pulled in by the intensity of his stare. "I like that about you. Quite a lot, as a matter of fact."

By the Sire. His words were making me feel all squirmy inside. I needed to change the subject.

"I'm off for Jaxminster."

"Still looking for a Lady Amelia?"

"Yes, unfortunately. The one in Jaxminster is my thirteenth attempt."

He let out a low whistle. "And what happened with the other twelve?"

"All dead ends." I wanted to scream with frustration. "The next one on my list is the Lady Amelia Masson. Does that name mean anything to you?"

"Not at all." Rowan's face became unreadable. I hated it when he did that. And since Rowan was a master spy for the Creation Casters, he did it quite a lot.

"Why are you *really* here, Rowan?"

He arched his right brow. "What if I said I missed you?"

"Liar. You're as single-minded about protecting your people as I am about rescuing mine."

"True. Even so, I still missed you."

I wasn't letting him off the hook that easily. "In other words, you'll tell me what you want when you're good and ready."

Rowan chuckled. "How do you read me so well?"

"Call it my gift." We followed a turn in the road. "How has your work been going?" Rowan also sought news of the missing Necromancers, but for a different reason. He feared the Vicomte gathering up their magick. If anyone wielded that much power, then they could attack Rowan's people. As a result, while I'd been hunting down Lady Amelias, Rowan was working on a diplomatic course between the Vicomte and the Caster's King, Genesis Rex. "Any luck so far?"

"We're seeing some initial success with diplomacy. Luncheons, balls, dinners. No word yet about the Vicomte's plans for the Casters."

"That's unfortunate."

"We've made allies with a few of the Royals, which is good. A handful are quite unhappy with the Vicomte. One in particular might be useful."

"Anyone I should know about?"

"Not at this time." His face became stony once more.

"You're doing it again."

"What?"

"Playing the spy."

"You know I'd tell you if I could, Elea." He gave me another one of his intense stares. "My first duty is to the throne."

I blushed and looked away. "I understand." And I did. When your uncle is your King, and that King orders you to keep a secret, then your follow those orders and keep your mouth closed.

We rode along for a few more minutes before Rowan broke the quiet. "Have you any ideas on how the Vicomte could wield Necromancer power?"

"I've been thinking about it." In fact, I'd been contemplating it quite a bit. "It would need to involve a totem ring." That was how we Necromancers stored spells. Totem rings enabled mages to cast lengthy incantations with a single word—there was no lighting up bones or creating colored smoke. Unfortunately, totem rings were incredibly hard to create and only stored one kind of spell at a time.

Rowan stared at my hands. "I notice you're not wearing any today." Normally, I had a totem ring on every finger of my left hand.

"Yes, I've had to set those aside. Wearing totem rings would be a clear sign that I'm a Necromancer. And the spells for creating new rings would attract too much attention." Sadly, I didn't have any old rings to use, either. They'd all been ruined during my last battle against the Tsar.

"The Vicomte using a totem ring." Rowan frowned. "It's possible. Although, how would he get the magick into his body? The man isn't a Necromancer. Totem rings only work for mages like you, right?"

Excitement fluttered inside my stomach. I loved these chats with Rowan. There were no other free mages around that I could discuss new magick with. Sure, I could transport back to my old Cloister, the Zelle, and chat with Petra, my Mother Superior. However, Petra was almost a hundred years old. Her mind was sharp when it came to traditional magick. But when I needed to think through new uses of power, no one was better than Rowan.

"What do you think?" Rowan spoke again, snapping me out of my thoughts. "How could the Vicomte take in power from a totem ring?"

"I do have one idea."

Rowan grinned. "I knew you would."

My body warmed under his praise. "The Vicomte has a number of adopted children. All of them are experts in machines."

"And?"

"He's not bringing in orphans out of the kindness of his heart. I think he's putting them to work. They're creating some kind of device for him. It's a machine about as large as a throwing stone. And if my guess is right, that device could transmit magick into a non-mage."

"Quite possible." Rowan nodded slowly. "The Vicomte's been obsessed with machines for years. We'll focus our spy work in that area." His voice took on a deep tone that I liked very much indeed. "Thank you, Elea."

I looked away quickly. Even with the space between us, being this close to Rowan made me all distracted. I needed to refocus on my mission. "I learned some news about my lost Necromancers. Perhaps you can shed some light on it."

"I'll do my best."

"The Vicomte is hiding my Sisters somewhere on Royal land."

"Not his own property?"

"It's someone from court. The thief back there confirmed it."

"I see." Rowan grew quiet. It was what he always did when thinking through a problem. "Not a lot of places could be used for draining magick. After the Tsar took power, my team canvassed all the known dungeons on Royal lands. None of them would have worked for such a purpose."

"I'm sorry to hear that." A sense of emptiness filled my soul. My people had been disappearing for years, and yet there was no sign of them.

"Take heart. I'll check around. One of the old dungeons could have been adapted for draining magick. Or perhaps a new one was built since the Tsar took power." He pulled off his glove, reached across the distance between us, and took my hand. The shock of his touch moved through me. Confidence and care warmed my soul.

Oh, you are dangerous, Rowan.

"If anyone can find them, Elea, you can."

Rowan gave my hand a gentle squeeze and then released me. My arm went cold without his touch. I hated admitting this, but I dearly missed Rowan. That simply wasn't right. Necromancers like me shouldn't form attachments. Still, when it came to Rowan, I couldn't help myself somehow. I cleared my throat and tried to put on a casual voice. "If nothing comes of this last Lady Amelia, perhaps I could aid you in your diplomacy."

He gave me another crooked smile. "You might expose me with your spells."

"A likely story. You just don't want me involved."

"That's right." His gaze intensified once again. "I want you safe. If this last Amelia doesn't work out, then I want you to return to Braddock Farm."

Naming my old farm made my chest ache. The servants who were working on it were good people. They sent me regular missives, and things were going well. Even so, that farm was my only home. Some days I wanted my old rocking chair and fire-lit hearth so badly, I could hardly stand it. And if I failed with the Lady Amelia Masson, then I was sorely out of other options and ideas.

I stared at the western horizon. Braddock Farm was that way. Maybe it was time to regroup for a while. I could harvest some grain. Read a few spell books. Plan other ways to find Ada.

When I spoke again, my voice was dreamy. "If I went back to Braddock Farm—and I'm not saying that I would—would you alert me of any news?"

"I'd even let you cast a compulsion on me."

I scanned his features carefully. A compulsion spell was no small thing, and Rowan's face looked open and earnest.

"In that case, I'll consider it."

His eyes glittered. "That's all I ask."

We reached the edge of the forest. A small town stretched out before us. *Jaxminster.* Here the buildings stood no more than two stories high. All of them were made of white plaster and framed by heavy wooden beams. A tall clock tower stood at the far edge of town.

I stopped my horse. "This is the place. Lady Amelia Masson lives in the estate beyond that clock tower."

"How do you know?"

"Amelia was adopted by the Vicomte. All his so-called children have extraordinary gifts in science or mechanics. They must build their own clock towers as an early project for him."

A flicker of unease crossed Rowan's features. "I hope it goes well for you."

"I've nothing to fear from her. The worst rumor I've heard is that she's a crazy recluse. At least, she's not one of the adoptees who builds weapons."

Rowan frowned. "What about the Fantomes?" It was a valid concern. Almost every Royal had a Fantome in residence. That was how the Vicomte controlled his court.

"Amelia's out of favor. She doesn't have any Fantomes around. I'll ask her a few questions and hope she has answers. Perhaps she'll share something useful."

Rowan's frown deepened. I knew he was still worried about my safety.

I lowered my voice to a serious note. "I'll be fine, Rowan."

"Still, I'd rather that you could easily contact me without attracting attention." Rowan raised his right hand. The veins there glowed red as crimson mist swirled about his arm. Within seconds, the haze solidified into a little robin that sat quietly on his palm. "This bird is one of my familiars. If you need to get a message to me, call her name, Tamu. My magick will do the rest."

The little creature hopped onto my shoulder. Her tiny claws pricked my skin before she flew away. "I will. Thank you."

Rowan opened his mouth to say something and then closed it just as quickly. I glanced over to his hands. He was wearing his heavy leather gloves once more. I couldn't help but wonder... Did he ever wear his mating band? For one full day, our souls had been connected through those rings. Did that mean as much to him as it did to me?

My hand settled onto the base of my throat where my own ring hung under my gown. I knew it was weak of me. Even so, I treasured this band. Wearing it with Rowan was one of the few moments in my life where I felt truly linked to another person.

Rowan noticed my hand, and his features became unreadable.

An itchy feeling moved over my skin. When we were talking just now, Rowan admitted to hiding something for his King. What could it be? Part of me wanted to press for a full answer, yet I held back. I couldn't afford to get any more involved with Rowan than I already was.

My mission lay elsewhere. I needed to save Ada and the other Necromancers. Straightening in my saddle, I nodded toward the town. "It's time for me to leave."

Rowan shifted his horse onto another path. "Be safe."

"And you as well." I clicked my tongue, and Smoke took off for Jaxminster.

—The End—

∿

To find out more about CONCEALED, visit:

http://monsterhousebooks.com/books/beholder/concealed

APPENDIX I - BONUS CONTENT

ON THE BEHOLDER WORLD

Folks have asked how I created the unique magical world of CURSED. It all began with a personal motto of mine...

There are four kinds of beauty: heart mind, soul, body. Of these four, only body gets worse as you age, no matter what you do.

Anytime I invest energy in my body, I remind myself to give equal time to my heart, mind and soul. Over the years, I started to wonder about a realm where people got equally obsessed with all four aspects (heart, mind, soul, body). I decided that such a quartet of factions would probably hate each other.

The world of Beholder was born.

Soul

In this universe, Necromancers value the pathway of the soul. *Raising the dead* felt a little overdone to me, so I have my Necromancers summon ghosts and skeletons by carefully controlling energy of the past.

Heart

Meanwhile, Creation Casters focus on emotion and heart. Their magick enables them to create new animals to do their bidding (among other things!).

Mind

The realm's Royals have no magick. Instead, they follow the beauty of the mind, which is why they're obsessed with machines.

Body

Commoners don't have any mage powers, either. They focus on the physical, especially in the sense that they must work hard to keep body and soul together.

With any luck, here's how it all comes together.

Story

Our main character, Elea, starts off as a farmer and then trains to be a Necromancer. By the time the series is over, she'll have experienced---and been changed by---each world. She'll also have to make some big choices on how to balance these four opposing energies.

If all goes as planned, Elea will be a new kind of Odysseus on a journey that's both modern and ancient. And because it's my series and I love this kind of stuff, she'll also have lots of fun, battles, and romance along the way.

~

RULES FOR WRITING FANTASY

I'm a big of fan using rules while I'm writing. Creating CURSED was no exception...

Set stuff up

If I mention something (such as an item, god or monster) that becomes important later, then I need to set it up at least two times earlier in the book. And it can't be an obvious drop in, either. I must tie it to another character point or emotion so it doesn't stand out.

Backstory, backstory, backstory

If I create a new world or people, then it gets a history back to at least three generations. I also assign a language base to the group. For example, the Creation Casters have a language base of Swahili.

Thoughts

In fantasy, it's easy to rely on amazing battles or unusual settings. I try to check in (meaning go inside the character's head) every three paragraphs or so. Why? I think people read for the internal journey as well as the external one.

Feels

Along the same line, it's easy to ignore the inner emotions of a character in a fantasy work. Again, the setting and battles can detract. All of which is why I make sure to express a character's feelings every three paragraphs. And yes, I count that stuff.

Limit those data dumps

Also on the fantasy vein, it's really tempting to spend pages upon pages explaining the history of a particular aspect of a world. I built this shizz up and want it in black and white, dammit! But that content drags the story down, so I limit any so-called data dumps to four or five sentences, tops.

Sensation

This is different from thoughts and feelings. I like to set each major scene with as many of the five senses as possible. Smell is the hardest to do and most powerful, IMHO.

Language

The written word is a unique toolset for creating scenes or emotions. For instance, I use longer words with more assonance for slower sequences. To build up action scenes, I use shorter words with consonants and more onomatopoeia. POW!

Voice

Every major character needs a unique voice, *especially the villains*. I ask myself: if this were an audio book, would I know just by a phrase or two of dialogue which character is speaking? If not, I need to go back and dig deeper on voice.

Reading aloud

Continuing with that thought, I read my work aloud. A lot. When I'm heavy into writing, I get stomach cramps from just talking all day long!

Have fun

Writing can be tough, so I try to remind myself to have a good time along the way.

Or at least, an extraordinary amount of mochas.

INSPIRATIONS FOR ELEA

$\mathcal{I}$n creating Elea, I listed out various medieval ladies that could serve as her role models. Here are some of my favorites.

Eowyn

Lord of the Rings fans know Eowyn as the badass chick who takes down the evil Nazgul king. Their interaction goes a little something like this:

LORD OF THE NAZGUL: Don't even try to hurt me. No living man may injure me. Nyah. Bleh.

EOWYN: But I am no living man. You look upon a kick-ass chick, you patriarchal dipshit. [KILLS HIM]

What I love about JRR Tolkien's medieval kick-ass chicks are that they always win in the end and act fabulous while doing so, which brings me to …

Galadriel

I can still remember the moment thirteen-year-old me read the passage in Lord of the Rings where Galadriel is tempted by ultimate power of the one ring. If Galadriel takes it, then…

"All shall love me and despair."

What a great line!!!

Galadriel then refuses the ring, which is one of the most heroic things in the history of ever. After reading that part, I sat straight up in bed and was like *damn, I want to write something like that too*!

Celaena Sardothien

I heart Sarah J Maas's Throne of Glass series and its heroine, Celaena Sardothien. The books are set in a super-cool medieval world with lots of dungeons and hidden royalty. And our heroine knows how to be sassy. Yes!

Eleanor of Aquitaine

For my next heroine, I'm switching gears to a real person. Eleanor of Acquitaine was the mother of Richard the Lionheart and a host of medieval English kings.

FUN FACT: Did you know that King Richard spent all of ten months of his rule in England? Eleanor actually ran the freaking country for fifteen years. And that was *after* her husband locked her up for a decade because she led too many civil wars against him. But Eleanor's hubby died and she took his throne. Now that's badass.

Queen Isabella of Castile

Another real person. Another total badass. In medieval Spain, some loser tried to steal Isabella's throne and she bitch-slapped him down with political and military smartassness.

My heroine.

Just like Elea.

~

NOT FOR ELEA

When creating a new character, it's key to have my inspirations ready. That said, it's also important to know what I *don't* want in her personality. With that in mind, here are some of the traits I tried to keep as far away from Elea as possible.

Whining

Ugh. I can't stand a whiner. And Elea doesn't whine. She pulls up her Necromancer robes and gets to work.

Cowering

I totally irks me when the female leads cowers in a corner while the guy fights. That shizz is just rude.

Tripping

We all run through uneven surfaces, especially in wooded

areas. We all do NOT have to fall on those surfaces. It's simply not a requirement.

Being a lump

Okay, okay. Despite our best efforts, sometimes we all do fall down while running. I get it. Buuuuuuuut if you do fall, don't stare at your attacker like a dumbass while they close in. Get back up and run. Or better yet, kick that attacking fool right in the face!

Love triangles

I know, this is a totally personal thing. As a writer, I can certainly do a 'love triangle lite.' However, I have issues with anyone who dithers around on making a decision about who she loves ... all while the people she supposedly cares about hang out in anguish. Not really love in my book.

Cheating

This one is another totally personal choice but yeah, this can really bug me. In my thinking, you can take two minutes to break up with someone before hooking up with someone else, especially if you have magick and can do it with an enchanted owl or whatever.

Developing your power

So you have a special power. It turns out that you can fly or something. Go you! In these cases, it irks me when the heroine doesn't go YES! MINE! and develop the crap out of that gift. What are you waiting for? YOU CAN FREAKING FLY. Do it already. Don't wait until the last chapter when you're about to die. Get organized, girlfriend.

Developing your partner's power, because you have ZIP

It bums me out when the heroine doesn't have a power, but her boo does. I'm a big fan of both partners working as a team and being equals. Again, I know that's a personal thing but there you go.

Lots of 'not talking'

Every so often, I have times when my protagonist doesn't tell her significant other something and wow, does that ever cause trouble. But I try to make that the exception rather than the rule because I like it better when couples share things.

Whining part 2.

I list this one twice because I really, really, really can't stand a whiner. When I write a whiny line for a heroine, I seriously want to punch myself in the face.

And then I click delete.

~

THE HEROINE'S JOURNEY

*I*n forming the character arc for Elea, I relied on my personal interpretation of what I call the *heroine's journey* (other people use this term too, so I wanted to get that out front). My particular interpretation of the heroine's journey was inspired by STAR WARS.

You read that right.
STAR WARS.
Chicks.
Myth.
Yeah.

STAR WARS creator George Lucas has gotten lots of air play for consulting myth expert and general smarty-pants Joseph Campbell, making sure Old Joe officially blessed the space epic as following the so-called *hero's journey format* from Campbell's book, THE HERO WITH A THOUSAND FACES.

About the hero's journey

IMHO, the hero's journey began with the work of Carl Jung, who said that humans are born pre-wired for what it means to be a mother, father, hero, warrior, healer, villain ... the list goes on and on. We even have pre-crafted stories about those ideas built into our noggins, which arise in our minds as dreams, or get triggered when we hear the *right* myth at the *right* time.

In this way, our brains can activate what we need to survive, be it our inner hero, warrior, mother, father — you get the idea. Campbell described the standard hero story that's built into our heads.

Caveat

Not everyone believes this theory, just like not everyone (myself included) sees Campbell and Jung as across-the-boards examples of awesome behavior. But hey, we all fall short in some ways, and mistakes shouldn't negate excellent work. Having said that, I'll now trash Joseph Campbell a wee bit.

Where Campbell missed the boat (to me, anyway)

Campbell wasn't exactly a feminist. Although he acknowledged that every psyche has both a male (animus) and female (anima) aspect, somehow that male and female stuff didn't get applied to the concept of a hero archetype. Mmmmmm ... not sure I'm buying that one, honey bunches. Methinks if there's a hero's journey, then there's a heroine's journey, too.

But this is a post about the heroine's journey and STAR WARS. Luke Skywalker is a DUDE, you dip!

Good point, mystery troll inside my head. In this system, female warrior energy can drive the life of a man as well as a woman. For example, the ancient fighting goddess Athena had both male and female worshippers, including the hero Odysseus

(who's arguably the ultimate example of female warrior energy in action.)

Back to STAR WARS

With that long intro behind us, here are four reasons why yours truly believes that STAR WARS is *not* the hero's journey, but the heroine's journey:

Reason #1: The ultimate thing you can become in this universe is a Jedi, and Jedis get to wear dresses

Come on, how much more obvious can the symbolism be? But wait, there's more. Jedis fight with their minds as well as their swords, which is (to me anyway) a classic sign of female warrior energy. It's true, they *are* running around carrying a huge electronic phallus, but I'm not necessarily convinced that's an uncommon female experience.

Reason #2: Jedis get powerful by trusting their feelings

And that's typical guy territory? Ahhhh, nope. Classic masculine warrior energy is Zeus's thunderbolt. You break the rules, you get a jolt of mega-electricity through your cranium, end of story. There's no complex assessment of feelings with old Zeus-y. Which is fine, really. There are times for the thunderbolt, and times for a sword-and-smarts combo.

Reason #3: Luke's journey from whiny farm boy to dress-loving Jedi involves changing the universe

Rescuing the world, killing the bad guy, search-and-destroy missions ... these are all the work of the hero's journey. Heroes don't reconstruct the very fabric of society; they rescue stuff that's under threat. On the other hand, in a heroine's journey, the story ends with the re-imagining society as a whole.

CASE IN POINT: At the end of STAR WARS, the Emperor's statues are a-falling down and the galaxy's ready to be re-built. It won't be the same Republic it was before the Empire ... it won't be the Empire all over again (whew) ... but it *will* be something new that affects every aspect of life. That's heroine stuff.

FOR THE RECORD: Saving the world is also very, very cool. Go heroes!

Reason #4: The heroine's journey ultimately benefits the character with positive female energy

And in the original STAR WARS, the one ultimately getting all the bennies is Luke.

Whoa, there. You can't say Luke ... The heroine's journey is for girls!

Why yes, random inner troll, it absolutely is. But it also addresses far more than the estrogen-set. In fact, the heroine's journey *most* benefits the good guys, what our founding fathers called a *gentleman*, as in being *gentle* and a *man* at the same time.

Let me explain. For centuries, the gentleman was society's ideal of masculinity. I'm talking here about guys who are intelligent, considerate, well-spoken, and yet able to fight the good fight. There's a balance in these men between masculine and feminine, and today, that's too often put down as weakness.

At least as a woman, I can complain about dumbass ideals for my femininity. The good guys don't have that luxury. They live in this secret guy-world that benefits a small percentage of men--- all of whom are far from the gentlemanly ideal---while most of the good dudes suffer in silence, always wondering if they're measuring up.

It isn't fair, and it's time it all changed.

That, IMHO, is what STAR WARS is really all about. It's why, despite the knock-offs and wannabes, no one has come close to its success. It's a story for the good guy. The gentleman.

It's the heroine's journey, and in the end, that's really a journey for all of us.

~

APPENDIX II

IF YOU ENJOYED THIS BOOK...

...Please consider leaving a review, even if it's just a line or two. Every bit truly helps, especially for those of us who don't *write by the numbers,* if you know what I mean.

Plus I have it on good authority that every time you review an indie author, somewhere an angel gets a mocha latte. For reals.

And angels need their caffeine, too.

ACKNOWLEDGMENTS

If you're reading my freaking acknowledgements, chances are, I should thank you for something. So, for the record: you are awesome, dear reader.

That said, huge and heartfelt thanks must go out to my husband and son for their rock-solid support. Writing the Beholder series meant a lot of early mornings, late nights, long weekends, and never-ending patience. You two are the best guys in the universe, period.

After that, I must thank the extensive network of reviewers, friends and colleagues who helped me build my writing chops in general. Gracias.

Finally, deep affection goes out to my late, much loved, and dearly missed Aunt Sandy and Uncle Henry. You saw the writer in me, always. Thank you, first and last.

COLLECTED WORKS

Beholder

Where a medieval farm girl discovers necromancy and true love

1. Cursed
2. Concealed
3. Cherished
4. Crowned
5. Cradled

Angelbound Origins

About a quasi (part demon and part human) girl who loves kicking butt in Purgatory's Arena

1. Angelbound
2. Scala
3. Acca
4. Thrax
5. The Dark Lands
6. The Brutal Time *(2019)*
7. Armageddon *(already here, long story!)*
8. Quasi Redux *(2020)*

Angelbound Lincoln

The Angelbound experience as told by Prince Lincoln

1. Duty Bound
2. Lincoln
3. Trickster *(forthcoming)*

Angelbound Offspring

The next generation takes on Heaven, Hell, and everything in between

1. Maxon
2. Portia
3. Zinnia *(forthcoming)*
4. Kaps *(forthcoming)*
5. Huntress *(forthcoming)*

Fairy Tales of the Magicorum

Modern fairy tales with sass, action, and romance

1. Wolves and Roses
1.5 Moonlight and Midtown
2. Shifters and Glyphs
3. Slippers and Thieves *(forthcoming)*
4. Bandits and Ballgowns *(forthcoming)*

Dimension Drift

Dystopian adventures with science, snark, and hot aliens

Prequels

1. Scythe
2. Umbra

Novels

1. Alien Minds *(forthcoming)*
2. ECHO Academy *(forthcoming)*
3. Drift Warrior *(forthcoming)*

ABOUT CHRISTINA BAUER

Christina Bauer thinks that fantasy books are like bacon: they just make life better. All of which is why she writes romance novels that feature demons, dragons, wizards, witches, elves, elementals, and a bunch of random stuff that she brainstorms while riding the Boston T. Oh, and she includes lots of humor and kick-ass chicks, too. Christina lives in Newton, MA with her husband, son, and semi-insane golden retriever, Ruby.

Stalk Christina on Social Media – She Loves It!

Blog:
http://monsterhousebooks.com/blog/category/christina

Facebook:
https://www.facebook.com/authorBauer/

Instagram:
https://www.instagram.com/christina_cb_bauer/

Twitter: @CB_Bauer

VLOG: https://tinyurl.com/Vlogbauer

Web site: www.bauersbooks.com

COMPLIMENTARY BOOK

Get a FREE novella when you sign up for Christina's newsletter: https://tinyurl.com/bauersbooks

BEVERLY HILLS VAMPIRE

A NOVELLA BY
CHRISTINA BAUER

www.ingramcontent.com/pod-product-compliance
Lightning Source LLC
Chambersburg PA
CBHW021701260626
47154CB00023B/2105